Readers love t
series by JAMIE
KIM FIELDING, AND ELI EASTON

Stitch (with Sue Brown)

"Reading this collection felt like my birthday on rewind, with each story as a new little gift for me."

—Boys in Our Books

"Four fantastic tales about forging Mr. Right."

—Prism Book Alliance

"The sheer diversity of these stories made for a delightful read. I liked the different variations on the same theme; no two stories are alike. There is absolutely something for everyone here. I really enjoyed it…"

—Joyfully Jay

Bones (with B.G. Thomas)

"This is a sinful, sensual treat for Halloween; like dark, bitter chocolate, it will melt on your tongue, making you crave more."

—My Fiction Nook

"All four stories taught me something… All were well written, creative, and enjoyable."

—Love Bytes

"Overall, this is a wonderful book, with just enough magic and mystique to keep me highly entertained. Thank you to Kim, Eli, Jamie, and Ben for their stories!"

—Rainbow Book Reviews

claw

gothika #3

eli easton
jamie fessenden
kim fielding

DREAMSPINNER PRESS

Published by
DREAMSPINNER PRESS

5032 Capital Circle SW, Suite 2, PMB# 279, Tallahassee, FL 32305-7886 USA
http://www.dreamspinnerpress.com/

This is a work of fiction. Names, characters, places, and incidents either are the product of author imagination or are used fictitiously, and any resemblance to actual persons, living or dead, business establishments, events, or locales is entirely coincidental.

ISBN: 978-1-63476-044-7
Digital ISBN: 978-1-63476-045-4
Library of Congress Control Number: 2014922892
First Edition April 2015
Printed in the United States of America

Printed in the United States of America

This paper meets the requirements of
ANSI/NISO Z39.48-1992 (Permanence of Paper).

Table of Contents

Isolation

Jamie Fessenden

THE OLD Mazda shimmied so much on the dirt road that Sean could almost forget his hands were trembling. But not quite. It had been so long. Would Jack be happy to see him? Sean felt as if they'd had a fight, but they hadn't. Not really. Things had just gotten... weird. Four years apart hadn't seemed like that long when Sean had set out to find Jack, but the closer he got, the longer it seemed.

He passed something that could have been a turnoff. It hadn't looked like much more than a deer track, but Larry had said it was easy to miss. Sean slammed on the brakes, making his worn tires skid on the dirt and gravel, then backed up. There was no way he could turn around without ending up in the forest.

He saw wheel ruts going off into the trees. That had to be it.

Sean turned onto the road—if it could be called that. It was more a trail of deep tire ruts on either side of a low ridge of grass and rock. He prayed his car wouldn't bottom out. He'd also been fretting about the gas tank the last few miles. What if this wasn't the right road, after all? Would he end up stranded in the middle of nowhere with an empty tank of gas and the sun going down?

When he was a teenager, he and Jack had spent a ton of time in the woods. They'd learned how to build a shelter and start a campfire and get drinkable water. But that had been a long time ago. He wasn't anxious to see if his wilderness survival skills were still up to par.

He thought about turning back as the road narrowed and the brush seemed to be closing in on him. But just as he'd decided he couldn't risk going any farther, he rounded a bend, and there it was: a log cabin with a broad front porch, just as Larry had described it. The clincher was the beat-up old black pickup in the yard with the words "Jack of All Trades" stenciled on the side in yellow letters.

Cute.

Relieved, Sean pulled his car alongside the truck and stepped out. The summer air was hot and muggy, and his T-shirt was already clinging to his torso. Now that he was standing still, mosquitoes began to ravage his skin.

"Jack?" he called out, feeling the need to announce himself before walking up to the front door. He opened the trunk and hoisted his suitcase out.

Jack wasn't inside the house, anyway. After a minute, he came around from the back, wiping dirty hands on the red-checked flannel shirt he was holding. He looked good; Sean couldn't help but notice. He seemed a little taller than the last time they'd seen each other, when they were both twenty—though he'd always been a few inches taller than Sean. He also looked more muscular. Working as a handyman around town appeared to have kept him lean and added some definition to his stomach and chest. His dark brown hair was a bit on the shaggy side, but it suited him. Right then, sweat was running in tiny rivulets from his hairline. It streaked down his face and neck to pool in the hollows of his collarbones before spilling down his naked torso.

Jack looked at Sean for a long moment, as if he couldn't believe what he was seeing. Then he wiped the sweat off his face and tossed the shirt over one shoulder. "Hey."

"Hey."

Jack glanced down at the suitcase in Sean's hand. "You moving in?"

"Well," Sean replied uncomfortably, "I was kinda hoping I could stay with you for a few days."

Jesus! What was I thinking? It was an absurd request, considering how long it had been since they'd seen each other. But the old Jack would have had no problem with it. Sean realized then how much he'd been counting on that.

Fortunately, the "new" Jack didn't seem too bent out of shape about it, either. He just nodded and asked, "You have a fight with Denise?"

Sean shrugged. "No fight. Just a divorce."

THEY SAT out on the porch for the rest of the afternoon, catching up, while they killed off the six-pack and a half that Jack had in his fridge. Aided by a pleasant buzz brought on by the beer, the conversation was deceptively easy—just like the "old days," as long as they were able to dance around the subject of Denise and how Sean had screwed everything up between him and Jack.

But they couldn't dance forever.

"So," Jack said at last, casting a glance at the sun as it sank behind the pine trees, "I know this is none of my business—"

"Everything's your business, man," Sean said quickly. "We're best friends."

He immediately regretted saying it, seeing the way Jack frowned and glanced away in response.

"Yeah, well…. Are you gonna tell me what went wrong? Between you and Denise?"

Sean finished off the beer in his hand, then shrugged. "I don't know. Everything seemed okay. I mean, we weren't fighting, or anything. Things were just…."

"Just what?"

Sean mulled it over a long time before replying, "Cold."

Jack nodded, then opened another beer and handed it to him.

The wind sighed softly through the pines on all sides of the cabin. There was a small front yard where the truck and Sean's car were parked—mostly dirt and mud—but on the other side of that were more pines. They were completely cut off from the world. Not even the sounds of traffic reached them from the highway five miles to the south.

"Remember all those times you dragged me off to the woods to camp?" Sean asked, as if he expected Jack to have forgotten half their childhood.

"'Course."

"This is what you always wanted, isn't it? To be out in the woods where no one can find you…."

"You seem to have managed it."

"Yeah," Sean said, feeling a little defensive. "Well… your dad told me."

"I'm surprised he knew." Sean knew Jack and his father hadn't spoken in years—not since Jack came out. The old man hadn't been happy about his son being "one of them." He'd given Sean an earful about it that afternoon.

"He said Larry told him where to find you." Larry was the local sheriff and a long-standing friend of the family.

"Ah." Jack took a swig of his beer. "That figures." He didn't state the obvious—Jack's dad hadn't bothered using that information to contact his son. From what Sean knew, they hadn't spoken since Jack came out.

"Honestly, I was surprised to find you in a cabin," Sean rambled on. "I kind of pictured you in a tent or a teepee or… maybe a cave."

Jack snorted. "This was for sale and it was cheap. That cave sure sounds tempting, though."

Sean laughed, hating how nervous he sounded. *Are you wishing I hadn't been able to find you?* He didn't dare ask. But there was one thing he'd been wondering about over the past four years, so even though he knew he might not like the answer, he asked, "Have you…. Did you ever find…."

"A boyfriend?" Jack asked wryly.

Just hearing Jack say the word made Sean jealous. "Yeah."

"Relax, dipshit. There was never anyone but you."

Sean felt a surge of hope at those words—and guilt. He knew now he'd always felt the same about Jack, even though he'd been too dumb to know it. And he knew how miserable it would have made him to learn Jack had married someone else.

"I'm—"

He wasn't sure what he'd been about to say. An apology? Something brilliant that would make it all better? But Jack didn't give him the chance.

He stood abruptly and went to open the front door of the cabin, pausing in the doorway to look back at Sean and say, "You'd better come inside. It's getting pretty late."

Sean glanced at the sky, which had barely begun to fade from orange to gray. Then he looked at his iPhone. No reception, of course, but it still gave him the time. "It's not even nine o'clock yet!"

Jack seemed uncomfortable about something, glancing almost furtively at the sky. "I have to crash early these days. I do a lot of yard work for people early in the morning."

Then he went inside.

Why Jack needing to go to bed early meant Sean had to do likewise didn't make much sense. But Sean wasn't keen on sitting around by himself on the porch, so he got up to follow his friend into the cabin.

IT WAS a nice place, for a man living alone. There were really only two rooms—a big living room with a kitchenette in the back and a bedroom off to the right. Furnishings were minimal. The living room had a big fireplace, with a wide couch in front of it and a large oak chest serving as a coffee table and footrest. There were some bookshelves on the walls, and that was about it. No television—it was a pretty safe bet no cable company ran their lines out this far. Sean was surprised, though grateful, when Jack flicked a switch and an electric light went on overhead.

The small kitchen area had a sink with a pump handle and a small wood stove. The refrigerator was small, like something a college student might have in his dorm room. There was a chest freezer out on the porch for storing things, in case he got snowed in for a while—Jack had shown Sean its contents, as if to prove he hadn't lost his mind out there in the wild and started chopping up hikers or something. Near the window was a small aluminum table and a chair. At least Jack had an electric coffeemaker on the counter.

Jack closed the front door behind them and, to Sean's surprise, threw the bolt on it. The door had a knob with a lock like any other house, and it was solid enough to keep anything shy of a rampaging bull moose out. Was he really that concerned about someone breaking in, way out here?

"The bathroom's over here," Jack said, walking past him and opening what Sean had thought was a closet door near the kitchenette. It contained a toilet and a shower stall. No room for a sink, but the kitchen sink wasn't far away.

Thank God it's not an outhouse.

"Cool."

As Jack went around the small space, pointing out where he kept towels and snacks and his favorite books, in case Sean felt like reading something, Sean watched the subtle shifting of the muscles underneath the tanned skin of Jack's naked torso. That old familiar feeling of arousal welled up inside him, making his crotch feel tight. Once upon a time, they would have played a bit before going to sleep. And though he knew it was wishful thinking, Sean couldn't help but feel anticipation at the thought of being invited into Jack's bed.

But the pleasant buzz Sean had gotten from the beer began to fade as he realized things just weren't going to be that easy. Jack was avoiding looking directly at him, and being careful to keep his distance. He had to have known what was on Sean's mind, but he didn't give any sign of interest.

When Jack opened the door to his own room, he stood in the doorway, blocking it, rather than holding it open for Sean to come in. "You can sleep on the couch. There are blankets in the chest. Or, if you want, there's a sleeping bag in there you can stretch out on the floor."

"You're making me sleep on the floor?"

"Or the couch." Jack hesitated, and then gave him a wry smile. "Sorry. There's only one bed, and I'm used to sleeping alone these days."

Sean felt as if Jack had just dumped a pail of cold water over his head. It had felt, out on the porch, as if Jack had wanted the same thing he did—to be together, finally. But it looked as if he wasn't going to make that easy.

Sean knew he wasn't always the brightest bulb in the pack. He was still trying to figure out how *he* felt about things, never mind sorting out Jack's feelings. But he knew marrying Denise had fucked things up between them, and he at least owed Jack an apology for that.

"I'm sorry," he said. "For… what I did. You know… for marrying somebody else, when I should have known better…."

Jack stood very still for a long time, looking directly into his eyes. Then he gave Sean a single nod. "I know you are. I just wish it wasn't too late."

Sean felt his insides grow cold, as if his heart had been beamed out of his chest like in *Star Trek* and dispersed into space, leaving his blood still and coagulating in his veins. He didn't understand. Did Jack hate him now?

"There's more beer in the fridge," Jack continued. "Help yourself to anything you want to snack on." Then, just before he closed the door, he added, "But stay inside."

Sean's head was still churning with confused thoughts, but he managed to choke out, "Why?"

"I've had bears prowling around here lately," Jack replied. "I don't need to be scraping your innards off the porch tomorrow morning."

Sean might not have spent as much time in the woods as Jack, but a bear wandering by the tent now and then had never alarmed them as teenagers—not much. It hardly seemed cause for barricading themselves in the cabin as soon as it got dark.

But Sean didn't call him on it, even when Jack closed his bedroom door and Sean heard him throw another deadbolt on the other side.

Does he think I'll burst in and try to rape him in the middle of the night?

Things weren't going at all like Sean had hoped they would. He'd expected Jack to demand an apology, maybe even make him grovel a bit. But to say it was too late? Sean didn't know how to process that. They were both single now, and they were out there away from their families and friends—everyone who'd tried to keep them apart. How could it be too late?

Maybe Jack just didn't feel it anymore, that bond they'd shared— what they'd felt for each other. The thought was disheartening. But Sean refused to give up so soon. There had to be a way to remind him, to make him feel it again. There was time, as long as Jack didn't tell him to leave. Sean could afford to go to a hotel if he had to, but he had the uncomfortable feeling this visit might be his last chance to make things right.

SEAN SAT on the couch, staring at the cold fireplace while the sky outside the window darkened, irritated that there wasn't even a DVD player to help him pass the time. He glanced at the bookshelves on the wall, but didn't bother checking them out. He didn't feel like reading. He was lonely and watching Jack run around shirtless all day had made him horny as hell.

When things had been good between them—when the intense relationship they'd shared since high school had begun to grow obvious to everyone around them—Sean had panicked. He'd gone off to college, hooked up with Denise, and let Jack fade into the background. Somehow he'd thought they could still remain friends, but instead they'd just drifted further and further apart. Jack had agreed to be the best man at his wedding during his sophomore year at UNH, but that was the last time they'd seen each other.

Four years. Four years of trying to make his marriage work, when Sean knew deep down he'd made a mistake. He'd been an idiot. His fear of what was happening between him and Jack had caused him to drag a third person into the mess he was creating. He'd never meant to hurt Denise, but of course he had. His only excuse—and it wasn't much of one—was that he hadn't known he was doing it. And now here he was, foolishly trying to patch things up with Jack by making an imposition of himself.

God, I'm pathetic!

Sighing in frustration, Sean got up off the couch. He needed to take a leak, but he was feeling too contrary to heed Jack's paranoid warnings and stay inside. There was no reason he couldn't just use Jack's tiny bathroom, but he'd be damned if he was going to cower indoors all night just because there might possibly be the slightest chance of a bear wandering by the cabin. He could understand Jack being pissed at him, but there was no reason to treat him like he was five years old.

He quietly unbolted the front door and slipped out onto the porch. It was a beautiful night. The sky was somewhat overcast, but the moon illuminated the clouds from behind as they slowly drifted by. The late September air was starting to grow cool, though it hadn't yet taken on the chill of fall.

Sean walked to the far edge of the porch, unzipped, and started pissing on the grass below.

He was almost finished before he heard it—a sound like faint whispering in the woods. He'd heard it once before. Just once. And it had chilled him then, just as it chilled him now. Then there was another sound—something more concrete—the crisp rustle of footsteps at the edge of the woods. Sean zipped up and peered into the shadows, trying to see if there was something there. A breeze sprang up, causing the trees and underbrush to sway and making it impossible to tell which shadow might be a moving animal. The moonlight faded as heavier clouds rolled by, and Sean could no longer see the yard clearly. Snapping branches indicated that the animal was moving closer. It sounded large—perhaps a bear or a coyote—and Sean began to back up across the porch, reaching behind him for the door.

Suddenly, it growled low and ominous, sounding like nothing Sean could identify—and an enormous black shape lumbered across the yard toward him. Sean panicked and ran for the door, yanking it open and slamming it behind him. He threw the deadbolt and backed away, his heart pounding in his chest.

Whatever it was, the animal didn't attempt to break the door down. After listening for a couple minutes and peering out through one of the windows in a futile attempt to see into the darkness, Sean took a deep breath to steady himself and laughed at how frightened he'd allowed himself to get. He might even have imagined the shadow running toward him across the yard.

"Fuckin' coyote," he muttered before turning away to search for the blankets Jack had told him were in the chest.

HE DREAMT of that night when they were camping near Cedar Pond. They were both fifteen, both randy as hell, and their friendship was still burning with an intensity few adults could understand. So it was little wonder that here, isolated from the rest of the world, they finally gave in to what they'd both been wanting for such a long time. They didn't talk about it. Sean, especially, was afraid to. Talking might have given it a name, and he was terrified of that name, of the contempt his father and uncle would have had for him if they'd found out. So he and Jack just did... what they did. And when it was over, they held each other in the darkness of their tent, caressing and kissing until they drifted off to sleep.

Later he awoke and was disturbed to find himself alone in the tent. It was still dark, and without Jack's body heat warming the tent, Sean felt cold. He hoped Jack had just crawled outside for a minute to take a leak or something, but he waited and waited and his friend didn't return. Finally, with growing trepidation, Sean unzipped the tent door and peered outside. The moon provided a faint light, though the forest floor was thick with shadow.

"Jack?" His voice sounded quiet and a little fearful. He couldn't shake the feeling that something was very wrong.

He crawled out of the tent and stood, wrapping his arms around his naked body in a vain attempt to stave off the cold night air. Then he saw Jack, standing silent and still about fifty feet away. He was naked, beautifully illuminated by a shaft of blue-gray moonlight. But when Sean called to him again, there was no response.

Cautiously, Sean walked on bare feet through the ferns and pine needles blanketing the forest floor. When he drew near, and Jack still hadn't moved, he reached out to brush Jack's bare shoulder with his fingertips. Only then did Jack turn his head to give him a strange, enigmatic smile.

"Listen," he whispered.

Sean was shivering and wanted nothing more than to crawl back into the warmth of their sleeping bags—both him and Jack together—but he cocked an ear and tried to listen. At first he heard nothing. Nothing, that is, except the usual sounds of a forest at night—wind in the trees, the rustling of leaves, the occasional snap of a twig as a squirrel or deer slipped past in the shadows. But then he caught something—a faint sound like people whispering. The voices were elusive and impossible to pinpoint. He couldn't be certain what direction they came from, or even if he was really hearing them.

"What is it?" he whispered back.

Jack's smile was rapturous, as if he were hearing the voices of angels. "It's calling to us."

"What is?"

"The forest."

THE NEXT morning Sean woke to the sound of a vehicle pulling into the driveway. It was light out, and the clock on the fireplace mantle read nearly ten. Bright sunlight was streaming through the open curtains.

Before he could decide whether he was really awake yet, the door opened and Jack came in. Once again he was shirtless, which was a pleasant enough sight to wake up to, but the damp, sweaty T-shirt he tossed at Sean's head was a bit less pleasant.

"Hey, deadbeat! You ever gonna wake up? I've been working for hours already."

"Fuck you," Sean muttered, but he sat up, tossing the shirt on the floor. "What have you been doing?"

"Landscaping at the Donnelly's," Jack replied cheerfully. He crossed the living room to turn on the water in the kitchenette sink, then started scrubbing his filthy hands. "They want to rent their house out when they move to Florida."

"Oh." Sean stood up from the couch, still fuzzy and half-asleep. He was wearing just a pair of tight briefs, and when Jack turned back to him, rubbing his hands on the dish towel, Sean was pleased to notice Jack eyeing his package a bit before looking away.

"Come on. It's hot as hell, and I've got two hours 'til I have to deal with that old bitch, Mrs. Westcott, and her damned flower beds. Let's go for a swim."

"Where?"

"There's a pond, just down the path behind the cabin."

Sean rubbed his face with his hands and glanced down at himself. "I didn't bring a suit."

Jack quirked an eyebrow at him and tossed the dish towel onto the counter.

BATHING SUITS didn't appear to be standard issue this far away from civilization. Jack didn't bother with one, and apparently he didn't expect Sean to, either, despite the wall he'd put up between them the night before. It was wonderful to see Jack naked again. He'd been making disconcerting appearances in Sean's masturbatory fantasies, even when Sean had thought he could make his sham of a marriage work. After the separation and divorce, Jack had moved to front and center. It was nice to see he'd improved over the past few years. His stomach was more sharply defined now, his arms corded with muscle.

It was a little embarrassing how quickly Sean got a semi after the clothes were tossed onto the rocks near the water's edge, but Jack didn't seem to mind. Once they'd waded out into waist-high water, Jack pounced and dragged him under. The pond was clean, but their bodies stirred up a cloud of silt when they hit bottom, so Sean quickly lost sight of his friend. But he could feel their bodies intertwined, rubbing hot skin against skin. The laughter died after they'd wrestled each other to the bottom a few times, and he could feel Jack's hard cock rubbing against his under the water, almost fucking, but not quite. Sean's frustration grew until he couldn't stand it. He tried to grasp Jack's cock with his hand, but Jack gently pushed him away.

Then he stood and squinted up at the sky.

"Is it noon yet?" he asked.

"How should I know? You want me to use my dick as a sundial?"

Jack sighed and rolled his eyes at him, then walked out of the water to go dig his cell phone out of his pocket. "I still have a few minutes," he said after glancing at it.

Rather than rejoin Sean in the water, he flopped down on his back on the grassy bank. Sean didn't see much point in swimming by himself, so he came out of the water to flop down beside him.

"Did you know my folks sold their place?" Sean asked.

Jack squinted up at the bright blue sky. "Yeah. I still run into your sister, now and then, when I'm in town. She keeps me up on what your folks are doing these days."

"It sucks," Sean said vehemently. "I loved the pond there. And the fields… and the old barn."

"Yeah."

Sean rolled over onto his side, giving Jack a sly smile. "Remember hanging out in the loft?"

Clearly, Jack did remember because his face grew flushed.

"You're turning red," Sean teased.

"Yes, I remember."

"I know *I* still remember."

Jack refused to look at him. "That's just… something kids do."

"Whatever you say, Dr. Freud. Think you can still beat me?"

Jack couldn't pretend he didn't know what Sean was talking about because he blushed even more. "I'm not in the mood."

He certainly had been in the mood a minute ago, judging by all the crotch grinding. And he still had a hard-on. "Why not?" Sean asked, grinning. "Nobody can see us."

"That's not the point."

"You're the one who wanted to get naked together and splash around in the pond."

"To cool off," Jack replied. "I wasn't trying to start anything."

It had certainly *felt* as if Jack was starting something. Maybe he hadn't thought it all the way through, but he'd been enjoying the eroticism of the situation as much as Sean. Still grinning, Sean slid his hand down the front of his body, and Jack seemed mesmerized as he watched it descend. Sean's breathing grew ragged as his fingers brushed through his blond pubic hair and slowly embraced the base of his swollen cock.

But apparently that was going too far because Jack suddenly jumped up and reached for his clothes. "I have to get back to work."

"I'm sorry. I just thought you were… holding back…." Hadn't Jack been horny just a minute ago? Hadn't they both been waving erections around?

Jack was fumbling to get his legs into his pants in a way that might have been comic, if Sean hadn't been so confused. "Maybe I *want* to hold back."

He took off for the house, still fastening his pants as if he were escaping a fate worse than death.

Sean growled in frustration and ran after him. "Why? Yes, I fucked up. I know that. I'll do anything you want—"

"I'm not trying to get you to grovel!" Jack protested, walking toward the house. "It's just… things are different now."

"I know! But I was hoping… I don't know. That we could *fix* it. That you'd *let* me fix it…."

"It's not that easy, Sean."

Sean opened his mouth to reply, but Jack jerked to a halt and Sean nearly collided with him. He looked up ahead and saw what Jack had reacted to.

There was a police cruiser parked in front of the cabin, and two officers were standing near it. Sean knew them both—Larry and Kelton. Larry had been elected sheriff when Sean was a kid, and he had yet to be unseated. He was a tall man with salt-and-pepper hair—a bit more salt than four years ago, but still pretty much the same. Kelton was short, darker-haired, and a bit on the rotund side. He'd come on board a bit later, but now it was hard to imagine the two not working together. They'd always reminded Sean of Abbott and Costello.

Kelton was regarding Sean and Jack—particularly Sean—with a startled expression, and that's when Sean realized he hadn't grabbed anything to put on when he'd chased after Jack.

Larry was unflappable, as always. He simply nodded at Jack. "Afternoon."

"Larry!" Jack said nervously. "Kelton. Hi."

Larry then said to Sean in an exaggerated country hick accent, "Yer *nekkid*."

"Be right back," Sean said. He hadn't brought anything but his underwear down to the pond, and walking around in his tighty-whities in front of the cops didn't seem like a good idea, so he scampered up the steps and into the cabin to grab his jeans. It only took a moment, and he could hear the conversation through the open window.

"What can I do for you?" Jack asked.

Larry answered, "Well… really we just stopped by to warn you about some large animal sightings in this area."

"*This* area? Who's sighting things out here? I'm out in the middle of fucking nowhere."

Sean came back out onto the porch in time to see Larry nod, conceding the point. "Well, within a few miles. Ellie Jacobs saw something out at her farm last night—it was pokin' its nose in her dumpster. And later on, Ben Thompson took a shot at something sniffin' around near his chicken coop. But that's just a couple miles from here, and animals roam."

"Bears?"

"More like wolves, from what they were describing. Or maybe just one."

"In New Hampshire?" Jack asked, the disbelief clear in his voice. "Not likely." Wolves had been extinct in the state for over a century.

Larry shrugged. "A gray wolf was killed just twenty miles over the border into Canada a couple years ago, and hikers keep claiming they've seen them in the White Mountains. Probably just coyotes, but you never know."

Sean wondered for a moment if the animal noises he'd heard the night before could have been the animal Larry was talking about. Could it really have been a wolf? He opened his mouth to mention it, then thought better of it. Jack would be pissed if he found out Sean had gone outside despite his warning. And really, Sean hadn't seen anything. Most likely it had just been a coyote.

Jack laughed. "This is the part where some crazy old coot cries out, 'That weren't no wolf! I seen it, and it walked like a man. I tell ya… it was a *werewolf*!'"

"Maybe," Larry conceded. One corner of his mouth twitched up a bit—that was about as close to a smile as the man ever got. "My life sure feels like a horror movie at times." He turned and headed back to the cruiser, Kelton falling in behind him like a faithful dog, and called back over his shoulder, "Anyway, just be careful. And let us know if you see anything."

"Sure."

As they opened the cruiser doors, Sean heard Kelton mutter, "Somethin' there's gotta be illegal…."

"You wanna give 'em a ticket?"

"No."

"Well, all right, then."

They climbed into the cruiser and drove off.

SEAN SPENT a boring day at the cabin by himself while Jack did a bunch of jobs in town. He scrounged up some lunch and went skinny dipping again, but it wasn't as much fun without Jack. He jerked off this time, but that didn't take long. He didn't have much interest in reading, so he didn't even bother looking at the bookcase. He thumbed through the music on his iPhone—pretty much the only thing it was good for, this far off the grid—but couldn't find anything he was interested in listening to.

He thought about driving into town himself, but the gas in his tank was so low, he wasn't sure he'd make it. He'd have to ask Jack later if he had a gas can, or could make a gas station run for him. Anyway, he'd grown up in Dunkirk. It wasn't much more interesting than the cabin was.

Finally, in an act of desperation, he split wood. Jack had a bunch of cut logs piled up behind the cabin next to a woodpile covered with a tarp. Sean hadn't used a maul in years, but it came back to him quickly enough. And it gave him a way to pass the time and work off some of his frustration with the way things had been going. He understood why Jack was hesitant to let him back into his life, but that didn't make it any easier to deal with. He couldn't stay there forever, mooching off Jack's food. But he was afraid to leave again without resolving things between them. He couldn't escape the feeling he wouldn't get another shot at it.

JACK PULLED in just as it was getting dark and a beautiful crescent moon was rising above the pines. Sean was ecstatic to see him—even more so when Jack carried a large pizza and a twelve-pack up onto the porch. They spent another pleasant evening together, shooting the shit until mosquitoes drove them inside.

They'd dirtied a couple of plates eating the pizza, so Jack washed those in the sink. While he was doing that, Sean drifted back to the small bookcase. He'd glanced at it earlier but hadn't seen anything interesting. Mostly horror novels. Now he noticed something he hadn't before—a lot of them were about werewolves. Like more than half. And they weren't all novels, either. A lot of them seemed to be books *about* werewolves, with titles like *Werewolves in Western Culture: a Lycanthropy Reader* and *The Book of Werewolves, Being an Account of a Terrible Superstition*. There were also a bunch of dolls and figurines of the Lon Chaney Wolf Man and wolves in general.

"What is all this shit you're reading?" he asked, picking up a book called *The Werewolf* by Montague Summers and flipping it open to see a bunch of entries in the Table of Contents like The Werewolf: His Science and Practice.

Jack glanced over and then took the time to dry his hands on the dishtowel before replying, "I like horror."

"Especially werewolves. You've got three shelves on them."

Jack came close to him and peered over his shoulder at the book. They were both shirtless, thanks to the muggy summer evening, and Sean was intensely aware of the heat coming off Jack's skin and the mingling of their sweat as his chest brushed Sean's shoulder.

He could feel a soft puff of breath against his neck when Jack spoke. "When I was a kid, I used to think it would be so awesome to be a werewolf, running free in the forest." He chuckled, a low, sultry sound. "*Naked.* Far away from people...."

This was a childhood fantasy Sean had never been informed of. At least all the stuff about werewolves. He'd always known Jack had an affinity for the forest, even before that odd night of the whispering. They'd spent a lot of time camping together in the little pup tent Jack's father had given him for his eleventh birthday. During the summers they'd practically *lived* in the woods. Jack had seemed to belong there, and he'd talked about going off into the forest to live someday. Sean hadn't been quite so enthusiastic about that idea, but he'd always felt *he* belonged with Jack, wherever that might be... until he'd panicked and run away.

"Well, you figured out the 'far away from people' part, at any rate," Sean said with an awkward laugh, closing the book and slipping it back onto the shelf.

Jack wandered away and flopped down onto the couch, putting his feet up on the oak chest. "Not far enough when it comes to Mrs. Westcott and her goddamn flower bed. Bring me another beer, will you?"

"Yes, master." They'd stashed the remaining few beers from the twelve-pack in the fridge, so Sean grabbed a couple of those and brought them over to the couch. He handed one to Jack and flopped down on the couch beside him. "You were social enough when we were teenagers."

"Since when? *You* were social—sometimes. You went to parties, and I went to parties because I was hanging out with you. But I always hated them."

Sean knew that was true. They'd both always preferred to be alone. He'd just never thought of it that way because they'd always been alone *together*. Now Jack seemed to have forgotten the "together" part. It occurred to him for the first time that Jack really might not want him there at all. Maybe he'd just barreled in and set up house without noticing how uncomfortable Jack was with the idea.

"Am I making a pest of myself?" he asked. "Would you rather I stayed with my sister?" He braced himself for the answer.

Jack paused, his beer halfway to his lips. "Where did *that* come from?"

"I just…. Well, I just thought… I kind of showed up on your doorstep and expected you to take me in. Maybe you're feeling put on the spot."

"Are you drunk?"

"No," Sean said, frustrated. "I'm just asking."

Jack snorted and took a swig from his bottle. Then he carefully lowered it to his lap before responding. "You can be a little pushy, at times."

"So I *am* being a pest, then."

"You're not being a pest." Jack grinned. "Or maybe I should say you're always a pest. But I don't mind. Really. That's just the way you are."

That didn't exactly sound flattering. But Sean had asked, so he wouldn't piss and moan if that's how Jack really felt about him. He asked, "Would you like me to go stay with Julie?"

Jack appeared to think about it for a good long time. Then he rubbed his chin with one hand and said, "I don't think that's really what I want."

"Then why am I sleeping on the couch?"

Jack gave him a long, hard look then, directly in the eye. Then he sighed and stood up. "Look, what happened when we were teenagers…. We were different people back then. Don't you get it? You can't just expect to pick up where we left off."

"You told your father you were gay," Sean pointed out.

"What does that have to do with anything?"

"I'm just sayin' what happened between us wasn't just kids fooling around," Sean said. "You're gay, and so am I. It took me a while to realize it—"

"The fact that we're both gay doesn't mean we were meant for each other."

"No," Sean conceded, "but we *were* meant for each other. You know it as much as I do. I know I hurt you by… what I did…."

"You did." Jack looked Sean directly in the eye. "You have no fucking idea." For a moment Sean saw so much pain reflected in those smoky hazel eyes that he was forced to look away. And in doing so, he knew he'd failed yet again.

Jack finished off his beer and got up to go rinse out his bottle at the sink.

"I'm sorry," Sean said quietly.

"I know. And I forgive you. Really. But it doesn't matter." Jack set the bottle down on the counter and walked to his bedroom door. He turned in the doorway and spread his hands in a gesture of futility. "It's too late to fix it, Sean."

Then he went into the bedroom and closed the door. Sean heard the bolt latch.

SEAN DIDN'T know what to do. He knew he'd screwed up—big-time. But he kept apologizing, Jack kept saying he forgave him, and nothing was changing. What else could he do? Wait it out? Give it time? He could do that, if that's what it would take. But would Jack let him? Sean couldn't stay in the cabin forever. Certainly, not without a job.

Maybe he could talk to Jack about that in the morning—finding a job, pulling his own weight. Jack said he didn't want him to leave, and Sean sure as hell didn't want to leave. If he found something in town to help out with groceries, maybe that would help. It was something, at least.

Sean felt incredibly frustrated right then. He needed air. And another beer might not hurt. So he grabbed one of the last two in the fridge and quietly let himself out onto the front porch. Larry's warning about animals in the area was still fresh in his mind, but by then he'd convinced himself people were probably just seeing coyotes and freaking out about them. Certainly what he'd heard last night had to have been a coyote. They could be dangerous, of course. But he'd seen them often enough in the forest. Usually they just skittered off.

He stood on the porch in the darkness, listening to the soft sigh of the wind through the pine trees and birches as he drank his beer. He was still shirtless, and the breeze caressed his bare skin and tickled his nipples, causing them to stiffen involuntarily. It felt good. Almost without thinking about it, he reached up with his left hand and circled his right nipple lazily, encouraging it to grow even harder. By the time he'd drained the bottle, he decided a quick wank might help him relax. He would have felt weird doing it in the living room, where Jack could walk through at any moment, but out there in the dark….

Thoughts of Jack's naked body glistening with moisture as he lay on the grass that afternoon were all it took to make his jeans feel they were ready to burst at the crotch. Sean set the empty bottle down on the wooden boards at his feet and walked to the far edge. He unfastened the button on his jeans and opened the fly, then fished his hardened cock out of his boxers.

It felt good, stroking himself languidly in the muggy night, a gentle breeze bringing the mingled scents of pine and dirt and grass to his nostrils, and caressing his sweaty torso like cool fingers. It didn't take long before he felt his orgasm building, so he picked up the pace. He clenched his teeth as he exploded, squirting his seed out over the edge of the porch into the darkness. Hopefully, it wouldn't be visible in the morning.

When he'd finished, he stood there a moment longer, catching his breath. Then he tucked himself back into his boxers—not bothering to refasten his jeans, since he'd be taking them off in a minute—and went back inside.

"DO YOU still hear it?" Sean asked.

They were eighteen now, though their lives had changed little since that night when Sean heard the whispering. They still spent most of their free time together in the woods, they still kissed and caressed and explored in the dark, and they still spoke little about it. The whispering had frightened Sean, but Jack had seemed delighted by it.

"I do," Jack replied, lying naked on the grass, the sweat on his skin glistening in the moonlight. It was a hot night in July, and the heat had chased them out of their shelter. The old tent had long ago worn out and been sacrificed to use as material in lean-tos and other types of shelters they'd learned how to build. "It's still calling to us."

A chill ran down Sean's spine despite the heat. He'd heard the whispering himself, so he didn't think Jack was schizophrenic or anything. But that didn't make the situation any less disturbing. He sat cross-legged beside Jack, lightly tracing the contours of Jack's stomach muscles with his fingers.

"What does it want?"

"It wants us to join it."

"Where?"

"In the forest."

Sean shivered slightly. "You aren't thinking of going, are you? How would you survive? Especially in winter?"

"I'll go someday," Jack said, smiling serenely, "but not until you're ready to go with me."

Sean wasn't sure if he'd ever be ready. Yes, he loved being in the forest. He felt comfortable in the woods, at least when he was with Jack. But Jack knew so much more than he did about what was edible and what was poisonous. He never got lost or turned around. He could build a fire without matches, trap rabbits, and he'd even learned to hunt with bow and arrow—one of the few things he and his father enjoyed doing together. Sean wasn't like that. He'd be lost out here if Jack wasn't with him.

"I don't know if I'll ever be ready," Sean said.

"You'll have to be if we're going to stay together. I can't wait forever."

SEAN AWOKE to a sharp bang.

His heart was racing in his chest as he listened in the dark. But he had no idea where the sound had come from. The cabin was completely silent. Had he dreamed it?

Something massive slammed into the front door, making it shudder in its frame and jostling the framed picture of a sunset on the wall beside it.

"Oh, shit!" Sean gasped.

He had only a split second to remember he'd forgotten to latch the bolt before the door slammed open, banging against the wall. The picture crashed to the floor, glass shattering. Something half crouched, half stood in the doorway, hunched over but definitely balanced on two legs. It was silhouetted against a cloudy sky lit blue-gray by the moonlight.

Sean screamed and scrambled over the back of the couch without thinking. He fell hard onto the wooden floor behind it, landing on his back and getting the breath knocked out of him.

Then the wooden feet of the couch scraped against the floor as something bounded over it and landed on top of him—something massive and hairy and reeking of damp dog. Its breath was hot against his face, and an enormous paw with sharp claws pressed down on the center of his chest, pinning him. The thing growled, and in the faint moonlight coming through the windows, Sean could see it draw back its lips to expose ferocious canines. Hot saliva dribbled down onto his cheek.

Sean finally found breath enough to scream, but it had little effect on the animal. It lowered its face, and Sean waited for the searing pain of teeth tearing into his flesh. But it didn't come. Instead the creature sniffed at him a moment, and then, to his intense disgust, it licked his nose and mouth.

Sean turned his face away in revulsion, but the creature continued to lick him, switching to his ear. Sean whimpered.

Nice doggie, nice doggie. Please don't eat me....

Then as fast as it appeared, the creature was gone. Sean felt it jump off him, and when he dared to look, it was nowhere to be seen. He lay on the floor, panting and listening intently for the sounds of an enormous animal moving around the room. But he heard nothing.

He sat up tentatively, and his hand touched the floor in a puddle of warm liquid next to his ass. He'd pissed himself.

Fuck.

The door was still open, but it didn't take long to determine he was alone in the sparsely furnished room. Sean leapt to his feet and ran to the door. Slamming it shut, he threw the bolt. He flipped on all the lights he could find, and then ran to Jack's bedroom door to pound on it.

"Jack! Get up! Now!"

There was no answer, so he pounded again. It seemed like ages before he heard a sleepy "What the fuck?" coming from the other side. A moment later the door opened and a completely naked and sleep-tousled Jack glared at him. "What the fuck are you screaming about?"

Before Sean could answer, Jack glanced down at his boxers and made a face. "Jesus! You're dripping!"

SEAN TOOK a quick shower while Jack mopped the floor. He did feel a little guilty about pissing on the floor and dribbling it all over the place, but he was irritated that Jack hadn't taken his account of the beast seriously. It wasn't exactly that he hadn't believed him—that might have been reasonable.

Instead, he'd listened to Sean's account, frowned at him, and said, "I told you to stay inside and keep the door bolted."

What the fuck! "Because of a *bear*! You told me there was bear! That was no fucking bear!"

Jack had just glared at him and said, "Go take a shower. You're still dripping all over the place."

So he had. He left his wet boxers in the shower stall to deal with the next day and walked out of the bathroom naked. It didn't seem to matter— Jack hadn't bothered to put anything on either. But neither of them was in a mood to find it sexy.

Sean watched Jack empty the mop bucket into the sink, his frustration mounting, until finally he demanded, "Are you gonna tell me what the fuck's going on?"

"What makes you think I know?"

"The fact that I was just attacked by this thing—"

"You said it licked your face," Jack interrupted, smirking. "That's not much of an attack."

"Jesus! You don't even give a fuck! Which means you either don't care if I get eaten, or you already know what this thing is."

Jack opened the fridge and found only the one beer left. He magnanimously handed it to Sean. "Of course I don't want you to get eaten," he said. Then he surprised Sean by kissing him lightly on the cheek. "Come on."

Sean watched in disbelief as Jack crossed the room and threw back the bolt on the door.

"What the hell are you doing?"

"It's okay," Jack said, opening the door and gesturing for Sean to follow him. "It's gone now."

BY THE time Sean worked up the courage to follow his friend outside, he found Jack sitting on the front steps, gazing out into the forest as if it was a peaceful, serene night, instead of a night full of monsters. Sean looked around cautiously, but in the dark, he couldn't see well enough to tell what lurked in the underbrush.

"There's something magical about these woods," Jack said quietly. "You know that as well as I do."

Sean sat down beside him. He *did* know it, but he was too unnerved to wax philosophical. The creature hadn't been some cute little pixie. "If by 'magical,' you mean 'evil'...."

"I don't think the wolf is evil," Jack replied grimly. "Just... untamed."

Sean felt a chill crawl up the back of his neck. The bastard knew what it was. He'd known all along what was lurking out there. "The 'wolf'?"

Jack shrugged, then held out a hand for the beer Sean was drinking. Sean let him take a sip and hand it back.

"Well," Jack said, "I call it that. But it's not really a wolf. You saw for yourself."

"It was a fucking *monster*!"

"You said it didn't hurt you."

"It licked my face!"

Jack snorted. "Better than chewing on it."

"That's not funny. You knew that thing was out there, and you didn't warn me."

"I told you to bolt the door at night."

"Like I was gonna listen to that if I thought it was just a bear or something," Sean grumbled. "You should've told me what the fuck it was."

Jack nodded and gave him a conciliatory smile. "I'm sorry. You're right. I just... didn't know what to tell you that would make sense. I was hoping you'd have enough brains to take my warning seriously."

Sean huffed out a breath. "So if it isn't a wolf, what the hell is it?"

"I don't know. It started coming around about a year after I moved in here. I guess that would make it... two years back. The first time... I was terrified." He gave Sean a gentle nudge with his elbow. "Although I don't recall pissing myself."

"Fuck you."

Jack chuckled. "I put bolts on the doors. I picked up all those books on werewolves, because... well, that's what it seemed to be, from what little I knew of it."

"It stood up!" Sean remembered. "On two legs!"

"Yeah, I know. Anyway, I hoped the books might tell me how to... banish it... get rid of it. Chase it off."

"I'm guessing they didn't," Sean muttered sarcastically.

Jack laughed and held out his hand for another swig of beer. "Nope. I tried a bunch of stuff, but nothing worked."

"Did you try silver bullets?" Sean was racking his brain for different ways to kill werewolves. All he knew was what he'd seen in a few werewolf movies, and they were probably full of shit, anyway.

Jack snorted. "Who around here makes silver bullets? Besides, I didn't want to kill it—just make it go away. After all, it never hurt me. Never hurt anyone, as far as I know."

"It slobbered all over me!" Sean said indignantly, as though a more heinous crime had never been committed. What he really meant, of course, was that he'd been terrified. The thing had literally scared the piss out of him. But he didn't particularly want to bring that up again.

Jack was unmoved. "You'll survive." He paused a moment, then added, "If this thing really is a werewolf, then it's also a man, right? Or maybe a woman. But in any case, a human being. I can't kill a human being—not just for being scary-lookin'."

Sean really didn't get why Jack was so protective of some slavering monster. Sure, it might be human during the day, but that wouldn't matter so much if it decided to chow down on their intestines tomorrow night. Still, he knew Jack could be ridiculously stubborn, so he let that drop for now.

"Who do you think it is?" he asked.

Jack looked uncomfortable. "Well… in a town this size, it's pretty much gotta be someone we know."

Shit. Sean hadn't thought of that. He'd been assuming it was some stranger from out of town wandering through. But that couldn't be the case, if the creature had been coming by Jack's cabin for two years.

"It's probably Tommy Cooper," he muttered.

Jack laughed. "Yeah, it probably is." Tommy used to harass both of them in high school for no good reason. He was a jackass.

"Look," Jack continued more seriously, "if you're really all that scared of it, you can leave. Nobody's stopping you." He handed the beer back to Sean and stood up. "Otherwise, just stay inside at night and bolt the door. You'll be all right."

He clasped Sean's shoulder a minute, then turned and went inside the cabin, though he left the door open. The knowledge that his escape route was easily accessible gave Sean the courage to remain outside a bit longer.

You can leave. Nobody's stopping you. That stung. It didn't feel so much like Jack was trying to get rid of him as he just didn't care, one way or the other. Sean finished his beer and mulled over whether Jack really wanted him there or not, and why his lack of enthusiasm was hurting so much.

Maybe I should *leave,* Sean thought. He'd expected Jack to welcome him with open arms and for things to go back to the way they'd been before. Now Sean knew he'd been naïve. Jack had been hurt a lot more by his misguided attempt to lead a "normal" life than he'd realized. He'd said he didn't want Sean to leave, necessarily, but was that the same as wanting him to stay?

The sighing sound made by the wind no longer sounded peaceful to him. It just sounded forlorn. And he was afraid the whispering might start again if he listened too long. He got up and went inside.

THE NEXT morning, Jack fried up some bacon and eggs while Sean sat on the couch, reading one of the books on werewolves. The subject had never interested him when he thought it was fantasy, but now that he knew it was real—at least, it seemed like the most plausible explanation for what the creature was—he found it much more interesting.

"You know," Jack said over his shoulder, "if you keep hanging out here, I'm gonna start making you do some of the housework, you lazy bastard."

I'll clean the whole goddamn cabin with a toothbrush, if that's what it takes to get us back to normal, Sean thought. But out loud, he just said, "I can cook better than you."

"Fine. You can cook dinner."

Sean grunted, but he was still engrossed in the book. "This says some people *deliberately* become werewolves."

"Sometimes. Other times it just happens to them."

"It says they can do it by performing magic rituals or wearing wolf skins. How the hell could *that* work? People wear wolf skins all the time—or they did before they became endangered. They didn't all turn into werewolves."

"Don't ask me," Jack answered. "I didn't write the book. Bacon's done."

"Or you can drink rainwater out of a wolf's paw print. That sounds disgusting!"

"Then don't do it. Now put the book down and come get your breakfast."

Sean closed the book and set it on top of the oak chest. But before he could do more than stand up, he heard the sound of a car pulling into the driveway. He walked up to the front window and drew aside the curtain.

"Oh, for Chrissake," he muttered. "It's Larry and Kelton again."

FORTUNATELY, JACK had made more than enough food. Kelton scoffed down a plate of bacon and scrambled eggs while his boss stood across the room, glowering at him.

"Are you sure you don't want anything?" Jack asked Larry. "A cup of coffee, at least?"

The sheriff shook his head and managed a polite smile. "No, thanks. My daughter stuffed me—and Kelton—" This with another disapproving glance at his underling. "—with pancakes a couple hours ago."

Kelton either didn't hear the disapproval in his voice, or he was ignoring him.

Larry returned to the question he'd asked earlier. "You're sure you didn't see or hear anything last night?"

"Not a thing."

It took all of Sean's willpower not to say anything, or give Jack a significant glance that Larry would surely have noticed. He wasn't sure he was fully on board with Jack's desire to keep the werewolf a secret, but he'd betrayed Jack once, and he'd be damned if he'd do it again. At least, not until the werewolf proved dangerous. So far, Larry hadn't reported anything serious—no people had been hurt, and no pets or livestock had been attacked.

On the other hand, the phrase "fool for love" did come to mind....

"Whatever that thing is," Larry said, "people are startin' to get scared of it. It came close to town last night. Knocked over Ronnie Leclair's garbage cans and set his dogs off."

"If all it's done is knock over a few trashcans, I don't see why everyone's getting so bent out of shape over it."

Larry gave Jack a sour look. "It's big. That's why. It's big and nobody knows what the hell it is—not for sure."

He glanced down at Sean, who was sitting on the couch, leaning forward to get at the plate of food he'd set on the chest. Larry seemed to notice the book beside his plate for the first time and stepped forward to pick it up. "*The Werewolf?*"

Sean laughed and tried to sound offhand as he said, "That mention of werewolves yesterday got me interested."

"Yeah," Larry said. He looked over at the bookshelves and said to Jack, "You collect stuff on that, do you?"

"Tons," Jack replied. "I love horror movies—especially werewolves."

Larry looked back at the book in his hand. "Well... I hate to disappoint you, but I'm pretty sure we're dealing with a *real* wolf. Or more likely a wolf-dog hybrid. Did I tell you we found a paw print?"

"No." Jack's voice sounded unconcerned—perhaps mildly interested—but Sean saw the muscles in his jaw tighten.

Larry set the book back on the oak chest. Then he held up his hand, fingers splayed wide. "Big as my hand."

"That's... pretty big," Sean said, struggling to keep the fear out of his voice as he recalled the creature pinning him down the night before, one of those enormous paws in the center of his chest.

"For a wolf, it's *huge*. Some dog breeds get pretty big, but that paw…. That was a wolf. No doubt in my mind."

A silence fell over everyone for a moment, while Larry appeared to be waiting for them to react, and Sean once more debated the wisdom of staying silent about the creature he'd seen last night. He had no idea what the hell Jack was thinking.

Fortunately, Kelton knew exactly what was on *his* mind. "Hey, you mind if I steal some more bacon?"

Larry frowned at him, but Jack answered, "Help yourself." Then he asked Larry, "If you find this thing, are you planning on shooting it?"

Again Sean could sense the tension behind his expression of mild curiosity.

"I hate to kill anything for no good reason," Larry said. "But people in town want it out of their hair, and they don't issue us tranquilizer guns."

AFTER THE officers finally drove off, Sean and Jack finished their breakfast and went around to the back of the cabin to finish splitting the wood. Sean had made a sizable dent in the pile of logs, and Jack seemed impressed. But he wanted to get it all taken care of by the end of the day, so they teamed up, taking turns at the splitting.

"Why don't you just tell him what you know about the creature?" Sean asked.

Jack swung the maul and wedged it firmly into a log, then lifted the two together and smashed the whole thing down hard onto the stump he was using as a base. The log split apart with a tremendous *crack*, the pieces falling to the ground on either side.

"I'm not gonna help them track it down and kill it," he replied, gasping. "I told you—it's a human being."

"That's what I'm saying. If you can convince Larry of that, maybe he *won't* kill it."

Jack split another log before replying. "Let me put it this way. That thing keeps coming back to this cabin, for whatever reason. If Larry *doesn't* believe me about it being a werewolf, but he knows I've seen it a bunch of times, he'll set up a stakeout here. Then he'll shoot it, and I'll be the one who led him right to it."

Sean didn't have a reply to that. Jack was probably right. But what if the creature did finally kill somebody? Then *that* would be Jack's fault, too—at least, indirectly. And Sean's.

"I thought you said it showed up two years ago," Sean said.

"It did."

"Then why hasn't anyone seen it before now?"

Jack paused and looked thoughtful. "I've been wondering about that. The truth is, there's a lot of forest between here and town. I figure his home base is nearby, so he's been sticking to the woods near here for a while. Something must have… agitated him or something. So now he's roaming farther away."

He said this last while looking directly at Sean, as if he thought Sean's arrival must have something to do with it.

Sean laughed nervously. "Are you blaming me for upsetting the local werewolf?"

Jack snorted and looked away. He thunked the maul into the base to wedge it there and said, "I'm beat. You up for a swim?"

CLOUDS HAD begun to roll in from the southwest by the time they'd had their fill of splashing around in the nude, and Sean thought he heard a rumble of thunder. But it didn't sound close yet.

Jack climbed out of the water and flopped down on the grassy bank. He put his arms behind his head to pillow it and gazed up at the sky. "Looks like it's gonna rain soon."

Sean got out of the water, straddled him, and then fell to his hands and knees like a dog. He shook his head violently, spraying Jack's shoulders and face with drops of water from his blond hair.

Jack laughed and scrunched his eyes shut against the onslaught. "Stop it! You mongrel!"

"What do you care? You're wet already."

"You're such a dick."

"Sorry," Sean replied with a wicked grin. "You want me to clean the water off you?"

Without waiting for a reply, he lowered his face to Jack's chest and ran his tongue along his breastbone. He knew he was taking a big risk doing that. But as he'd hoped, Jack groaned—a sound full of arousal and pent-up sexual frustration. Jack might not want to go there—not yet—but that sound left little doubt in Sean's mind that there was still desire lurking under the surface, if nothing else.

"Will you knock it off?" Jack growled.

"If you tell me you don't like it."

Jack took a very long time to respond. "I never said I didn't like it."

"Then what's the problem?"

Jack sighed and fixed him with a look. "Tell me you love me."

Now it was Sean's turn to feel uncomfortable. Men didn't say things like that to each other. He'd had that drilled into him his entire life by his father, his uncle, his classmates…. He knew it was stupid to feel that way after coming out here determined to get Jack back. He knew he *wanted* Jack. He knew he *needed* him. He'd finally been able to say "I'm gay." But "I love you"? Even knowing how much Jack needed to hear those words from him, they still stuck in his throat.

"You know I care about you," he hedged. "You know I *want* you."

Jack frowned. "That was good enough when I was eighteen. It's not anymore."

"I used to say it to Denise. But it never meant anything—it was just what husbands are supposed to say to their wives, and I knew it's what she wanted to hear…." It didn't feel right to think of saying those words to Jack, who meant everything to him. Not when they'd become tainted by so many years of falsehood. He hadn't wanted to lie to Denise. He'd *wanted* to feel what the words were saying. But he couldn't. And when he'd finally admitted it, she'd been so hurt….

He opened his mouth, trying to find a way to articulate what he was feeling, but he stopped when he heard another rumble of thunder. It was ominously close. "Shit," he said quietly, "I guess we better get inside."

Jack merely looked back at him with a sadness in his eyes that tugged at Sean's gut. *I don't want to hurt you,* Sean thought. But it was exactly that thought that prevented him from saying what he knew Jack wanted to hear. Those words had hurt Denise a lot when she'd discovered they weren't true.

He got up and began walking toward the house as the rain came down in a light summer shower. When he didn't hear Jack following, he turned to look back. Jack was still lying on the grass, his eyes closed, rainwater sprinkling against his face.

Sean waited for a while, until it was clear Jack needed some time alone. Then he turned and walked to the cabin.

Sometimes, he really hated himself.

EVEN AFTER Jack came inside and the rain began to pour down around them like a waterfall, things remained uncomfortable between them. Not exactly hostile—they spoke to each other and the conversation was friendly. But it wasn't easy. Sean was almost glad when Jack said good-night and locked himself away in his room. It still irked him that Jack seemed to think he couldn't be trusted not to sneak in during the night, but he figured they both needed a little time alone to think.

He stripped to his shorts, turned off all the lights, and lay on the couch for an hour or so in the dark, mulling things over and listening to the rain battering the shingled roof of the cabin until he finally drifted off.

THEY WERE nineteen, and the summer was coming to an end. Sean would be leaving for college in a week. It wasn't more than twenty miles away, but he'd be living in a dorm and he didn't have a car. He'd be back for holidays, but... it wouldn't be enough.

They lay in their shelter on a bed of moss and leaves, arms and legs intertwined, skin against skin. It was a chilly night, but they were warm. This was the closest Sean would ever come to heaven, and he knew it. But he was going to leave it behind because his family wanted him to go to college. He had no idea what he would study. He didn't even want to go. But he was going anyway.

"I don't know what I'll do without you here," Jack whispered.

"I won't be gone forever."

"You'll meet someone there," Jack prophesied. "You'll probably get married and have twenty kids, and I'll never see you again."

Sean laughed, but it was an awkward sound. Jack was perilously close to saying things they'd never said, and it was making him uncomfortable. He tried to make a joke out of it. "I'll name all of the kids after you—Jack, Jacqueline, Jackie, Jack Frost, Jack the Ripper...."

"I love you," Jack said suddenly.

Sean fell silent. He knew Jack wanted him to say it back, but when he opened his mouth to respond, he heard the voice of his Uncle Greg in his mind, telling him how disgusting fags were, and he shut it again. He couldn't say it. Men didn't say it to other men.

But he leaned over and kissed Jack on the mouth. He could do that.

HE WOKE to another loud bang on the door.

His first thought—felt more than articulated—was that the creature was trying to break in again. His body trembled all over as he listened for another bang, wondering if the wooden door could hold if the thing really wanted to get inside. The bolt was fastened, at least. He could see that, even in the darkened room. The rain had died down, so some moonlight was filtering through the windowpanes.

There was another bang, which made him jump, and it was followed by the door latch rattling. Then, to his surprise, he heard Larry's voice. "Jack! Sean! Are you in there?"

Jesus! Are you trying to give me a heart attack?

He jumped up, only dimly aware he was in his boxers, and unbolted the door. When he opened it, Larry burst in so fast he almost knocked him over. The officer whirled around and shined his flashlight directly in Sean's face—which caused him physical pain this soon after waking—and then spun around to scan the room with it.

"Where's Jack?"

He sounded frantic. He was also soaking wet, just like Kelton, who'd followed him inside.

"Sleeping," Sean said, pointing to the bedroom door.

Larry rushed to the door and pounded on it with his fist. "Jack! Are you okay in there?"

"Why the hell wouldn't he be?" Sean was back to being alarmed.

While Larry continued to pound on the door and shout for Jack to open up, Kelton explained breathlessly, "We came across that thing in the woods near here and shot it! Then it took off in this direction. We caught up to it just as it jumped through one of the cabin windows!"

"What?" Sean gasped.

But there wasn't time to think about the implications of that before Larry kicked the bedroom door hard with a muddy boot and splintered the bolt. The door swung inward, and all three men rushed to see what lay on the other side.

Sean was terrified they'd find Jack torn to shreds, the creature hunched over him with gore dripping from its fangs. But apart from the wide open window, and the water all over the sill and the floor near it, nothing seemed amiss. Jack was there, lying naked on the bed, the sheets and blankets kicked off in his sleep.

He was facing away from them, but as they entered, he turned his head to look over his shoulder and asked sleepily, "What the hell are you guys doing in here?"

"Oh, jeez!" Kelton whined, shielding his eyes with one hand.

Larry looked back and forth between Jack and the open window, dumbfounded. Sean wasn't sure he knew what to make of the situation either, especially the fact that Jack was still lying there as if two police officers bursting into his room was nothing unusual. He wasn't making any move to cover himself, or jumping up and shouting for them to get the fuck out, or anything.

Why is he just lying there?

"Sorry," Kelton said uncomfortably. "Uh… maybe we should go…."

Larry ignored him. He swept the flashlight beam around the room, bringing it to rest on the windowsill. There was something dark there.

"Uh…. Larry?"

Larry moved into the room, his eyes focused on the windowsill, and Sean followed him, a knot of dread growing in his chest. The smudge on the sill was mud. Sean was no detective, but he knew there was no way it could have gotten there without someone—or some*thing*—coming in from the outside.

Larry directed the light to the floor, where it revealed massive muddy paw prints. Worse, there were spatters of blood on the floor around them. As the sheriff moved the light along the floor, it became clear that the trail of prints led directly to the bed. Larry and Sean approached the bed until the flashlight clearly illuminated Jack. From this angle, he was unable to hide the blood that pooled around his body on the mattress.

The three men stared at each other silently—Sean, and probably Larry as well, struck dumb by the sheer horror of the situation, and Jack trembling in obvious fear.

Fear of us, Sean thought. Afraid Larry would raise his gun and empty the magazine into Jack's gut. *He's the monster!* Sean felt his world spinning, and he had to brace himself against the dresser to keep from falling over. Even at that, his knees still threatened to give out underneath him.

Finally, Larry spoke, his voice quiet and surprisingly gentle. "Is everything all right, son?"

Jack glanced at Sean, his eyes pleading, though for what, Sean wasn't sure. "Yes."

"You sure?"

"Yes. Everything's fine." He was gritting his teeth against the pain, making his voice sound strained and clipped.

Larry gave him a long, evaluating look. Abruptly, he said, "Sorry for disturbing you. We'll let you sleep."

He gripped Sean's elbow and yanked him away from the dresser, forcibly steering him around the bed toward the door. The two of them practically ran over Kelton in the doorway.

When the door was closed behind them, Larry pulled Sean away from it and asked in a low voice, "Do you want a lift into town, son?"

Kelton looked completely baffled. From his vantage point in the doorway, he couldn't have seen the blood or Jack's injured state. "Why would he want that in the middle of the night?"

Larry was looking intently into Sean's eyes. They knew. They both knew. And while Sean's head reeled with the knowledge that Jack and the beast were somehow—impossibly—one and the same, and Jack was now seriously wounded and possibly dying in the next room, he had enough presence of mind to recognize what Larry was really asking.

Do you want to escape before he changes again and maybe kills you?

Would Jack really kill him? He'd been lying to Sean for the past few days—pretending he had no idea who the werewolf was. Had he also lied about it being harmless? Was he capable of killing people? Had he *already* killed people?

Is he planning on killing me?

Even as the question flashed through his mind, Sean knew he didn't believe it. Not Jack. They'd been best friends all their lives. *Lovers* ever since that fateful camping trip. Sure, things were strained between them at the moment, but.... Jack? A killer? It didn't register.

It must not have made sense to Larry either, or he wouldn't have left the bedroom without arresting Jack. Or at least doing *something*. Instead he'd hid it from Kelton, protected Jack. He'd known Jack and Sean for their entire lives, and right then he seemed to be gambling on what he knew of Jack's character. But he also seemed to be assuming Sean was an innocent bystander in this little horror movie drama, and he was offering Sean a chance to escape, if he wanted it.

"Thanks," Sean heard himself saying, almost as if it was somebody else talking, "but I think I'm okay."

Am I?

Larry nodded slowly and turned to walk out of the cabin. Kelton still seemed baffled by his partner's behavior, but he gave Sean an embarrassed wave and said, "Sorry to disturb you."

"No problem."

Sean stood in the open doorway a moment, watching the two policemen get into their cruiser and drive off. He needed to get back to Jack, see what he could do to help him, but it was hard to move from that spot. He was acutely aware that there was no cell phone reception out there, no landline, and his car probably didn't have enough gas to make it to town if he needed to escape.

WHEN HE returned to Jack's bedroom, Sean found Jack sitting up in the bed with the reading lamp on the nightstand turned on. He was sitting in a pool of blood, and it was more or less all over his body and hands, but he was conscious, examining the wound in the lamplight.

He looked up when Sean approached and said, "I think I need some help."

Sean gazed back at him, the horror of the scene making his skin prickle, before the more practical part of his brain was able to assert itself and send him running for a clean washcloth and a bowl of warm water. And maybe some rubbing alcohol and bandages.

The wound turned out to be far less severe than it seemed. Once the blood was washed off, Sean discovered it was just one gash in Jack's side. It was deep and probably needed stitches, but he was able to sterilize it somewhat with the alcohol, making Jack gasp in pain, and then put a large bandage over it with antiseptic ointment on the inner side. He fastened that in place with gauze bandaging, wrapped around Jack's middle.

While he was taping that in place, Sean tried to joke about the whole situation. "I thought werewolves couldn't be harmed by regular bullets."

"That would be incorrect," Jack said, wincing. Then, after a long uncomfortable silence, he added, "You seem to be taking this well."

"Am I? I suppose this is better than having a giant monster chase me around the cabin until I piss myself."

Jack grunted and looked away, as if embarrassed. "I'm sorry about that."

"Why did you lie to me?" There was a note of shrillness in Sean's voice. He felt as if he might lose it at any second.

"I guess I was hoping I could introduce you to the idea gradually. I didn't want to scare you."

"Well I'm scared *now*, okay?" Sean snapped. "I have no idea how dangerous you are when you change into that thing."

"I could never hurt you, Sean. You saw that for yourself."

"Maybe you just weren't hungry that night."

"Or maybe I just *love you*," Jack said impatiently, "and I would never hurt you."

For all of Sean's agonizing about not being able to say those words himself, he realized this was the first time *Jack* had said them since he'd arrived here. It was good to hear.

"How did this happen, Jack? Did you learn some kind of magic spell from those books?"

Jack shook his head. "No. It was the forest. I told you it was calling to us. All those years camping out in the woods when we were kids, I could hear it calling to me—to both of us—and there were some nights when it felt like the only thing keeping me from getting up and just walkin'... never coming back... was I didn't want to leave you."

Sean felt a twinge of fear at that—at the thought of Jack disappearing from his life forever. He realized he'd always been afraid of that, of Jack just walking into the forest and never coming back.

"Then I ended up out here on my own," Jack went on. "And I was more or less completely isolated. I barely saw anyone except for the work I did now and then to get a little cash—that, and Larry swinging by to make sure I hadn't shot myself in the head or something."

"I'm sorry," Sean said.

Jack quirked up a corner of his mouth at him and shook his head. "No. That's the thing. I didn't mind it. I felt at home out here. At peace. And at some point... it was like it took me over. When I said the creature started showing up a couple years ago, what I really meant was... that's when I started to *change*."

"How?" Sean asked.

"I don't know. But I'd go to bed and wake up outside, naked. At first I didn't remember anything the next morning. But eventually things started coming back to me, like remembering a dream."

Jack's face lit up while he talked about it, as if he were describing a religious experience. And maybe, for him, it was. The spirit of the forest had finally revealed itself to him and made him one of its own.

"Are you fully conscious now, when you're the wolf?" Sean asked.

Jack shook his head. "Not really. Nothing real clear, or I wouldn't have come in and scared you that night. I just… wanted to be with you."

Sean laughed. "Jesus." That was oddly sweet, though still terrifying.

He stood up and began to pull the bloody sheets off the bed, more for something to do than anything else. He felt as if his brain was overloading with all of this. Jack lifted his ass so Sean could get the sheets out from under him.

"In the beginning," Jack went on, "I was pretty frightened. That's when I bought most of those books, hoping I could find a way to cure it. But most of them say the only cure is death, or permanent maiming."

"Maiming?"

"In folklore, a hunter often cuts off the paw of a wolf, only to find the wolf transforming into a naked human being—missing a hand, of course."

"That would suck."

"Pretty much," Jack agreed. He hesitated, then said, "After a while I stopped looking for a cure. I wasn't killing people, and I enjoyed being a wolf."

"Why?"

Jack's face took on that vaguely religious look again. "It's wonderful, Sean. You have no idea! The things you can see, the smells on the wind, the strength and energy flowing through you! The *freedom*!"

"The bullet wounds," Sean replied sarcastically.

Jack raised a hand to touch the bandage, a bit more subdued. "It barely grazed me."

Part of Sean understood. He'd always loved the time they'd spent in the forest when they were boys. Partly because he'd been with Jack, of course, but also he'd loved the scents of pine and earth, the sounds of wind in the trees and the streams near their camping places. And the peace he'd always felt there.

Sean lifted the bloody sheets in his arms. "Look at this!" he exclaimed, trying to shift the conversation back to something less ethereal. "How can you call yourself a gay man, when you don't even care your best sheets have been ruined!"

Jack laughed. "I'm not that kind of gay man. Are you?"

Sean smiled back a little ruefully. "Probably not. But I've been fucking around with you since we were fifteen. I guess that makes me *some* kind of gay man."

"It never mattered to me what we called it," Jack said. "But there's one thing I want stated out loud, and you know what it is."

Sean did. And he thought maybe he could say it now. But the moment he opened his mouth, there was a knock on the front door.

SEAN DARTED out into the living room and peered through the curtains at the window. "Shit! Larry's back!" He turned to see Jack standing naked in the bedroom doorway, clutching his bandaged side. He was still pretty bloody, despite Sean's attempts at wiping him off. "You'd better cover that bandage up."

Jack shook his head stubbornly. "No."

"Well, at least put some pants on, dumbass. Larry probably doesn't want to see your dork twice in one night."

While Jack disappeared back into the bedroom, Sean went to the door and opened it. Larry was caught in the act of raising his hand to knock again. He hesitated, then put his hand down.

"Evenin'."

"Hi," Sean replied.

"Sorry to bother you again at this hour, but somehow I figured you'd still be up."

Sean nodded and stepped aside. "Come on in."

"Thank you."

Larry entered as Jack came out of the bedroom, still shirtless, but at least wearing jeans. They glanced at each other uncomfortably, and Jack started to raise a hand to the bandage, but stopped himself. Larry nodded at him, as if everything was normal. But all three men knew things had shifted radically that evening.

"What can we do for you, Larry?" Jack asked.

"I told Kelton I was going home after I dropped him off," Larry said, "but I thought maybe you and I should have a little talk instead."

"About what?"

Larry glanced at Sean, and then his attention seemed to be caught by Sean's hands. Sean looked down to discover they were still covered in Jack's blood. "Uh… excuse me."

He walked over to the sink in the kitchenette while Larry continued, "I shot something tonight—something I know wasn't a man. It was dark, sure, and it was raining. But… that thing wasn't human." As he spoke, he began to drift around the living room, glancing at the couch, the oak chest, as if he were taking in the décor. "I followed it right to this cabin here. I saw it jump in through the window. But you know what I found when I went inside? Not an animal. Not a… *monster*. Just my good friend, Jack." He paused when he reached the bookcase. "Who happens to have a pretty impressive collection of stuff about werewolves. And who, coincidentally, has somehow been injured in his left side—the exact same spot I could swear my bullet grazed that animal."

Jack did bring his hand up then to rest on the bandage. "It's just a nick. I'll be fine."

Larry picked up one of the figurines on the bookshelf, a werewolf that appeared to be lunging and snarling ferociously. "I'm glad to hear that."

"Larry…." Jack took a step toward the sheriff. "You've known me my entire life. You know I'd never hurt anyone."

Larry's attention appeared to be occupied by the figurine's vicious countenance. "Not under normal circumstances…."

"*Never.*"

Larry placed the figurine back on the shelf and turned to face Jack. "This is a rural area, son. Everybody and his kid brother owns a gun. Even if Kelton and I stop hunting… this thing… sooner or later, if it keeps showin' its face around here, somebody's gonna put a bullet in it." He paused, distracted by Sean tossing the towel he was drying his hands on down and coming to join them. Then he looked back at Jack. "If this thing really is harmless, then that would be pretty tragic. Don't you think?"

Sean felt a twinge of fear at that. Larry was right. Jack didn't appear to have any supernatural healing abilities or immunities to weapons. If that bullet had hit him in the head….

Jack nodded slowly. "Yes. I do."

Larry sighed and walked to the front door. He placed a hand on the handle but paused to say, "I don't know what can be done about that. It's just what I'm thinking about right now." He smiled sadly. "Anyway, I should be getting home to bed. You two have a nice night."

"Good night," Jack said.

A moment later, the sheriff was gone.

"WELL, THAT was fucked up," Sean muttered.

"He's right. People are on the alert now. I'm gambling with my life every night I stay in the area." He turned and walked into the bedroom.

Sean called after him, "Can't you just stick close to the cabin?" When Jack didn't reply, he followed him into the room. He found Jack trying to lift the edge of the mattress, but not having an easy time of it. "Stop that, you jackass! You're gonna make yourself bleed again!"

Jack eased up, wincing against the pain. "I'm just trying to flip it over, so I don't have to sleep in a pool of blood."

"Get out of the way. I'll do it."

Wrestling with the mattress was really a two-man job—it was more of a heavy futon than a mattress, and annoyingly floppy—so it was a pain in the ass doing it by himself. But better that than Jack bleeding all over the place and dying. So Sean managed.

Jack stood there watching him, looking frustrated. "No, I can't just stick close to the cabin. If I had that much control over what the beast does, I wouldn't be rooting through people's garbage at night."

"Dude! That's disgusting."

Jack shrugged as if to say, "A werewolf's gotta do what a werewolf's gotta do."

"You just started doing that," Sean pointed out. "Ever since... well I guess since I showed up."

Jack kept his expression blank, but he glanced away guiltily, and Sean knew he'd been thinking the same thing.

Sean didn't want to say it, but he had to. "Maybe if I go away.... Maybe that will calm the wolf down, so he'll stop roaming."

"No," Jack said adamantly. "It won't."

"How do you know?"

"Okay. Yes. Maybe you showing up put me off balance," Jack said. "But it'll just get worse, if you leave now."

"You don't—"

"Sean!" Jack practically snarled. "Do you really think the wolf will be happy if you walk out on me... *again*?"

That brought Sean up short. He looked away, embarrassed. In the uncomfortable silence that fell between them, Jack went to the closet and pulled some fresh sheets off a shelf.

"I just... I thought you loved this place," Sean said quietly.

"What I love is the forest. I only love the cabin because it's in the forest." Jack tossed the sheets on the bed. "The forest has been calling to me since we were kids. You know that. I kept asking you to come with me. After you left... I wanted to just give in, run off into the woods and never come back."

The thought of Jack disappearing—really disappearing, forever—made Sean's stomach clench. "That's pretty much what you did, isn't it?"

"No. I bought a cabin in the woods, but it's not the same. As long as I stay here, I still have ties to people in Dunkirk."

"That's not so—"

"I kept those ties because of *you*," Jack interrupted, sounding impatient, almost angry. "I was afraid to go somewhere you could never find me again, because I was stupid enough to think you'd come back for me someday."

That revelation dropped between them, cold and hard like a stone, causing both men to fall silent again. Jack busied himself with flipping the sheets open onto the bed. It wasn't that Sean hadn't known how much Jack needed him. They'd just never laid it out like this, raw and exposed. Sean felt his face stinging as if he'd been slapped.

But I did come back, even if it took me a while. I'm here!

Jack said gruffly, "Help me with this."

Sean obeyed, finding a corner of the fitted sheet and hooking it over one corner of the mattress, while Jack did the same with the opposite corner. They fastened down the remaining corners, and then Jack picked up the top sheet. He held on to one corner and tossed another to Sean, but when he moved to tuck it under the mattress, Sean pulled on his end, drawing the sheet taut between them.

"What are you doing?" Jack asked.

Sean's gaze fixed on his, and he said softly, "I want to sleep in here tonight."

Jack was silent for a long time before finally wrenching his gaze away from Sean's. He let out a breath and replied, "God, Sean. You don't know how much I want that. But I can't. The change tends to come over me while I'm sleeping...."

Sean pulled gently on the sheet, reeling it in until Jack was forced to kneel on the mattress to avoid falling face forward onto it. Sean met him halfway across. "Then how about I go back to the couch after I've had my way with you," he said, trying to sound lighthearted, though he felt as if he'd fall apart if Jack locked him out one more time.

"I'm injured."

"I'll be gentle."

Jack gave him a tolerant smile. "You're such an asshole."

Then he leaned forward and kissed Sean on the mouth.

SEAN TRIED to do all the work. He laid Jack out on the mattress and kissed and caressed every inch of his smooth, sun-bronzed skin, wanting to keep him still so he wouldn't make the injury worse. But when he took Jack's thick, hardened cock into his mouth, relishing the familiarity of it, Jack grabbed his hips and pulled him around so Sean could straddle his head. Sean felt the hot dampness of Jack's mouth engulf him, and he moaned.

God, I've missed you. How could I have ever thought I'd be happy without this?

As teenagers, it had been enough to bring each other off with their mouths or their hands, but Sean yearned for more now. They caressed each other's thighs and hips and asses, but the touch wasn't enough. Sean could feel a hollowness in his belly, a longing to merge their two bodies together. It was so powerful it ached.

He let Jack's cock slip from his mouth in order to lick farther down, bathing Jack's tightened ball sac with his tongue. When Jack lifted his legs on either side of Sean's head, Sean didn't hesitate to move lower, lapping along the hardened muscle there until his tongue plunged into Jack's puckered hole. Jack's moan vibrated his cock and rippled up the length of his body. Sean plunged his tongue in deeper, savoring the sweet muskiness he found there.

It wasn't the first time they'd done this. Both had tasted the other intimately. But there was one thing they'd never done with each other. It had seemed too forbidden.

But now Jack pulled his mouth off Sean's cock for a moment to gasp, "Fuck me."

"Have you ever done it?" He felt a surge of jealousy at the thought of Jack with another man—especially doing *that*. But he could hardly have blamed him.

"No," Jack sighed. "But I've always wanted you to do it. I've fantasized about it forever."

Sean had never done it either, but he was fine with the idea of trying, if it would make Jack happy. He licked his forefinger and slowly slid it into Jack's slicked hole, eliciting another moan.

"Yes," Jack breathed.

They did that for a while, Sean uncertain how much preparation Jack would need to take something as thick as a penis. He tried adding fingers, but discovered saliva didn't quite make it slippery enough.

"Do you have any lube?" he asked.

"No. See what you can find in the kitchen."

It was hard to stay aroused while searching cupboards, but fortunately it didn't take long to locate a bottle of vegetable oil. Soon Sean was back in the bedroom, his cock quickly hardening again in Jack's mouth while he slid two greased fingers into his friend's backside. After he'd worked his way up to three fingers, he figured Jack should be able to take him.

Since Jack was already lying on his back, Sean simply kneeled between his legs, then moved forward until Jack's thighs were draped over his and Jack's ass was lifted slightly, his hole positioned near Sean's crotch. Sean entered easily, grunting as Jack's body squeezed his shaft tightly. Jack gritted his teeth and hissed.

"Are you okay?"

"Yes," Jack said. "Give me more."

Sean pushed in deeper, moving slowly, watching Jack's face closely as he tried to keep him on the thin line between pleasure and pain without going over it. Every time he paused, Jack would breathe a moment and tell him to keep going, until Sean was completely inside. Then Sean began to move.

It was amazing. Yes, Sean had fucked before, but it had never felt like this. It had been something physical, and it had felt good, but nothing more. Now he felt a surge of energy and emotion building in every part of his body, spreading from his groin into his torso, filling up his chest with a warmth and so much joy and love—yes, love!—for this man it was almost agonizing. It spilled over and flooded his limbs, making his arms quiver as he balanced on one hand and stroked Jack's cock with his other.

Jack erupted first, crying out as he sprayed his stomach and Sean's arm, coating Sean's hand with thick cum. They hadn't used a condom. Neither had even thought about it. So when Sean shuddered a moment later with his own release, it felt as if he were flooding Jack's insides and claiming him.

I love you! I will always love you!

But he couldn't speak it. He was unable to speak at all.

LATER THEY lay together in the dark, the sheets thrown off skin damp from making love on a muggy summer night, but arms and legs intertwined because the contact mattered more than the heat. Sean had been craving Jack's touch ever since he'd arrived—ever since the last time they'd been together in the forest, really. Though maturity and awareness of his feelings had lent an intensity to this night that he'd never felt before. He hadn't known what he was doing, fumbling around with Jack as a teenager. Now he knew. And it was so much better, knowing.

"Don't fall asleep," Jack warned.

"You're the one who can't fall asleep, Fido."

Jack snorted. "Jackass."

"Spot."

"Asshole."

"Tintin."

"Tintin's human. I think you mean Rin Tin Tin."

"That too," Sean said, giggling like a little kid.

Jack ended the game by leaning in to kiss him. Sean savored the kiss for as long as possible before Jack pulled away.

Then Sean whispered as he trailed his fingers along the curve of Jack's naked hip, "You didn't make me say it."

Jack didn't pretend not to know what Sean meant. The moonlight coming through the window illuminated his face as he gazed back at Sean. "It doesn't matter now."

"Why not?"

"Because what I wanted when I told you to say it… I know I'll never have that now."

"What did you want?"

"For you to come with me."

Sean didn't know if he could do that. It was one thing to live in the woods for a summer. Sure, that could be fun. But all the time? "Can't we just move somewhere else?" he asked.

Jack shook his head.

"Or maybe I could lock you up at night," Sean said, "so you couldn't get out."

Jack looked appalled at that. "Every goddamn night? Chained up while the forest is calling to me? You don't know what you're asking."

"Then…." There wasn't any other option. Sean knew that. He didn't want to lose Jack again—certainly not forever—and he sure as hell didn't want some idiot putting a bullet through his skull. "Fine," he said. "Take me with you."

Jack looked at him for a very long time. Then he climbed out of the bed and walked over to the window. It was still open, and he stood, looking out at the woodpile behind the cabin and the forest beyond.

At last he said, "I want to. But you've never been out there in the winter. You don't know how rough it can get."

"You haven't been out in the winter either."

"Yes, I have," Jack replied, turning back to look at him. "Not for more than a week or so at a stretch, but I've done that much."

"So you'll teach me what you know, and we'll figure out the rest. But at least we'll be together." When Jack still seemed uncertain, he added, "I love you, Jack."

Jack didn't react the way he'd hoped he would. There was no rushing into his arms, no ecstatic "I love you" in return, no tears of joy. Just a noncommittal "huh" as Jack directed his gaze out the window again.

"What do you mean, 'huh'? I thought you wanted me to say it."

"Only if you meant it."

Sean growled in frustration. "I *do* mean it, you idiot!"

"We just had sex," Jack replied. "Everybody loves you after you fuck them—or let them fuck *you*. Wait until morning, and then see how you feel."

"I don't need to wait. I know how I feel." Sean sat up on the edge of the bed. "Look, Jack. I'm sorry I panicked when you asked me to say it down by the pond. But for four years I slept with a woman I *thought* I loved, except that it never felt right. We never connected. I thought for a while it was her fault—that she didn't love me. But it wasn't her." He stood up and took a couple tentative steps forward, feeling as if Jack might leap out the window and bolt if he didn't approach slowly. He gestured back toward the bed. "Laying there with you tonight... I was in heaven. I wanted to stay there forever, pressed up against you. I'm not confused at all anymore. I know I'm in love with you. I was in love with you when we were nineteen. I was just too stupid to know it."

He was close enough now to see Jack's face in profile as he smiled sadly and shook his head. "Even if... that's true... I'm talkin' about going way up north, Sean, deep into the forest, as far away from people as I can get. And half the time I'll be an animal. If you came along, you'd be isolated from everybody—even from me, a good bit of the time. It would be a lonely, miserable life for you."

"What if I was like you?" Sean asked in a last fit of desperation.

"Like me?"

"A werewolf. Can't you make me one? Then we'd both change at night, and you wouldn't have to leave me behind when you hunted."

"You've lost your mind."

"Why?" Sean asked. "Didn't you say it was wonderful?"

"It is."

"Then let me experience it!"

Jack sighed and frowned. "I don't know how, even if I wanted to. I already told you, nobody made me a werewolf. It just happened. I have no idea how to make you one too."

"You could try, couldn't you?" Sean pleaded. "You could bite me or something." He wasn't a total coward. He could handle a single bite wound.

Jack seemed to be mulling it over. In the silence that fell between them, Sean became aware of the sounds of the forest outside the window—the wind in the trees, the hooting of an owl, even the sound of water still dripping off branches. And beneath it he could hear the faint whispering again. Would this be the soundtrack of his life from now on? The music of the forest replacing the music he had on his iPhone? Forever?

Will we never have beer*?* That was almost incomprehensible.

"You're not ready," Jack said, as if he'd been reading Sean's mind and watching the doubts scroll by.

But that just made Sean stubborn. "That's my decision, isn't it?"

"I suppose," Jack said doubtfully. "But it isn't easy, Sean. Becoming a wolf…. That scared the shit out of me, even though I always thought I'd like the idea."

"So you'll help me through it."

"You're just being contrary."

"You bet your sweet ass," Sean said. "Now change me into a werewolf before I punch you."

That made Jack laugh and broke some of the tension. He groaned and leaned forward to rest his forehead against Sean's. "I want to…."

"Then do it."

NEITHER OF them really thought it would work for Jack to bite Sean when he was human, but they decided to try it anyway. Jack brushed his teeth first to hopefully decrease the chance of infection. It felt ludicrous.

The whole thing did. But Sean knew it was the only way they'd be able to stay together.

It hurt like a son-of-a-bitch. Jack bit him on his left forearm, where it would be easy for Sean to clean and dress the wound, and he bit *hard*. There was no point in being half-assed about it. It bled a lot, and even after they'd cleaned the bite with rubbing alcohol and covered it with bandages, Sean could feel it throbbing.

But he didn't change.

"Maybe I have to sleep on it," he suggested.

"Maybe," Jack said dubiously. "Or maybe it just didn't work."

"Have you ever read anything in those books about someone becoming a werewolf like this?" Sean asked. "By being bitten by someone who's a werewolf, but when they're in human form?"

Jack sighed and shook his head. It was beginning to grow light outside, and they were both getting tired. Not to mention the fact that they were now *both* injured and in pain. "Not that I remember. People in the folktales are always bitten by an animal and then discover afterward that the animal was a werewolf."

"Then you'll have to change."

Jack seemed to be thinking it over for a bit before he said, "I might be able to. I tried a couple times, and it seemed like the change *started*, at any rate. But I'm afraid I might hurt you."

Sean was afraid of that too. But he didn't want Jack to know that. "You said you remember things from when you're… transformed. Do you remember the night you licked my face?"

"Yeah," Jack said, smiling. "I remember that."

"What was going through your head then? Did you want to hurt me?"

Jack shook his head adamantly. "No. I was curious about you. You seemed familiar. And I liked the smell of you."

"Then doesn't that mean you won't hurt me?"

Jack gazed intently into his eyes, perhaps trying to divine how much faith Sean really did have in his ability to keep him safe. They'd turned on the table lamp earlier, so they could see to tend to the bite wound, but now he leaned over and flicked it off.

"Go stand near the window," he said.

Sean obeyed, a nervous quivering welling up in his stomach as he stared out into the gray predawn light. The bullfrogs had gone silent, but some of the morning birds had begun chirping. There was a thick mist hanging over everything. He felt as if he'd just agreed to surgery without anesthetic. Had he really asked Jack to turn into a monster and *bite* him? He remembered the sight of that mouthful of fangs snarling at him just before the creature—Jack—had licked his face. Knowing that it had been Jack only made the memory slightly less terrifying.

I must be insane.

Jack came up behind him and said in a low voice, "Try not to move. I need to sort of… meditate. Don't make any noise."

It wasn't like any meditation Sean had ever heard of. He could hear Jack breathing behind him, slow and deep, but while he was doing that, he was pacing slowly back and forth. He was very close to Sean, and his warm, naked body frequently brushed against Sean's ass or back. When it did, Jack seemed to be sniffing him, running his nose along Sean's shoulders and up Sean's neck into his hair. It was intensely erotic, and Sean's cock grew harder with each featherlight touch. Almost against his will, Sean closed his eyes, carried off into a meditation of his own, a trance induced by gentle caresses.

Jack ran his tongue along the base of Sean's neck, and Sean couldn't help shivering. "Is that part of the meditation?"

"Shh…."

Chastised, Sean shut his mouth against the desire to moan as Jack licked him again.

Jack began to run his fingers along Sean's arms, tracing paths along them with his fingertips… or rather his fingernails… while he nuzzled Sean's neck. It felt good, even when the nails began to scrape a bit, as if they were lengthening, growing sharper. Jack's breathing grew stronger, more like panting.

A low, soft rumbling behind Sean set his hair on end. It wasn't a human sound. It was the sound an animal like a wolf or a dog made deep within its chest, a menacing sound, a warning before the attack. Jack's breath was hot against his bare flesh, but it no longer felt sexual.

It felt hungry.

The creature snarled, and Sean wrenched himself away, screaming in terror. There was no place to go. He slammed into the wall beside the window and turned, quivering with fear, expecting fangs and claws to fall on him and rend his flesh.

Jack stood still in the moonlight, his hands clenched into fists as hair grew *into* his body, withdrawing into his naked skin like the hair on the giant doll's head Sean's sister had played with as a kid. Sean might have found that thought funny, but his heart was racing, and he was too horrified by what was happening to Jack's *face.*

A second ago, it had probably looked more like a wolf, but now it was in the process of retreating back to the visage of a man. The resultant half-wolf, half-man he saw now nauseated Sean more than the twisted things he'd once seen in jars at a freak show—made worse by the fact that it was *changing*, contorting as he watched, making him want to scream in the most primal depths of his consciousness....

Then it was over. Jack was Jack again, naked and glistening with sweat in the moonlight. He was panting, and when he took a step forward, he staggered and had to grasp the window frame to keep from collapsing.

I failed. The realization washed over Sean with a sickening certainty. He'd had the chance, but he'd lost his nerve. His voice was small and defeated when he said, "I'm sorry...."

"It's okay."

"I'm so sorry—"

"I understand." Jack took a deep breath and steadied himself. Then he reached out a hand.

Sean took his hand, but when Jack tried to pull him forward, he held back, trembling. Jack gave him a wounded look, and that broke through the fear. He folded himself into Jack's arms and buried his face in Jack's shoulder.

"I'm sorry," he whispered, his eyes stinging with tears.

"Shh," Jack hushed him, petting his hair affectionately. "It's okay."

But Sean knew it wasn't okay. It was good-bye.

SEAN WOKE to discover the sunlight coming into the room was almost directly under the window, which meant it had to be nearly noon. He and Jack had fallen asleep just as the sky had turned rosy at sunrise. He still felt as if he could sleep several more hours, but a vague sense of alarm filtered through his grogginess and jolted him wide-awake.

He was alone in the bed.

"Jack!"

No answer. Sean sat upright and called again, but he knew—the cabin was empty. He could *feel* it. The small trash can beside the bed held the bandages he'd used on Jack's wound the night before, balled up and spattered with dried blood.

Then he saw the note on the night table.

Sean, I'm sorry. I have to go, and we both know you can't come with me. I love you—you know that, right? More than I can put into words. But I can feel the forest calling me. I can feel the wolf pacing inside me, wanting to be let out. I think it might take me over completely someday. And if that happens, I don't think I'll mind.

But it means we can't be together. I know it's cowardly to disappear without saying good-bye, but I knew I'd never be able to do it if you woke up and begged me to stay.

Don't feel guilty anymore. I forgive you, and I know how you feel about me.

I'll always love you. Nobody but you.

Jack

Sean ran out into the living area, and then flung open the door to burst naked out onto the porch, shouting though he knew it was futile. Jack's truck was still parked in the driveway, but nothing came back from the surrounding forest but the songs of birds and the nattering of squirrels. Jack was gone. The bastard had left him behind.

The pond! He didn't know why he thought Jack might be there. It made little sense. But maybe he'd stopped to get a drink of water or… something….

Holding on to that ridiculously scant fragment of hope, Sean ran down the path, his bare feet slipping in the mud. Everything was wet from last night's rain—the earth, the leaves that whipped his naked body as he ran, the grass near the water's edge.

Jack wasn't there. Of course not. Why would he be? By now he was probably miles away, running on all fours.

Sean collapsed on his knees, despair overwhelming him. *Why was I such a fucking coward?*

He'd had the chance, and he'd blown it. A few seconds longer, the pain of one bite—that's all it might have taken. And then he'd be with Jack right now.

Jack, who'd always been the center of his life, even when Sean was too stupid to see it, the one person Sean had thought he could always come home to. Sean knew he was self-centered, a bit of an asshole. But Jack had always been there for him—even this time, when Sean had shown up on his doorstep unannounced, not having talked to him for almost four years. The thought of him being gone forever was excruciating.

The one time I tried to sacrifice my own needs for his, and I failed.

Perhaps it was his self-centered nature, but Sean refused to accept this. He refused to believe it was over, less than twenty-four hours after he'd finally wrapped his head around the fact that he was in love with Jack—that he'd always been in love with him.

The books.

People didn't have to get bitten to become werewolves. There were all kinds of ways. Some of them were pretty much impossible for Sean— he wasn't likely to find a wolf skin to wear or make a belt out of. At least not in a reasonable amount of time. He needed to do it fast, if he were to have any hope of finding Jack before he disappeared up north into hundreds of miles of forest in New Hampshire or Maine or the thousands of miles of forest in Canada.

He took a step on the rain-drenched grass, and the answer came into his head immediately. Turning, he raced back to the cabin.

It was there, in the mud near the woodpile—one massive footprint. Or rather, paw print. Just as Larry had described it—as large as Sean's hand with the fingers splayed out. There were other prints, of course, running between the forest and the open window to Jack's bedroom, but this one was clear and unmistakable. It could be nothing other than a massive wolf.

And it was full of rainwater.

Still naked, Sean fell to his knees, and then leaned over the print on all fours. Part of his mind was yelling at him to get up out of the mud, clean himself up, and put some goddamn clothes on, but he forced himself to ignore it. He'd chickened out once too often. Not this time.

The rainwater tasted exactly as he'd expected it to. Muddy. But he drank as much as he could. He felt ridiculous, but he kept at it until he was licking up more mud than water.

He lifted his head, unsure what to do next, but he didn't have to think about that for long. Something was different. He was hit with a wave of smells, as if he'd opened a window and a fresh breeze had carried the scents of mud and pine and cut wood and... *everything*... to his nostrils. It was overwhelming at first, making him dizzy.

Then the sounds. He heard a cardinal flutter down onto the woodpile, then take off again. A chipmunk scurried along the base of the pile and *chittered* at him a moment. The wind in the branches, the rainwater still dripping off the eaves of the cabin roof, the drone of a plane high overhead, the cawing of crows in the front of the cabin, the cabin door softly banging in its frame because Sean hadn't closed it properly and the wind was agitating it....

And the whispering, growing in volume until it was louder than he'd ever heard it before. It came from the forest on all sides of him, and now he could distinguish words—*Come, Sean! This is your home! It has always been your home!* He'd never heard voices so beautiful. They seemed to reach into his soul and tug on it. This is what Jack had been hearing all this time. It was what he'd been feeling. Sean finally understood.

As he lowered his head again, he detected a scent to the paw print. It had been hidden beneath the smell of mud and water before, but now it came to Sean's nostrils as clear as strong perfume—the smell of Jack, the smell of the *wolf.*

Sean was barely conscious of his nasal passages lengthening as he inhaled the scent, of his face elongating. He was too excited by the smell. He could smell it coming from the bedroom window, and it was all around the area near the woodpile. He moved to follow it, his gait becoming more fluid as his arms and legs evened out, as the muscles grew larger in his shoulders and hips, and fingers withdrew to make forepaws more suitable for running.

He ran then, around the woodpile, following the scent. At the edge of the forest, he paused, snuffling around on the ground until he found it— a trail of odors leading off to the north. The scent of Jack's paws on the ground, of his fur brushing against the witch hazel bushes, of a spray of urine where he'd marked an oak tree. Without a second's thought, Sean plunged into the undergrowth. He ran, exhilarated, sniffing frantically at everything he passed, the path Jack took as clear to him as if it had been marked by blazing torches.

There was little thought in the mind of the wolf that had been Sean. All else had faded away, leaving just the one driving need—a need no longer able to be expressed in complex human terms.

Find Jack.

JAMIE FESSENDEN set out to be a writer in junior high school. He published a couple short pieces in his high school's literary magazine and had another story place in the top 100 in a national contest, but it wasn't until he met his partner, Erich, almost twenty years later, that he began writing again in earnest. With Erich alternately inspiring and goading him, Jamie wrote several screenplays and directed a few of them as micro-budget independent films. He then began writing novels and published his first novella in 2010.

After nine years together, Jamie and Erich have married and purchased a house together in the wilds of Raymond, New Hampshire, where there are no street lights, turkeys and deer wander through their yard, and coyotes serenade them on a nightly basis. Jamie recently left his "day job" as a tech support analyst to be a full-time writer.

Visit Jamie: http://jamiefessenden.wordpress.com/
Facebook: https://www.facebook.com/pages/Jamie-Fessenden-Author/102004836534286
Twitter: https://twitter.com/JamieFessenden1

By JAMIE FESSENDEN

Billy's Bones
By That Sin Fell the Angels
The Christmas Wager
Dogs of Cyberwar
The Healing Power of Eggnog
The Meaning of Vengeance
Murder on the Mountain
Murderous Requiem
Saturn in Retrograde
Screwups
We're Both Straight, Right?

GOTHIKA
Stitch (Multiple Author Anthology)
Bones (Multiple Author Anthology)
Claw (Multiple Author Anthology)

Published by DREAMSPINNER PRESS
http://www.dreamspinnerpress.com

Transformation

Kim Fielding

Chapter One

THE UNFAMILIAR bristles on Orris's chin scraped the back of his hand. Despite the lingering bitter taste of vomit, he tried to keep his voice even. "What did this?"

Samuel prodded the mangled remains of the lamb with his boot. When he pressed his lips together into a thin line, he bore a disturbing resemblance to their father. "Coyotes. John Dunning lost a goat to 'em last week."

"Are they dangerous?"

Samuel curled the corner of his upper lip. "Not for a grown man, they ain't." He used to speak as well as Orris—as well as any educated man in 1880s New York. But twelve years in Oregon had coarsened his speech as well as his features. Perhaps someday Orris would talk like that as well and his stomach would no longer roil at the sight of a mauled animal.

"What will you do?" he asked.

No doubt figuring the cost of lost livestock, Samuel shook his head. "Dunning bought a pair of guard dogs. They ain't grown yet. Says when they breed he'll trade me a pup for some work."

"That won't do you any good now."

"Then you can be my guard dog. You'll keep watch at night until the lambs are bigger."

Orris blinked at him. "But I don't...."

"Won't take much to scare a coyote away. Even you can do it. Just have to yell at 'em, maybe fire a shot or two."

Fire a shot. Right. "I need to do more to earn my keep," Orris said softly, not meeting his brother's eyes.

After a brief pause and another kick at the lamb's corpse, Samuel gestured at the tree-covered hills behind him. "The coyotes are coming down from there, most likely. The vermin find our livestock easy pickings, and then they slink back up there to hide. No farmsteads in them woods yet. Now there's just a couple of hunters up there. Someday, though. Soon."

Orris squinted at the distance. "You think so? People would have to clear the whole forest to farm up there."

"People will. It's the way of things, Orris. We conquer the wilderness, or it kills us." After a final glance at the pathetic pile of fleece and blood, he stomped toward the house.

THE SOUND of cutlery on china echoed in the cramped dining room, which always smelled of onions and damp.

Lucy swallowed a bite of bread and wiped her mouth. "Mary Ann Dunning said we'll have a doctor in town soon. He's having a house built near the general store."

"Too far for us in an emergency," Samuel responded.

"But close enough if it's not an emergency. You could use the help sometimes." Samuel had gotten partway through medical training before fleeing the city. Lucy glanced down at her belly. "He might make it in time when the baby comes."

"Not if this one comes as fast as the others." Samuel spared one of his rare smiles for his daughters, who smiled back. They were serious little girls, plain and sturdy like their mother, and both very bright. Orris had taken over their schooling since he'd arrived, freeing Lucy for her many other tasks. It was probably the only reason Lucy had agreed to allow Orris to live with them.

"I think this one's a boy," she said. "Perhaps he'll take his time."

Samuel shrugged at his wife before cutting a hunk of meat and stuffing it in his mouth. "Lost a lamb," he said with his mouth full.

"It's not the scours?" she said, sounding alarmed.

"Coyote."

"Ah. Like at the Dunnings. He's been sitting out at night with his shotgun."

"I know." Samuel took another big bite. "Me and Orris will be doing the same."

Lucy cut her eyes at Orris, then away. "He's just as likely to shoot one of us as he is to shoot the coyote."

Orris scowled but didn't say anything, in part because she was right. He'd never learned to use a gun.

With a snort, Samuel reached for another piece of bread. "Maybe I'll just give him some pot lids to bang together." Everyone except Orris laughed, and Orris ducked his head. Samuel used to tease him when they were boys too. He took it as his right, being eight years older. Their five other brothers used to chime in. Orris should probably be grateful that now it was only Lucy and the girls.

After dinner, Orris helped with the washing up. Samuel scoffed, claiming it was women's work, but Orris didn't mind scrubbing pots and dishes. When the kitchen was clean and Lucy and the girls had settled in the parlor with their sewing, Orris wandered outside. A light mist fell, the moisture and the gray evening light softening the edges of the outbuildings. Orris could sometimes swear that moss would grow on him if he stayed still too long in this climate.

Samuel knelt in the mud outside the small barn, inspecting a cracked wooden board. He didn't look up when Orris approached, but he gave a soft grunt. "I'll have to replace this. I'll show you how in the morning, after I teach you to use my gun."

"But it's just one board."

"Just one, or soon another." Samuel stood and wiped his hands on his trousers. "You have to keep on top of it, or it all goes to hell."

"How can you… how can you stand it? There's always something breaking, something dying…."

"How could *you* stand breathing musty old books all your life? And listening to asses in tight collars and ridiculous hats jawing on about nothing, day in, day out?" Samuel shrugged. "I'd choose a barn that needed mending any time."

Orris nodded at him. Samuel had always seemed too big for stuffy rooms and crowded city streets. He'd always stomped around with his hair mussed and his clothes slightly askew. He looked more at home here, with muck on his boots and bits of hay caught in his collar.

"Do you want me to keep watch for the coyote tonight?" Orris asked. "I can shout if I see it. Or bang pot lids."

"No. Not tonight. But tomorrow night you will because the day after that I'll be riding into Portland."

"Portland?" Orris had seen the city only briefly, when he'd arrived via the new railway line. But he'd been exhausted from the long journey and overwhelmed with the turn his life had taken. He'd barely registered the muddy streets, the squat buildings with false fronts, the tall-masted ships crowding the river, and the rough-looking locals. He'd worried then about being shanghaied—he'd read lurid stories about the practice in the New York newspapers—but Samuel had met him at the train station and whisked him away as quickly as a one-horse buckboard permitted.

Now Samuel toed at a small rock. "I need supplies. Lumber, mostly. Want to get the house addition built before we get too busy with growing season."

Orris's heart made a funny little hitch. "House addition?"

"I reckon you're getting tired of sleeping in the parlor. Sofa's lumpy. Your room will be a small one, but we can fit a bed in it. Give you some privacy. You'll have to help me build it, though, so you'd best learn to use a hammer well."

"So I can... I can stay?" He hated the way his voice cracked over the words.

Samuel smiled at him. "Didn't let you travel all the way across the continent just so I could turn you away. You're not—well, you're not well suited to our life here, but you'll learn to manage. And you're my baby brother."

Orris was not going to cry. "Thank you," he rasped, staring at his shoes. They were badly scuffed. He needed boots like Samuel's.

"I don't give a damn about your proclivities, you know," Samuel said, making Orris snap his gaze up in surprise.

"Most people say my... my proclivities are an abomination."

"Father said that, I suppose. And our brothers." Samuel scowled and shook his head. "Fools, the whole lot of them."

"The Bible says—"

"I don't give a fig what the Bible says! The Bible says a man can take a harem's worth of wives, but I doubt Lucy'd much approve of that. It says men can be sold into slavery; that they ought to take a blade to their sons' necks if a voice tells them to. It's a bunch of stories believed by people too weak to trust their own morals. But *I* know what's right and what's wrong, and I don't fear facing the Almighty when my judgment comes."

While Orris was slightly scandalized to hear Samuel utter these words, he wasn't exactly surprised. At age twenty-one, Samuel had steadfastly refused to attend church. He'd scoffed at their father's accusations of blasphemy, collected a few belongings, and headed west. Meanwhile, Orris had faithfully attended services every Sunday, even though he'd known he'd be condemned were his secrets discovered.

As they had been, eventually.

Orris scratched at his small beard. "Even so, they say it's unnatural."

Samuel snorted. "Unnatural! A few years ago, I had a pair of rams who had eyes only for each other. Couldn't interest either of 'em in a ewe until I sold one ram away, and even then, the other was never very eager in his duties. I got a pair of drakes right now who are plenty cozy with one another. I even seen them sitting on eggs. If sheep and ducks can hanker after their own sex, there's nothing unnatural about it."

"I'm not a sheep or a duck," Orris said.

"No. You're a good man, Orr. You've always been kind, and you're the smartest among us. There's nothing immoral or wrong about you. You were only... you were born like this, I reckon. Just like William was born left-handed. Damned inconvenient sometimes, but not evil or unnatural."

Orris had never had a conversation like this with anyone. Even when he'd faced his father after having been expelled from the university—even when they both knew very well *why* he'd been expelled—they'd addressed the topic only obliquely, as if it were too shameful even to name. Maybe it was easier to talk about these things standing in a muddy farmyard than in a gilded parlor on Fifth Avenue.

For a few moments, Orris and Samuel were silent, both staring at the clouds. Night would fall soon. The darkness here was so much more profound than it had ever been in New York. It scared Orris a little, and yet it was somehow also comforting. He felt that here a man might be able to keep his secrets to himself.

In a quiet voice, Orris admitted his greatest sorrow. "I'll never be loved. I'll never belong to someone, or have him belong to me."

Samuel didn't answer at once. Perhaps he was thinking about their father's disapproval of Lucy, still expressed in his letters even though he'd never met her.

Finally, Samuel cleared his throat. "We have rules, Orr. You know I got no patience for the spectacle that calls itself society back east, but even here we got rules. They keep us civilized, even if they don't always make much sense. Not too long ago, the girls were complaining to me, asking why they couldn't wear trousers like the boys. Skirts get in the way, they said. I s'pose they do. And it's stupid and it's not fair, but the rules keep the wilderness at bay." He gestured west toward the hills, although it was too cloudy to see them.

"I understand," Orris said. And he did, even though his heart ached and his soul despaired.

"There's a place or two you can go in Portland. Never been myself, of course—not my taste, and anyway I have Lucy—but I've heard rumors. Places where folks look the other way if the rules get bent a bit. Maybe you'll pay them a visit once in a while. I can send you into the city when I need things. I don't much like going myself."

Orris nodded slightly. Portland was full of sailors, frequented by men traveling alone and far from family and home. At least a few of them would be interested in other men's company. The same had been true on a larger scale in New York. But although he might wish to venture into the city eventually, he would not seek out the places Samuel referred to.

With a heavy sigh, Samuel again wiped his hands on his trousers. "I'll need some coffee if I'm gonna to be up all night." He turned and walked back to the house.

RAIN PATTERED against the windows as Orris squirmed uncomfortably on the sofa. He felt guilty for being wrapped like a mummy in several quilts, warm and dry indoors while Samuel guarded the livestock outside. And he knew he ought to sleep while he could, because Lucy and the girls would be downstairs before dawn, setting the fire and beginning the morning chores. He couldn't help but long for the times when he'd lazed comfortably in his feather bed well past sunrise, knowing the servants would be taking care of things and Cook would make him breakfast whenever he was ready for it.

Even better, though, had been those few delicious mornings spent in Daniel's wide bed, their limbs entwined, their skin sticky with sweat and spend. After their ardor was sated, Daniel liked to play with the messy strands of Orris's red-gold hair. They'd use the soft pillows to muffle their laughter at the silly impressions of their pompous old philosophy professor. And Daniel liked to tickle Orris under his arms and on his ribs, and—

Now he was somewhere in Europe, and Orris had been banished an additional three thousand miles away. They would never see each other again.

Exile sounded very romantic when one read about it in stories. But the reality wasn't romantic at all, especially when one was scrunched on a narrow horsehair sofa, yearning for something that would always be denied.

The floorboards overhead creaked as someone walked across an upstairs room. Lucy, probably. She wasn't sleeping well with the discomfort of her pregnancy. Besides, Samuel had told Orris that Lucy often woke up to check on their daughters, as if something might have happened to them during the night. The house was safe enough, but her worries were understandable. She'd lost her first daughter to fever when the girl was but an infant.

With Samuel on guard for dangers outside, and Lucy being watchful for problems indoors, Orris felt especially irrelevant. He was immensely grateful they'd been willing to take him in despite his disgrace, but he doubted he'd ever fit in any better here than he had in New York. He was the seventh son of a seventh son. Possibly cursed, definitely extraneous.

And good Lord, so lonely.

If he'd had his own room, he might have taken himself in hand, both for the comfort of touch and for the sleepiness he'd feel after his release. But he wouldn't dare here in his brother's parlor, with his sister-in-law pacing just over his head.

He finally drifted off and dreamt that he was dressed in thick woolen clothes that weighed him down as something chased him. He couldn't see the monster behind him, but he could hear it—snarls and growls and nasty laughter. It chased him up Fifth Avenue, where people stood to watch and the buildings closed in tightly, trying to trap him. He darted down a side street where dark churches loomed, and even as he ran, he desperately shed his clothing. Soon he was naked, and that was wrong; and being nude felt *good*, which was worse. Then he came across a human corpse blocking his way, and although it was horribly mangled, he recognized it as Daniel. But Orris simply leapt over the bloody body, not feeling any regret over Daniel's death, and that was the worst of all. No. No, it wasn't. The worst was when he turned another corner to find his family huddled together. When they saw him, they screamed and began to run away. And Orris chased them, snarling and growling and laughing with glee.

Chapter Two

ORRIS'S BEARD didn't grow in particularly quickly, but in New York he'd visited the barber three times each week. Here in the wilds of Oregon, the nearest barber was a half-day's journey away. Perhaps he could have shaved himself, but he didn't trust his hand to be steady with the blade and so he'd grown a beard. He often caught himself stroking his whiskers when he paused to rest. He was doing it now, in fact—running his fingers through the coarse hairs as Samuel inspected his novice repair work.

Orris wondered whether any of his friends in New York would recognize him now. Former friends. All of them had turned their backs on him when his disgrace became known. Even Hugh Price, who spent most of his waking hours drinking and whoring in the Bowery. And even John Bernard, who sometimes visited the bathhouses for trysts with other men. Ah, but the Prices were obscenely wealthy, and the family's donations to the university were generous enough to permit Hugh's atrocious behavior and worse marks to be overlooked. And Bernard's habits were whispered about, but unlike Orris, he'd never been caught in bed—in flagrante, actually—with the son of a titan of industry.

"Not bad," Samuel said, nodding slightly at the barn repair. "The boards are a little crooked, but they'll do. The nails are set true, and you didn't waste many."

"Thank you," said Orris, smiling. He didn't often receive praise.

"By the time you finish helping me build the addition, you'll be an expert. Who knew? All these years wastin' time with your dusty books when you could've been a carpenter."

"I hardly think Father would have approved of that profession."

"Father." Samuel waved his free hand dismissively. "You could fill a library by listing things that man disapproves of. He's certainly not pleased that I became a farmer. As if there's shame in bringing food to people's tables. Father and our brothers, they sit indoors all day, pushing around pieces of paper and thinking themselves important. I work damned hard here, Orris. You seen that already. But I'd rather spend my days digging up stones and wading through sheep shit than to become a banker or a lawyer like the rest of 'em."

"Or a professor," Orris added quietly.

Samuel clapped him on the back. "You'd have been a good professor, Orr. But now you can be a good farmer or carpenter or…. It's the advantage, you see? I know you didn't wanna come here. I know this was your last resort. But this is a *new* place. A chance for a fresh start. You'll get your feet under you soon, and then you can decide what to make of yourself."

Orris managed a wan smile. He deeply appreciated his brother's confidence and support, but Orris wasn't sure he'd ever know what to make of himself. It was terribly spoiled of him to think so, but he wondered if he wouldn't have been better off born in a tenement than a mansion. If he'd spent his boyhood laboring instead of in school, if his father and brothers were rough workers instead of blue bloods, would he have turned out better? With a means to support himself, he'd at least have been free to tell his father that he'd sleep with whomever he wished.

"Come on," Samuel said, tucking the hammer into a pocket. "I'll show you how to shoot. Let's see if your marksmanship is as promising as your carpentry."

AS IT turned out, Orris's marksmanship was terrible. He flinched just hearing the gun go off. And when it was his turn to pull the trigger, he tensed his muscles and squeezed his eyes shut, scattering the shot everywhere.

After several attempts that entirely missed the target—a tree near the edge of the farm—Samuel sighed and took the gun. "Well, as long as you know how to work the thing, that's what's important. The noise will scare a coyote away."

"I guess I shall have to cross sharpshooter off my list of possible professions."

"I reckon you'd better."

They walked back toward the house, past a large plot planted with onions, their feet sinking into the rain-soft ground. The air smelled of onions and manure, with the tang of fir trees adding a fresh note. Better than the sewage-and-smoke reek of the city, at least.

In the small anteroom next to the kitchen, Samuel hung the shotgun on hooks. "I'm going to go make sure the wagon's ready for the trip tomorrow."

"Can I help?"

"No. Go get some rest before supper. You'll be up all night watching the sheep."

Orris shivered slightly. "You didn't see anything last night?"

"Not a thing. You probably won't either. But I can't afford to keep losing lambs."

"I know." Money was tight already, with an extra mouth to feed and a baby on the way. Orris's small efforts to help didn't begin to pay for his room and board.

He waited for Samuel to go back outside before shedding his hat, coat, and shoes. He slipped on the spare shoes he kept for indoor use. They'd been a gift from Daniel, and they were nearly as soft as slippers.

Lucy was in the kitchen, kneading a ball of dough. She had a light dusting of flour on one cheek, and a few strands of mouse-brown hair had escaped from her bun. Her older daughter was chopping vegetables while the younger scrubbed an immense pot. They all stared expressionlessly at him.

"Can I help?" Orris asked.

Lucy's reply was sharp as a blade. "No." And then, as if grudgingly granting a bit of courtesy, she added, "Thank you."

"I, um…. Samuel recommended I take a nap. So I'll be wide awake tonight."

He received no response.

He cleared his throat. "So I'll, I'll be in the parlor. If I'm needed." And he scurried out of the kitchen.

The parlor's window faced north, and the room was dark even at midday. It wasn't a large room, and the furniture crowding the space looked as if it had been dragged thousands of miles via wagon or ship— which it had, of course. The furnishings were plain and sturdy, serviceable but without ornament, very much like the pieces crammed into the servants' rooms in the attic of his father's house. Aside from the dark green wallpaper, the only attempts to decorate the room were a few framed embroidery pieces—presumably the work of Lucy and her daughters—a red tasseled pillow that looked completely out of place, and two framed floral designs made from locks of human hair.

A fireplace dominated one corner of the room, but since Orris's arrival, it had never been lit. Samuel and Lucy preferred to use the stove in the kitchen, since it was good for cooking as well as heat. At night they took heated water bottles up to their rooms while Orris made do with a pile of quilts and whatever heat drifted into the parlor from the kitchen.

His new bedroom would be built on the other side of the kitchen, and he already planned to place his bed as close to the stove as the wall permitted.

Ah, a bed. It would be lovely to sleep in one again. He thought about this as he took off the shoes he'd put on only moments before, loosened his tie, and then lay on the sofa. He would like to be able to uncurl his legs, stretch out his arms, and extend his body to its full length. And by Jove, he'd like to be rid of the damnable lumps that dug into his flesh.

He fell asleep to the homey sounds from the kitchen next door.

NEW YORK was never truly dark. No matter how late the hour, there were always streetlight flames flickering inside their glass prisons. Occasional windows in the residential areas would be alight with candles or lanterns or gaslights. And in the rougher bits of town, taverns spilled out a brassy light from windows and open doors, creating sharp shadows in the alleyways.

Oregon, however, was a different story. Although the moon was full tonight, the clouds were much too thick for anything but the faintest smudge of moonlight to shine through. The darkness seemed to swallow all the sounds around him.

He felt ridiculous, marching up and down the sheep paddock with a lantern in his hand and the shotgun under his arm. But at least it wasn't raining. And Lucy had even made him a pot of strong coffee and given him a small smile before he walked out the door. "I'll keep some soup on the stove," she'd said. "Come in for a few minutes if you need to warm up." She was no doubt pleased to have her husband beside her in bed tonight, and Orris was proud to have found another way he could help out a little.

With the mud squelching at his feet and the sheep breathing peacefully nearby, he could almost imagine himself the only human on the planet. Disturbing as that thought was, it was better than the alternative, which was wondering what Daniel was doing this very moment. It would already be the next morning in Europe. Perhaps he was waking up in a Parisian garret, yawning as he made plans to visit a café for crusty bread with butter and jam. Perhaps someone was waking up with him, a pretty French boy with a charming accent and fashionable clothing that didn't smell like dirt and onions and sheep. Or perhaps—

Something made a faint noise up ahead, on the small rutted pathway that led to the onion field and then to the tree-covered slopes beyond. It was an animal sound, a sort of muffled *humph* that somehow seemed deliberate. It reminded him of the satisfied little chuckle his father emitted whenever he felt he'd gotten the upper hand in a business dealing.

"Who's there?" Orris called, feeling more ridiculous than ever. At least his voice didn't quaver.

He was answered by another bestial laugh, this one possibly closer.

He stooped and carefully set the lantern on the ground. The light was steadier that way, but it mostly illuminated the area around his feet, which wasn't helpful. He drew the shotgun from under his arm and held it against his chest. He stood there, silent except for his harsh breathing and pounding heart.

For what seemed like a long time, nothing happened. He'd been accused of having an overactive imagination, and he was almost ready to believe he'd hallucinated the noises. But just as he was about to pick up the lantern, the animal chuffed at him again. There was no question that it was closer this time. Very close. In fact, if he lifted the lantern high and squinted, he might be able to see what was there.

He had no desire whatsoever to do so.

"It's nothing," he muttered. He'd seen enormous rats in New York, and probably this was something no more terrifying than that. He had no notion what sorts of creatures roamed this area at night, though. Coyotes, yes, but Samuel said they wouldn't be dangerous to a grown man. Bears? Were there bears?

"Go away!" Orris said, but didn't quite shout it. The creature answered him with another amused sound.

Perhaps he ought to fire the gun. But that would wake the entire household, and Orris didn't want to face Samuel and Lucy's scorn if he was panicking over nothing. Instead of being merely useless, he'd graduate to full-fledged nuisance.

In the darkness ahead of him, a footstep rustled on leaves. Orris realized he'd backed up against the fence and was in imminent danger of kicking over the lantern. His hands ached from clenching the gun.

Deliberately deepening his voice, he called out again. "Go away! Leave! You don't belong here!"

The creature growled.

It was a low sound—Orris could almost feel the vibration through his feet—and it ignited every one of his atavistic reflexes. His lips pulled back from his clenched teeth, his spine tingled as the hair on his neck tried to rise, and his bowels felt watery and loose. He imagined the sharp stare of the unseen animal and pictured bloody fangs and tearing claws.

Never mind Samuel and Lucy's potential contempt. He was going to fire the gun.

He willed his hands to unclench, and he brought the stock to his shoulder. But now his hands shook—his entire body shook—and his grip fumbled. He dropped the weapon, and it landed at his feet with a soft thud.

Not knowing whether to curse or pray, Orris bent to pick up the gun. He was still stooped and reaching when he saw the creature's eyes. They were close and glinted green in the lantern light.

Orris's legs gave out, and he sank to his knees. He stopped his desperate scrabbling for the gun and simply froze. Even his lungs stopped working.

The animal stepped closer, very slowly. Not as if it were frightened, but rather as if it enjoyed stalking him, the way Cook's cat liked to play with mice in the pantry. Soon it was near enough that Orris could make out the dim outline of its body. It looked like a large dog, he thought. Heavy, with a thick ruff of fur at its neck. In one large leap, it could be on him.

But it didn't leap—at least not yet. It stared at him and Orris stared back, and although he could sense little else of the animal, its eyes gave the impression of keen intelligence.

"Imagine when Daniel hears I've been eaten by a wild beast," Orris whispered. "Won't he be jealous. This beats a whole slew of handsome French garret-mates."

The animal—was it a coyote?—cocked its head slightly, which brought a burst of hysterical laughter from Orris. "Are you having second thoughts? Maybe a sorry thing like me will give you indigestion. I suppose you'd rather have a nice supper of tender lamb."

It came a step closer. Orris smelled it: wet fur, pine sap, and something else he couldn't name. The scent of the wilderness, perhaps.

And then a strange thing happened. Well, stranger. While Orris's heart still raced, he realized that the terror had fled, and what he was feeling now was… excitement. He was nearly giddy with it, actually, like the first time Daniel had interrupted their studies with a kiss and then dragged Orris willingly to his bedroom.

Why would a man feel excited when he was about to be killed?

Orris had no real answer for that. Maybe the animal could hypnotize its prey with its gaze, or maybe Orris had simply lost his sanity. In any case, he took a deep breath and tilted his head to the side.

"All right, then," he said.

The animal's muscles bunched. But just before it leapt, a strident bark burst from the darkness behind it. Orris startled, and the animal yelped with surprise before whirling around.

Good Lord. There were *two* of them.

The new one was snarling, but as it moved closer to the lantern, its attention seemed focused less on Orris than on the first beast. The new one growled, and the first yipped slightly before hunching its shoulders and dropping its gaze. Without another glance at Orris, the first animal trotted away. But the other one—the new one—it did not yet leave. It looked at Orris, but without menace. And there was something so compelling about it that Orris had to stop himself from crawling forward to meet it.

"You're beautiful," Orris rasped. He couldn't see enough detail to support such an assertion, but there was something about those glowing eyes, the confident set of the large body, that suggested power and... majesty, even.

The animal blinked at him. It stretched its head forward, and Orris thought it would close the space between them. But then it snarled—fast and sharp—before spinning around and bounding away into the blackness.

Chapter Three

"YOU LOOK tired, Orris. You should go back to sleep." Samuel glanced at Orris quickly before slightly adjusting Beau's harness. The horse stood patiently, breathing plumes of warm moisture into the morning air.

"I probably will, in a bit. But I wanted to tell you about last night."

Samuel paused. "What happened?"

"I saw it. Them. There were two of them."

"Coyotes?"

"I… I suppose so. It was hard to see in the dark. They looked like big dogs."

"Two. Probably means there's a den nearby, and soon, pups to feed." Samuel scowled and then squinted at Orris. "You didn't fire the gun."

"No. I, uh, I shouted at them. They ran away." Not quite the truth, but near enough. Orris hoped he hadn't missed any spots when he wiped the mud off the weapon before hanging it on its hook.

"Well. That's good enough, I reckon. We didn't lose any lambs. We'll watch a few nights more. These varmints are smart. Once they realize we're keeping an eye on things, they'll move on. Look for easier pickings."

Orris ignored the way his pulse quickened at the thought of seeing the animals again. "You'll be exhausted by the time you get back from Portland. I'll watch tonight."

"Thanks, Orr." Samuel gave the harness one more tug before nodding slightly and patting Beau's flank. "All right, then. See you this evening. And tomorrow we'll get a start on the addition."

Orris stood and waved as Samuel clattered away in the cart.

Although he wasn't as tired as he should have been, Orris went inside and lay down on the sofa. Lucy made a point to tell the girls to keep quiet, which was largely unnecessary; they were quiet children to begin with. But Orris appreciated Lucy's rare concern for his comfort. He pulled the quilts up to his chin and tried to nap, but he couldn't.

He closed his eyes and counted sheep, but pretty soon his imaginary sheep were pursued by shadowy beasts with slavering jaws and glowing eyes. Orris's feet twitched under the blankets as if they wanted to run too.

God, when was the last time he had run? When he was a boy, he used to rush up and down the sidewalks, ignoring his nannies' cries to slow down. He'd been so happy then. But he'd never been much for sports when he was in school, and a grown man couldn't break into a sprint on Fifth Avenue unless he wanted to alarm the passersby.

He could run here if he wanted to, though, couldn't he? Could dart across fields and through the ferny forest, and there'd be nobody to see and criticize. Ah, but if only he had a companion to run at his side....

These were very strange thoughts.

He kicked off the blankets, straightened his clothing, and slipped on his shoes. In the kitchen, Lucy leaned against the table, deep shadows under her eyes. "I thought you were sleeping," she said.

"Too restless. Can I help with anything?"

She shook her head. "The girls are outside with the chickens, and I'm going to start a stew for tonight's supper, and then I've the sweeping to do."

"I can sweep," he offered, although he never had.

"There's no need."

"All right, then. I think... I think I'll take a walk."

She gave him a skeptical look, then shrugged. Leisurely strolls weren't a common occupation here, he surmised. People walked only when they needed to get somewhere and didn't have a horse—not for recreation.

In the cramped anteroom, he switched to his muddy outdoor shoes and donned his coat and hat. Venturing outside, he was pleased to discover patches of blue sky visible through the iron-colored clouds. He might get caught in a downpour later, but for now he would be dry.

His nieces were laughing on the other side of the house, where the henhouse was. Orris headed past the barn to the sheep paddock, where the fleecy animals stared placidly at him. He leaned against the fence and watched them for a while, but they weren't very interesting. True, the lambs pranced and gamboled, but he wouldn't have felt too bad if Samuel and Lucy had announced they would be eating lamb chops that evening.

A raven landed on a nearby tree and made a few raspy calls before flapping heavily away.

Orris walked slowly along the fence just as he had the previous night, only now he didn't carry a gun, and there was no need for a lantern. The territory that had seemed so mysterious and wild in the dark was quite prosaic in the daylight. Farm animals, mud, weeds. The thick smell of growing things.

But then he came to a spot at the corner of the paddock, where the soil near the fence line looked freshly disturbed. He paused to look at his own blurry footprints. And then he took a few steps away from the fence and saw animal prints, a few quite distinct. They were large, with four broad toes, each topped with the point of a claw. Well, at least he had proof that he hadn't imagined last night's encounter. Not that he needed proof—those few minutes had felt more real than most of his life.

Tonight he'd be out here again. His heart sped at the notion, and not with fear.

IT WAS dusk when Samuel arrived home, and he looked drawn. "I hate that road," he said as he dismounted from the wagon.

Orris nodded. He'd traveled the Great Plank Road only once, but he remembered it as a harrowing journey—rutted where no planks were laid, winding, squeezed between steep hillsides that looked ready to swallow travelers whole.

"But you were able to get everything you needed?"

"Yes, I think so." Samuel stretched and then shook the kinks from his legs. "And I'm famished. Can you unload the wagon while I take care of Beau?"

"Of course."

Samuel had already bought some building supplies at the local general store. They were piled alongside the house, covered by a large sheet of canvas. Orris pulled the canvas away and began adding the new boards. He wished he'd thought to wear gloves—he kept catching splinters in his hands—but he enjoyed the smell of freshly cut wood, and he was quite happy that he was able to perform this physical task successfully. By the time Samuel emerged from the barn, the buckboard was empty.

"Good work, Orr. I'll put the wagon away tomorrow. Now I just want to eat and fall into bed."

When they entered the kitchen, Lucy kissed Samuel's cheek. Orris always blushed at these open displays of affection, but he was also gratified by the reminder that his brother was truly loved. Samuel was a good man who deserved a loving family.

Lucy's stew was flavorful and hearty. Orris surprised everyone by eating two large bowls. "Hauling lumber must be good for your appetite,"

Samuel said with a grin. "Maybe you should be a lumberjack instead of a carpenter."

Orris imagined himself out in the wilderness, surrounded by strapping men who wielded axes and saws as if they were playthings. "I think I'd make a sorry lumberjack."

"You never know. I can see you felling those trees, some as wide as a house. Sitting around a campfire with pine needles in your hair."

The girls giggled and Orris smiled at them.

After the meal was finished, Orris didn't offer to help wash up. He hurriedly lit a lantern and readied himself to go outdoors. He even refused Lucy's offer of coffee. "In a little while, maybe."

"I'll leave the kettle filled with water."

He thanked her, took the gun from its hooks, wished everyone a good night, and went outside.

A misty drizzle was falling, slowly soaking his trouser legs. His toes began to squelch inside his sodden shoes. Moisture gathered on his hat and dripped off the edges, making him feel like the world's most ridiculous fountain. He wondered if he would ever get used to the ever-present clouds and rain in this place. At least Samuel said the winters were rarely harsh and the summers rarely stifling.

Orris walked slowly, his head bowed, watching the little circle of lantern light sway near his feet. When he came to the far end of the sheep paddock, he paused for a while, listening to the *plink-rustle* of raindrops on leaves. He had no sense of being watched—not even by the sheep. He held the lantern high, trying to see as much as possible in the direction of the hills, but the light didn't travel far and the rain obscured the view even more.

Eventually he lowered the lantern and turned back toward the house.

He paced the paddock edges all night, his feet growing heavier and heavier by the hour. But he never even saw the sheep, let alone any predators. Bone-weary, he trudged inside at dawn. He hung up the gun and shed his outdoor clothes, then dragged himself to the sofa. He hoped Lucy, Samuel, and the girls would be quiet when they woke—which would be any minute. He fell asleep quickly, still refusing to admit that the emotion heavy in his gut was disappointment.

Chapter Four

A DAY later Samuel and Orris began the addition to the house. Mist again settled on their clothing, making Orris feel cold and miserable. But if they waited for dry weather to build, his bedroom might never be done. Samuel seemed cheery enough, at least, whistling happily as he worked and patiently instructing Orris in what to do.

They went inside for lunch. As they undressed in the anteroom, Samuel frowned at Orris's sodden shoes and raw hands. "You can't work like this," he said.

Orris shrugged. "I'll get used to it."

"Don't be stupid, Orr. A man needs to be properly fitted out for work." Still frowning, Samuel strode into the kitchen.

Lucy served them heaping plates of potatoes and meat, with steaming mugs of strong coffee to wash it down. She didn't eat with them, but she rarely did at lunch. In fact, as far as Orris could tell, she never sat down at all until suppertime. While they ate, she bustled about, alternately supervising the girls' studies and tending to some of her chores.

When one of Lucy's circuits brought her near the kitchen table, Samuel gently caught her arm. "Do you want anything from town?"

"You're going today?"

"Yes. Orris needs a few things."

Orris ducked his head, embarrassed.

But Lucy didn't admonish him. "We're running low on sugar and coffee," she said. "And I could use a spool of good white thread."

"Of course." Samuel lifted her hand to his mouth and kissed the back of it. Then he stood. "We should go now if we want time for more building today."

Obediently, Orris prepared for the journey. He tried to help Samuel hook Beau to the wagon, but horses made him uneasy and Beau didn't seem all that fond of him either. So Orris ended up standing back and simply waiting.

The ride to town took about an hour, the wagon jostling violently over rocks and muddy ruts. But Samuel was used to it. He chattered about their building project and about his plans to eventually expand the house's second story as well. "If Lucy's right and this one's a boy, he won't wanna share a room with the girls. More breathing room would be nice for us all."

"You've made yourself a good home. You and Lucy."

Eyebrows lifted, Samuel shot him a quick look. "We're not exactly wealthy."

"But you have food on the table. Your house is comfortable. Your daughters are smart, and they seem happy. And you... you care for each other, all of you."

Samuel seemed to think for a while. Then he nodded slowly. "You know, with all the rooms in father's mansion, and all the fancy things his money could buy... I was never a fraction as content as I am here. Even when I'm soaked and blistered and sore." He shook the reins, urging Beau to walk a little faster. "Maybe someday you will be too."

Orris made a noncommittal grunt in reply.

Soon they drew close to the town. Orris felt that the settlement's name—Beaverton—was an intentionally cruel irony. Trap all the beavers to make fashionable hats, drain their ponds, and name the town after them. And it was barely a town in any case. Just a few streets of modest houses, a white clapboard school, a general store, a feed store, a restaurant, and a small wooden building that served as the terminus for the railroad. The train ran from Portland and was the primary reason for Beaverton's existence, allowing farmers to easily transport their goods into the city.

Samuel stopped the wagon in front of the general store and dismounted. He patted Beau's shoulder before tying the horse to a rail. Two similar wagons were already there, as was a roan horse with a saddle. Orris clambered down and followed his brother into the building.

Orris had been in this store only once before, a few days after his arrival. He was surprised again at how many goods could be crammed into a relatively small space and how varied those goods were. Shelving lined the walls all the way to the ceiling, the wooden boards sagging under stacks of jars and tins, folded fabric, pots and pans, and sundry kitchenware. Small boxes and fabric sacks made a mystery of their contents. Long cabinets with glass fronts displayed more goods, and barrels held various foodstuffs and nails and... and a thousand other things, it seemed. An enormous iron stove squatted in the center of the room and heated it nicely, while a set of scales and a cash register dominated one corner.

"Good afternoon, Mr. Spencer," called the tall man near the cash register. He was busy weighing something for a woman in a calico dress. "I'll be with you shortly."

Samuel smiled at him. "No hurry, Mr. Allen, no hurry." He wandered over to a display of cigars, where he fell into conversation with another customer, a slight man with a bushy gray moustache. Orris hovered near the door, pretending a great interest in tins of fish.

Soon Mr. Allen came out from behind his counter. "How can I help you?"

Samuel cocked his head in Orris's direction. "My brother needs boots and some heavy gloves. And we need a few other things besides."

"Of course."

The selection of footwear was limited, but Mr. Allen found a sturdy pair that fit Orris well. He also found a pair of thick leather gloves. He placed those items on the counter near the cash register and gathered Samuel's other items: the coffee and sugar, thread, and a few pieces of candy for the girls. Then—with more ceremony than was strictly called for—he totaled the purchases on his cash register.

Although Samuel acted as if the matter were nothing, Orris felt his own cheeks heat. He literally hadn't a penny to his name. His father had driven him away with just enough money for a train ticket and expenses along the way, and since then Orris had been forced to rely on the charity of Samuel's family.

Samuel and Orris gathered up their purchases and headed to the exit. Before they could leave, though, they nearly collided with a man who came barreling inside.

"Hello, Dunning," Samuel said.

Dunning was a large man, tall and solid, with greasy hair hanging down beneath his hat. The first time he'd met Orris, Dunning hadn't bothered to hide a sneer of contempt. This time he didn't even glance Orris's way.

"Spencer," Dunning grunted. "You lose any livestock this week?"

"A lamb a few nights back. Been keeping watch since then. But my brother saw 'em. Two coyotes."

Dunning made a disgusted face. "There's only one of 'em. It came to my place last night, and I got a good look at the bastard. Wasn't no coyote." He dropped his voice dramatically. "Was a wolf."

Orris gasped so loudly that both Samuel and Dunning turned to stare at him. "A w-wolf?" he stammered, blushing furiously.

Samuel was frowning. "You sure? Nobody's seen a wolf 'round here in years."

"Just because we ain't seen 'em don't mean they ain't here. Told you. I saw it real good."

"It was raining last night."

"Critter came real close. Those useless curs I bought went squalling away like the devil himself was chompin' at their tails." Dunning gave an oily grin, revealing yellowed teeth. "I shot the son of a bitch, though."

Orris's heart sank so suddenly and so heavily into his gut that he nearly vomited. He felt all the blood drain from his face, and he had to steady himself on a nearby counter. "Shot?" he rasped.

Judging by the look Orris received, Dunning wouldn't have minded shooting him as well. "You got a weak temperament, boy. Maybe you should oughtta skedaddle back east, where you belong."

Samuel stepped forward, placing himself between them. "Leave him alone, Dunning. He's still adjusting, and he hasn't had much sleep lately. He'll do fine."

"So *you* say. He ain't my problem anyway."

With a shake of his head, Samuel seemed to dismiss the subject. "Well, I'm glad you killed the wolf. I'm tired of keeping watch at night."

"Didn't kill it. Least, not right away. I hit it, though. It screamed and ran off. Close as I was, I reckon it slinked off somewhere to die."

Orris couldn't even name the many emotions that stormed through him. He pushed past Samuel, skirted Dunning, and then rushed out the door. He continued running until he came to the wagon, where he leaned forward against the worn wooden side, his head hanging down.

A few minutes later, Samuel came up behind him, set their purchases in the back of the wagon, and covered everything with a square of heavy canvas.

Then he gave Orris a quick pat on the shoulder. "I'm sorry about that, Orr. Dunning's a miserable bastard. Never has a good word to say about nobody. I would've fought him over what he said to you, but what's the point? Even if I beat him bloody, he'd *still* be a miserable bastard. It's a shame he's our nearest neighbor, unless you count the Bonn brothers up in the hills, and we hardly ever see them."

"I... it's all right. It's nothing." Orris meant it. He didn't care what Dunning said about him. Orris had endured much harsher words from his own family.

He took a deep breath and let it out, then turned to look at Samuel. "There were two of them. I'm sure of it. They might have been wolves instead of coyotes, I suppose. It was dark and I don't… well, I don't have the experience to distinguish them. But there were two."

Samuel nodded. "I wouldn't be surprised if Dunning was too drunk to see straight last night." He sighed. "I guess we'll keep watch, for a while at least."

"I'll do it."

"We'll take turns."

They spent the return ride in silence, their heads bowed to the rain. Orris couldn't have hazarded a guess as to Samuel's thoughts, and his own were nearly as obscure. He could understand being startled to learn that he'd apparently been at close quarters with a pair of wolves. Surely even the staunchest frontiersman would quail a bit over that. But although fear was definitely a part of what he was feeling, he didn't fear for his life. The wolves were gone—one of them probably dead.

Why did he feel as if he'd lost something important?

Chapter Five

ORRIS SPENT the next few days feeling sore and bleary-eyed. Bleary-minded, too, which was perhaps a blessing. During the day he helped with the farm chores and assisted Samuel in building the addition. At night he patrolled the edges of the sheep paddock. Samuel tried to take turns at night, but Orris refused.

"Let me do this, Samuel. Please. It's something I can do to truly help you." Which was true enough. But if Orris had been honest with himself, he'd have to admit that his motives were decidedly mixed.

Samuel kept urging him to rest during the day. Even Lucy insisted that he lie down early in the morning and again after lunch.

But Orris couldn't manage more than short stretches of sleep. He had dreams full of jumbled images of blood and fur and forests and running. Worse yet, he dreamt of sex. As he slumbered, he rutted against a naked male body, hard and strong. He never saw the man's face—just glowing green eyes—but he felt the man's urgent need. And good Lord, he felt his own. He woke up aching and sweaty, worrying whether anyone had heard him moaning in his sleep.

The one small miracle was that he continued to show some skill at construction. Building was a bit easier with gloves and boots, and he found himself enjoying the work. It was satisfying to make something from nothing, to have a tangible result for his labors.

"This has gone a lot faster than I figured," Samuel said one afternoon as they paused to drink the coffee Lucy brought them. He leaned against a newly constructed wall while Orris sat on a section of felled log.

"That's good. Then we'll be done before you start planting."

"Oh, easily. You'll be moving into your new room by the end of the week. Of course, we'll have to find you some proper furniture...." He scratched his beard thoughtfully.

"You've spent so much money on me already."

"You're not a horse, Orr. We won't bed you down in straw. Don't worry. I can get Mr. Hall to order a bed frame and mattress, and you don't need much more than that. You ain't got enough clothing to fill a wardrobe."

That was true. A few hooks and a shelf or two would suffice. "A bed costs money."

"I have some saved." Samuel sighed. "You've been a real help, Orr, whether you know it or not. And I'll be leanin' on you after the baby comes. If you were my hired man, I'd be payin' you a dollar a day."

"But you wouldn't be giving me room and board. Or buying me boots and—" Orris stopped when Samuel abruptly straightened, staring at something over Orris's shoulder.

Orris twisted around to see.

A man loped toward them at a rapid pace. He was hatless, his hair long and pale, and his face clean-shaven. He wore buckskin trousers and vest and a grayish shirt but no coat, and even from far away he was clearly quite muscular.

"Who's that?" Orris asked, noting Samuel's posture. His brother didn't seem alarmed, just… alert.

"Henry Bonn. Him and his brother Charles live up in the hills. They're hunters."

Orris remembered Samuel mentioning the brothers a few times, but before he could ask any more questions, Bonn came to a panting halt in front of them.

Without preamble, he said, "Need your help. Please." He was flushed from his exertions, and his jaw was set in a desperate way, but he was also thrillingly, breathtakingly handsome. He had green eyes and a long nose, a square chin with a small cleft, and a wide mouth.

"What is it?" Samuel asked.

"My brother. He's… he's hurt. Bad. I've done my best for him, but I can't…. Will you help?"

"Of course. Let me fetch my things." Samuel turned to Orris. "Will you come with? It's a distance, and another pair of hands might help."

Orris couldn't imagine how he'd be of assistance. Samuel had briefly studied medicine, but Orris's specialty had been Latin and Greek. He doubted any man could be saved by the application of classical languages. But still he nodded.

"Yes. Whatever I can do."

While Samuel hurried inside, Orris waited awkwardly with Henry, who stared at him in an unnerving manner. "You're new," Henry said.

"Yes. I'm Orris Spencer."

"From back east."

"New York."

Henry didn't reply, but he continued his sharp scrutiny. Orris had to fight hard not to duck his head and shuffle his feet. It wasn't only those green eyes that made him uncomfortable, or Henry's handsome face. There was something more—an odd feeling that he'd met this man before, although Orris knew he had not.

"Why did you come here?" Henry finally asked.

Orris lifted his chin. "I was sent. I disgraced my family."

Any response was lost as Samuel came rushing out the door carrying a small leather bag. Lucy was right behind him, her brow furrowed with concern. She didn't say anything as Henry turned away from the road, toward the hills, with Samuel right behind him. Orris hurried to catch up.

The sheep bleated and galloped to the far end of the paddock as the men passed. They were unused to seeing them in such a hurry.

Orris hadn't ventured past the edge of the farm to where the slope began, so he hadn't realized there was a path leading into the hills. It was narrow and steep, studded with roots that threatened to trip him and overhung by branches that required careful maneuvering. Saplings and ferns blocked the way at times, and thorny berry canes with a hint of new leaves reached for him.

"What happened?' Samuel asked when they were well on their way. He sounded slightly out of breath, which made Orris feel a little better about his own labored breathing.

Henry's answer was terse and a little hard to hear since he was ahead of them. "He got shot."

"Shot? With a gun?"

"Wasn't an arrow."

"But… how?"

He didn't answer at first, and Orris thought he was ignoring the question. But finally, Henry grunted. "Stupidity."

And that was that, apparently, because he moved ahead so rapidly that Samuel and Orris had to hurry to avoid losing sight of him.

By the time they reached a clearing, Orris's muscles were heavy and his lungs felt like jagged glass. He figured they'd been traveling for an hour at least. A small log cabin squatted in the center of the clearing, its roof so heavily festooned with moss and pine needles that it resembled an odd sort of plant. There was a bare spot of ground adjacent to the structure—probably a vegetable garden—but no other signs of civilization.

Henry didn't pause to let them catch their breath. He pushed the cabin door open and strode inside. Samuel and Orris followed.

Orris nearly gagged. The close air of the cabin reeked of sickness and rot. The interior was stifling as well, no doubt due to the large pile of glowing coals in the fireplace. The single room was dim even with the lantern light. Henry moved to the side of a narrow bed where a man lay unmoving on his back, and Samuel pushed him slightly aside so he could examine the injury.

"How long ago was he shot?" Samuel asked after a few minutes. He'd moved blankets and clothing and bandages aside, but his patient hadn't so much as twitched.

"Several days ago. Week, maybe."

Samuel shot Henry an angry look. "And you waited 'til now to do something about it?"

"I didn't know. Not at first. He didn't tell me."

"How could you not notice your brother was wounded?"

"It wasn't… it wasn't so bad, at first. He knew I'd be angry, so he hid it from me. I reckon he thought he'd heal on his own." Henry's voice was subdued, full of sorrow and regret.

"Fetch some clean water, please," Samuel said. He sounded weary.

Henry grabbed a tin pot from near the fire and left the cabin. He came back a moment later with the pot full. "Should I heat it?"

"In a few minutes."

Orris still felt ill, and since he wasn't sure what to do with himself, he peered around. He saw another bed against the opposite wall, piled with neatly folded blankets. Near the two chairs and small table of rough wood were several shelves stocked with foodstuffs, tools, dishes, and cups. That was nearly the limit of the cabin's contents, but for a tall stack of cured animal skins tottering just inside the door. There were no decorative items at all, not even a rag rug on the packed-earth floor.

Samuel sat in one of the chairs and worked in near silence while Henry stoked the fire, fetched more water, and heated it. At Samuel's request he tore some cloth strips. Meanwhile Orris paced until his stomach finally settled.

They had been in the cabin for quite some time when the patient made a horrible, high-pitched moan and began to flail violently. "Hold him still!" Samuel shouted.

Henry threw himself across his brother's chest and tried to pin his arms down. Hoping he was doing the right thing, Orris rushed over and put all his weight on the man's legs. *What was his name again?* Orris thought inanely as he struggled to remain in place. *Ah, Charles. That was it.*

Even with Orris and Henry holding him down—and Samuel doing something to his belly that Orris didn't want to see—Charles still bucked frantically. He was screaming now, his animalistic howls deafening in the cramped cabin, but Orris wasn't sure he was truly conscious. His movements, while incredibly strong, seemed uncoordinated.

"Dammit! Hold him!" snapped Samuel after one particularly vicious jerk of Charles's body. Samuel's voice was ragged and his brow sweaty. Orris did his best to hold on.

The convulsions ended as abruptly as they had begun, Charles going instantly limp and silent on the bed. Orris would have thought him dead but for the thin wheeze of his lungs. When Orris stood, he finally got a good look at Charles, from the awful mess at his midsection to his face. Even as sick as Charles was, his resemblance to Henry was clear.

"Give me a little space, please," Samuel said quietly. "And something to drink."

Orris backed away and watched as Henry brought a tin cup of water, holding it as Samuel drank. Orris felt an irrational stab of jealousy.

Eventually, Orris sat in the remaining chair, while Henry sat on the empty bed and watched his brother worriedly. But sometimes Henry looked at Orris instead, and every time he did, the temperature in the cabin seemed to increase. Nobody had ever scrutinized Orris so closely.

Then Henry surprised him with a gesture toward the shelf with the bottles. "Do you want something to drink?"

"No. Thank you," Orris replied, although his mouth was dry.

"Food?" Henry barked a humorless laugh. "My first guest in a long time, and I'm being a poor host."

"Don't concern yourself with me. I'm not important."

"Whoever taught you that was a liar. But I reckon now's not the time for that discussion." Henry shook his head slightly before returning his attention to his brother.

After what seemed like a very long time, Samuel stood and wiped his hands on a rag. He gathered his things and tucked them into his bag and then, without saying anything, walked out of the cabin. Henry followed him at once; Orris hesitated a moment before following suit.

Orris took in several lungsful of clean air. In the gray light of late afternoon, Samuel was pale and solemn. "I don't know how he's lived this long," he said.

Henry answered. "He has a strong constitution."

"I'm... I'm afraid it's not enough. Even if I were a real doctor, I don't think there's much I could do for him now."

"There's no hope?"

Samuel shook his head grimly. "He's badly infected. His organs are already... I'm sorry."

"There's nothing I can do?"

"Try to keep him as comfortable as possible. I... I doubt he'll regain consciousness. He hasn't much longer, Mr. Bonn."

Orris was distantly aware that Samuel had temporarily lost his rough frontiersman's twang and had reverted to his old way of speaking. He sounded like a gentleman who lived in a mansion on Fifth Avenue and studied medicine at the university. It was a strange juxtaposition, with his farmer's clothes and the towering fir trees that surrounded them.

Henry licked his lips and set his jaw. "I understand. Thank you for your efforts. I truly do appreciate them."

"We're neighbors, Mr. Bonn. We do what we can for each other. You certainly helped us in the past. I'm just sorry I couldn't do more."

"Let me take you home before it gets dark."

"I can find our way back. Stay here with your brother."

After a brief hesitation, Henry nodded. For just a split second, raw grief washed over his face. But his expression was composed when he turned to Orris. "I'm sorry we didn't meet under better circumstances. Maybe we'll see each other again, sometime."

Orris tried to ignore the way his heart leapt at those words. This was hardly the time or place for happiness. He mumbled an awkward combination of apology and condolence. Then Henry shook hands with Samuel and Orris before ducking back into his cabin.

It would have been hard to converse during the journey home, if Samuel and Orris wanted to, because they were forced to walk the narrow path single file.

But when they came to a passage where the trail widened slightly, Orris stepped forward and caught Samuel's arm. "Are you all right?"

"Yes. Just tired." He gave Orris a quick sideways glance. "I've seen dying people before. It happens, especially when there's no real doctor nearby. I watched my own child die and couldn't save her."

"But you tried to save her. And you tried today. You... you did your very best. Nobody can ask more of a man than that."

Samuel sighed. "Thanks, Orr." He ducked under a branch and then glanced at Orris again, this time for longer. "Are *you* all right? You're not used to death yet."

Yet. Orris didn't care for the implications of that word. But he had other concerns at the moment. "I'm fine. Who are those men, Samuel? Why do they live... as they do?"

"The Bonns were here when Lucy and I first settled on our farm. I don't know their history. They keep to themselves, mostly. Make a living off hunting and trapping, I reckon. Those first couple of winters here, when times were rough, the Bonns traded us some meat. They didn't ask much for it either—just enough that I wouldn't feel like it was charity."

"It seems a strange way to live. Alone in the forest like that."

"I reckon some men prefer solitude. Maybe they were brought up like that. They'd probably find New York City just as strange."

"Maybe," said Orris, stepping over a large fallen branch.

"I see Henry or Charles once or twice a year. They don't have much to say, but they've always been pleasant enough. I get the feeling they ain't real happy with folks movin' in and building towns 'round here."

The path narrowed again and Orris stepped behind Samuel.

The last of the day's light was laboring through the clouds when they descended the hills and walked alongside the sheep paddock. The sheep still huddled on the far side, eyeing the men distrustfully.

"Samuel? How do you suppose Charles got shot?"

"Dunno. Ain't my place to ask."

"But aren't you curious about it?"

"Not really. Maybe it were an accident. Happens. Maybe they got into a fight and Henry shot 'im." He shrugged. "That happens too."

Orris supposed Samuel was right. He knew from his own experiences that fraternal love had its limits—and sometimes those limits were quite narrow. But as he slogged his way toward the house, he realized that he hadn't seen a gun inside the cabin. He would have expected a pair of hunters to have their weapons prominently in view.

Still pondering, Orris picked up his pace. He was hungry and exhausted, and soon he'd have to patrol the farm. Lucy stood waiting for them at the anteroom door, the aroma of dinner in the air and her arms folded over her swollen belly.

Chapter Six

ORRIS WASN'T sure which he appreciated more: the luxury of a private room to himself, or the ability to stretch out on a real, lump-free mattress. The knowledge that he'd built a substantial portion of that bedroom was a bonus, leading to a warm feeling of satisfaction. The separate room was particularly nice given the odd sleeping hours he'd been practicing these last two weeks. At his own insistence, he'd continued to guard the sheep every night, snatching a few hours of rest after dawn and after the noontime meal. When he wasn't sleeping or patrolling, he helped with the farm chores.

He felt ragged and blurry, as if he were slowly growing transparent. Which was odd, because in reality he was slowly developing hard muscles. He'd never be as brawny as Samuel, but his labors came ever more easily and his body felt sleek and sinewy under his skin.

Even when he took to his new bed, Orris didn't fall asleep at once. He ached with need in a way he never had—either before or after becoming Daniel's lover—and he took himself in hand shockingly often. Maybe the people who said masturbation leads to insanity were correct. His mental equilibrium was certainly unbalanced. But his own touch felt too good to forgo.

And when he did finally succumb to sleep, he dreamed. More of those strange, tumbled visions of hunting and being hunted, of forests, of a naked body embracing him, of blood and glowing green eyes. The dreams simultaneously terrified and thrilled him.

One drizzly morning, Orris helped Samuel harness Beau to the plow. The horse waited somewhat impatiently, snorting frequently as if to hurry them along. He seemed happier once he began to till the field, plodding back and forth in straight lines with Samuel at his side. Orris took in the scent of rich, freshly tilled earth and the cacophony of several bird species that feasted amid the overturned soil.

The field was nearly finished when Samuel's younger daughter came running full-tilt in their direction, braids flying out behind her. "Papa! Papa! The baby!"

Samuel went instantly paper white. "Orris," he groaned.

"Go. Go tend to her. I'll take care of the horse."

Samuel ran to the house without looking back.

Orris and Beau looked at one another. Over the past couple of weeks, they'd reached a fragile truce, although both were still nervous around the other. But perhaps Beau realized that without Orris's help, he was likely to be stuck in his traces for a very long time, so he stood still as Orris fumbled to unhook him from the plow. Orris didn't even need to lead Beau back to the barn—in fact, the horse led him. Once they were inside, Orris made sure Beau had food and water, but he didn't try to brush him down as Samuel would have. He hoped Beau wouldn't be too much the worse for wear; at least, he seemed content enough.

Orris washed up at the pump and then, with considerable trepidation, entered the house. Heavy footsteps sounded on the upstairs floorboards, and the girls huddled wide-eyed at the table, but nothing else seemed amiss.

"Do you need anything?" Orris asked them.

The older one shook her head. "Mama said there's bread and butter if we get hungry."

"*Are* you hungry? I can help you rustle up a meal."

"No."

He combed his beard with his fingers. "Would you like to do some lessons?"

The girls exchanged quick glances before the older one said, "No thank you, Uncle Orris. Not now."

"All right."

He stood in the middle of the kitchen, unsure what to do. He had no notion of how long babies took to be born. A few minutes? A day?

When he realized he was pacing restlessly—probably making his nieces even more worried—he stopped and sighed. "I'm going to step outside. But I'll stay close to the house, so if you or your parents need me, just call."

The girls nodded in unison.

Orris was thankful to leave the claustrophobic confines of the kitchen and breathe fresh, cool air. He wandered to the front of the house—the side facing the road—and climbed onto the rarely used porch. Everyone who lived in the house came and went through the anteroom, where coats and hats and muddy boots were kept. And in the time since Orris had arrived in Oregon, not a single visitor had come to the front door. It wasn't that his brother's family was reclusive, but their farm was fairly isolated, and they and their neighbors tended to be too busy to socialize.

The front porch was covered, and there were two slightly rickety wooden chairs. Orris sat on one of them and watched the clouds scud across the sky.

Perhaps he dozed off, because a man stood on the porch in front of him with such suddenness that Orris yelped and nearly fell out of his chair.

"Sorry," Henry Bonn said quietly. "I didn't mean to scare you." He was dressed in buckskin again, hatless, his long blond hair tied with a cord. He held a fabric-wrapped bundle.

"You didn't scare me. I was just... distracted, I suppose." Belatedly remembering his manners—and hoping his legs would hold him—Orris stood and held out a hand.

Henry's hand was large and rough and very warm. He shook Orris's hand firmly, but without making the little interchange feel like an attempt to prove his strength. "It's good to see you again, Mr. Spencer. Under less stressful circumstances."

"Orris. And, um, yes." Orris wasn't sure how to phrase the next question, so he blundered ahead. "Your brother...?"

"He was dead by the time you reached home."

"I'm... I'm so sorry. Please accept my condolences for your loss." The words seemed stiff and meaningless. Certainly insufficient to soften the grief etched on Henry's face.

But Henry bobbed his head. "Thank you. It was his own damned stupidity that killed him, but he was my brother and I loved him."

It was slightly shocking to hear a man speak of loving another man, even if the love was fraternal. Orris had never spoken those words to or about any of his brothers—not even Samuel—nor had any of them. But he could tell Henry's statement was honest and heartfelt.

"You did what you could for him," Orris said gently.

"And so did your brother. That's why I'm here. Wanted to thank him properly." Henry hefted the fabric-wrapped bundle slightly. "Just some deerskins. A token. 'Cause there ain't many folks 'round here who'd go out of their way for me, and your brother did. You too."

"Oh. Well, I'm afraid Samuel's... occupied right now. But I'll be happy to pass your message to him."

"Thank you." Henry set his burden onto the splintery porch floor. But he didn't seem eager to leave, and Orris... good Lord, Orris could look at him all day.

"Would you like to sit awhile?" Orris asked. "I can get you something to eat or drink."

Henry's broad smile was enough to make Orris weak at the knees. "I'll pass on the food and drink, but I wouldn't mind sitting for a spell. I don't get much conversation." He sat in one of the chairs.

Orris sat too, thinking how lonely it would be to live all alone in the forest, nothing but a ghost for company. Orris didn't much care for crowds, but even he wouldn't fancy complete solitude.

For several minutes neither of them said a word. Henry seemed comfortable, though, and his gaze was frank and friendly. Finally, he grinned slightly. "Do you like it here, Orris? Or do you miss the city?"

"I'm getting used to it. It's very different, of course. But beautiful."

Perhaps that was the correct answer, because Henry gifted him with that stunning smile again. "I've never seen a big city. I'd be uncomfortable."

"Where are you from?"

Henry leaned back in his seat as if he intended to stay there awhile, which pleased Orris so much he couldn't hide a grin.

"My parents sailed to California in 1850," Henry said.

"Were they looking for gold?"

"No," Henry replied with a small chuckle. "Money ain't important to us."

"Then why did they come?"

With a sad smile, Henry looked away, staring across the road at a muddy field. "Used to be more of us," he said quietly. "Never a lot, but more. We had… communities. But that was a long time ago. Men started burning the forests to make cities, and they invented guns. Machines. Life got harder for us."

Orris wondered exactly who "us" was. A small religious sect? A persecuted community like the Gypsies? He didn't ask, because it didn't seem right to interrupt Henry's story, especially when the story seemed to bring him such pain.

But when Henry remained silent a long time, his eyes focused far away, Orris cleared his throat. "So your family immigrated for a better life?"

Henry returned his attention to Orris. "Yes. My parents and a few others came to California. Me and Charles were born a few years later. But it turned out things in California weren't that much easier. We still…." He rubbed the back of his neck. "My folks died. Some of us moved up here. But now it's me and Char— It's just me left."

Orris was used to longing for things he couldn't have. But he'd never wanted anything as badly as he wanted to rise from his chair and draw Henry into his arms, to offer him the comforts of flesh and blood.

"Do you still have people in California? Or in Europe?"

"Dunno. Maybe."

More silence passed between them. Orris didn't know what thoughts passed through Henry's mind. It seemed presumptuous to even speculate. But Orris had an odd certainty that a particular part of Henry's heart was mapped exactly like his own: a barren land that despaired of experiencing anything but loneliness.

And then Henry shocked Orris by reaching over to squeeze the top of his hand. "Tell me about New York, Orris. What's it like?" He took his hand away, but Orris could still feel the warmth.

"It's crowded. Dirty. Dangerous, sometimes."

"Where did you live? I heard of buildings five, six stories tall. Like mountains full of people. Did you live in one of them?"

"No. Our house had just two floors, plus a cellar and an attic. The attic was always miserably cold in the winter and like an oven during the summer. I felt sorry for the servants who had to sleep up there."

"Servants." Henry had tilted his head quizzically. "So you have a lot of money."

"No. My father has a lot of money." Orris shrugged. "I quite literally haven't a penny to my name."

"Me neither. Money, gold... they're hard. Lifeless. Smell bad. Got no use for 'em."

"I wish I could say the same," Orris replied a little wistfully. "But I'm afraid I can't hunt for my suppers as you do."

A strange intensity burned in Henry's eyes. "Maybe not now. But you could."

"Are... are you offering to teach me to hunt? Because I'm not good at all with a gun. Samuel tried to teach me and was not at all successful."

Henry's teeth flashed white when he smiled. "I don't need a gun to hunt."

Orris didn't know what to make of that statement. Really, he didn't know what to make of Henry at all. The man seemed uneducated, almost feral, and yet his intelligence shone through his simple words. And everything he said seemed to have a dual meaning, like a secret language that Orris couldn't quite understand. Orris felt an almost physical tug toward Henry and wanted to believe Henry felt the same—but couldn't possibly hazard finding out if that were so.

"There must be something good about the city, Orris. Tell me."

Because Henry seemed sincere, and because it had been a very long time since anyone had seemed particularly interested in what Orris had to say, Orris complied. He spoke about museums and concerts, about restaurants and theaters. He described Central Park, with its polite facsimile of the wilderness. And he talked about the jumble of languages one heard on the street, the shops with every imaginable luxury, and the people who were heartrendingly poor.

Orris spoke longer than he had in years, but Henry appeared fascinated by his words, asking many questions. Orris had never before felt so… interesting.

He was in the midst of discussing one of his university classes when he accidentally mentioned Daniel's name. His tongue stumbled, causing him to blush.

Without Orris noticing, Henry had managed to move his chair closer and had angled it a bit so they were facing each other more than they faced the road. Now Henry leaned forward until he was close enough for Orris to see the little specks of blue and gray in his eyes.

"Why did your family send you away, Orris?"

"I told you. I disgraced them."

"How?"

Orris did not owe this man an answer. They barely knew each other, after all. He could refuse to respond. He could generate a falsehood, reinvent his own history. He *should* do this.

Veritas liberabit vos, said the Bible—*the truth shall set you free*. But that was a lie because the truth had sent Daniel far out of reach and banished Orris to the opposite end of the continent.

Ah. But wasn't that a kind of freedom too? Freedom from starched collars and droning sermons, freedom from his father's disdainful glares.

Orris looked Henry steadily in the eyes. "I disgraced my family by being a sodomite," he said—quite loudly.

Henry did not flinch or sneer, nor did he move away. "What happened to your lover?" he asked.

It wasn't the response Orris had expected, and it took him a moment to answer. "He's gone." He didn't explain the rest—how in the few dizzying, terrifying days after they were discovered in bed together, Orris overheard a servant saying that Daniel was being sent abroad. Orris had hurried the several blocks to Daniel's house, harboring visions of running away together, sharing a life in Germany or France or Italy or… or anywhere. But Daniel had turned him away. It seemed he couldn't abide the thought of losing his family's financial support. Orris boarded a westbound train just two days later.

"Good," Henry said, which wasn't at all the proper answer. Except then he stood—quite suddenly—and grasped Orris's upper arms, drawing him out of his chair. And then Henry gently but firmly pushed Orris back until he was pressed against the white-painted wall of the house, until their bodies were flush, until the scent of leather and sweat was thick in Orris's nose.

"You can say no, and I'll stop," Henry whispered into Orris's ear. Good Lord, he was so solid and strong and sure.

Orris took a deep breath before tilting his head slightly. "I won't say no."

Henry growled. The sound came from deep in his chest, and it made Orris's entire body vibrate. And when Henry licked him—his tongue moving slowly from Orris's ear down the taut curve of his neck to the edge of his collar—Orris very nearly lost his mind. But what truly undid him was when Henry kissed him. No chaste brushing of lips; no tentative fumbles. Henry pressed his tongue into Orris's mouth and his groin against Orris's hip. Orris clutched at him and pushed his own body forward.

He'd never kissed outdoors. It was wonderful. The road was very lightly traveled—sometimes days went by with no passersby. But as far as Orris was concerned, the entire population of New York City could have been gathered there in the mud, goggling at the porch, and he wouldn't have stopped what he was doing. Why would he when need thrummed through his body and Henry's, as natural and primal and huge as the mountains themselves?

Without breaking their kiss, Henry fumbled at Orris's shirt buttons. Good. They would have skin. Orris wanted to taste every inch of him.

But then Henry froze and pulled away, his head tilted upward. "You have a new niece or nephew, I think." His voice was raspy.

"I…. What?"

"Healthy, judging by the crying. Sounds strong."

Orris heard nothing but his own thudding heart and coarse breaths.

Henry took a step backward. He let one hand linger on Orris's arm for a moment before drawing farther away, just out of reach. "No," Orris protested.

"I reckon your family will be looking for you soon. Orris, I want—Well, don't matter what *I* want. I know your life changed pretty drastically when you came out west, but what I have to offer, it's a whole different world. You shouldn't accept my offer lightly."

"I don't know what you're offering."

"Exactly." Henry smiled. "I'll give you some time. Time to make choices. You gotta know what you really want, Orris. Someday you could get on a train and head back to New York. But sometimes when we travel, we can't go back. So we better make damned sure that's where we want to go."

"But I do—"

"Time, Orris. Ain't no hurry to do it all at once."

Henry stepped off the porch, then turned back to look at Orris. Unnoticed by Orris, the rainfall had increased, and now the water darkened Henry's hair and ran down his face. He pointed at the fabric-wrapped bundle of deerskins. "Thank your brother for me. Wish him well with the new baby." And then he loped away.

Chapter Seven

JESSE ORRIS Spencer was a screamer. Although he wasn't an especially large baby, one wouldn't know that based on the volume and vigor of his bellowing. His parents were delighted with his vocal outrage over hunger and discomfort; they said it was an indication of his health. But Orris— who'd cried a bit himself when he learned he was to be his nephew's namesake—secretly wished Jesse could be healthy a little more quietly.

Late winter might have been a slow season on the farm, but spring was not. Ploughing and planting needed to be done, and then the fields needed weeding. More lambs were born, and chicks and ducklings hatched, which meant more time spent feeding them and caring for their varied and inevitable ailments. Everyone would have been exhausted anyway, even were it not for Jesse's interruptions of their sleep.

They lost a few birds to raccoons or foxes, but no more lambs, and Samuel suspended the nighttime watches. Orris fell into bed each night sore and bone-weary, and if he dreamed, he didn't remember it when he awoke.

It was a happy time for all of them. Samuel and his family were thrilled with the new baby. Even Lucy smiled more often, and once or twice she even cracked a small joke. The girls were pleased to help care for their brother and proud to be taking on more of the household chores. Samuel strutted around, grinning more widely than any Fifth Avenue millionaire.

And oddly enough, Orris was happy too. For the first time in his life, he felt pride in his body. He would never be as well built as Samuel, but Orris had developed strong muscles on his arms, chest, and legs. Physically, he could do far more than he'd dreamed. Sometimes in the chill mornings, before he dressed, he ran his hands over the flat planes of his belly and the new contours of his upper body, and he smiled as he imagined Henry's hand instead of his.

Even these many weeks later, he could still taste Henry's kiss.

The rigors of farm life didn't give Orris much time to think about Henry, at least at a conscious level. And perhaps that was just as well, because Orris's thoughts on the matter were... murky. When he tried to understand what Henry was offering him, Orris's mind flinched away, as though he was keeping secrets from himself.

So instead of contemplating the matter as a scholar might, Orris remembered the taste of Henry's mouth, his intoxicating earthy scent, and the press of their firm bodies together.

Dinner came later now that the days were longer, and by the time food was served, everyone was famished. Tonight Orris had a third helping of meat and bread and a second generous slice of pie. Afterward he and Samuel ambled outside to the porch to watch the stars peek through tattered clouds. Orris sat in the same chair Henry had, and imagined he could still feel Henry's warmth.

"I reckon in the fall we'll send the girls to school in town," Samuel said without preamble.

"I can teach them here."

"I know. But they're getting older. They should spend more time around other young'uns. And I could use your help for other things. You're right handy to have around."

Orris smiled. "Thank you. But it's far for them to walk, isn't it?"

"There's children 'round here who walk farther. I reckon once in a while I can give them a ride, when I have to fetch something from town anyhow."

They watched the breeze pick up and set the treetops aflutter. An owl called from somewhere close.

Samuel cleared his throat. "I want you to know something, Orr. Me and Lucy, we weren't all that excited about taking you in. We figured you'd be a burden."

"I'm sorry," Orris said, not looking at him.

"Me too. I mean—you were still just a boy last time I'd seen you. And you were always off with your nose in a book. I didn't picture you adjusting well to farm life. Sure didn't picture you mucking out horseshit or lugging lumber around. But you've done those things, Orr. Done them well. You ain't a burden. Not even close."

Now Orris did look at his brother, and if Orris's eyes were slightly watery, well, perhaps that was understandable. "Thank you. And thank you for... for giving me a place when I had nowhere else to go."

"Well, that's what I'm trying to tell you. You got your feet under you now. Maybe you'll decide one of these days that you want to strike out on your own. Someone like you—smart, strong, willing to work hard—he's got plenty of opportunities out here. But you're truly welcome in this household. Stay forever and that ain't a problem. And if you leave, you can always come back. Anytime. This'll always be your home too." Samuel smiled. "You helped build it."

Samuel's words dulled a pain Orris hadn't even realized he'd been suffering. "Thank you. I'm grateful to you and Lucy."

"Maybe someday you'll find a woman and—"

"I won't."

"You don't have to…. It doesn't have to be about that kind of love. Maybe you just find someone who you feel comfortable with. Someone to work at your side, keep you company in the evenings. That's not such a bad thing, is it?"

Orris thought for a moment. "Would it be enough for you?"

"No," Samuel answered with a sigh. "I reckon it wouldn't."

JESSE'S CRIES woke Orris in the middle of the night, and he couldn't fall back asleep. He ended up getting dressed—fumbling for his clothes in the darkness—and heading outside. The wind had cleared the clouds away, and a nearly full moon shone brightly. Orris didn't need a lantern to make his way to the sheep paddock.

The animals were awake, huddled together at the spot farthest from the forest. Every now and then, one of them baaed. He felt a little sorry for them, always having to fear predators. Yet he couldn't blame the predators, who had to eat. Besides, Orris and the rest of the household had dined on lamb themselves the night before—and it had been delicious.

If Orris stood in a particular spot near the corner of the fence, he had clear views of both the house and the wooded hills. The house glowed slightly in the moonlight. It was a very modest structure; in New York he'd seen grander carriage houses. But even with the windows dark, this house looked safe and welcoming. His own bedroom was plain but cozy, with a good bed, a colorful rag rug on the floor, and a few of his nieces' drawings tacked to the walls. Right now the walls were whitewashed, but Samuel and Lucy had discussed with him the possibility of wallpapering them soon.

And then there was the forest, which rose up the hill and, as far as Orris knew, continued forever. He'd walked into those trees only once, when he'd accompanied Samuel to Henry's cabin. They'd been walking quickly then, and he hadn't had the chance to take in many details. He wondered what mysteries were hidden there, what creatures stalked through the green.

He wondered whether Henry was in his cabin right now, maybe thinking of him. Instinct told him not—he believed that Henry was probably outside under the same sky as him.

Orris turned around and gazed into the paddock.

He didn't startle when a soft *chuff* sounded behind him. In fact, he realized he'd almost expected it. He turned back unhurriedly.

A wolf stood perhaps fifteen feet away. Orris hadn't seen the wolves clearly last time, but this was a magnificent animal, large and powerful without being bulky. It held its head erect, with pointed ears cocked slightly forward and eyes gleaming brightly. The fur around its neck formed a thick mane. Orris wondered what it would feel like to bury his fingers in that pelt. Would it be soft?

There was nothing aggressive or threatening about the wolf's posture, nor did it seem afraid.

"You're beautiful," Orris said softly, even though he wasn't sure whether his voice would alarm or incite the creature.

The wolf twitched its ears slightly and took a small step forward. Then it stopped again.

Orris did not want to die. But there was something so entirely compelling in the wolf's eyes that, had he been asked, he would have willingly laid himself out before the beast as a sacrifice.

Instead he fell to his knees and reached out with his hands. "Please," he croaked.

The wolf took another step closer. But then it froze. It was saying something to him, without words, and Orris was too stupid to understand. He didn't understand anything anymore… except that he yearned for the wolf.

He would have crawled to the animal on his hands and knees, but it gave a soft growl. Without breaking eye contact, it swiveled its head in the direction of the hills. Then it turned and ran away.

Chapter Eight

"ARE YOU all right, Orris? You seem off this morning."

Orris realized he'd been standing motionless for some time, a shovel in his hand. He leaned the tool against the barn and shook his head. "I'm fine. A little tired, I expect."

"The baby's been keeping you up. I'm sorry." Samuel wiped his forehead with the back of his hand. "He'll be sleeping through the night soon."

"It's fine. I mean, it's not Jesse. I'm feeling a bit restless."

Samuel gave him a long look. "You could go into Portland for a few days. I've been meaning to talk to you about a small salary. Ain't much, but—"

"I don't want money. Or the city." What he wanted—no, what he *needed*—was the forest. The wild. He realized it quite suddenly and with a certainty that made his heart race. "Samuel? Can you spare me for a few hours today? I'd like to take a walk."

"A walk?"

"Yes."

Samuel looked troubled, but he nodded. "Sure, Orr. You go ahead. Clear your head."

Mumbling his gratitude, Orris headed in the direction of the forest.

"Where are you going, Orris?" Samuel called after him.

Orris pointed vaguely, but didn't reply.

"Be careful!"

Finding the narrow trail through the woods wasn't difficult. Staying on the path was harder. There was much more plant growth than last time, forcing him to clamber over and around many obstacles. At times the way was obscured entirely, leaving him briefly wondering if he was lost. Oddly, he wasn't frightened by the notion.

By the time he reached the clearing with the cabin, he was slightly winded and quite thoroughly dirty. He paused at the very edge of the woods. A few green shoots showed in the little garden plot and a hoe leaned near the door.

After taking several deep breaths for courage, Orris marched forward. His fist was raised to knock when the door swung open, startling him.

Henry was entirely naked. Orris could do nothing but goggle at him. At his wide shoulders and muscular, lightly haired chest. At the flat belly and narrow hips. At the plump, flaccid penis and pink scrotum nestled among golden curls. But even as he watched, the penis twitched and lengthened until it was partially erect.

"Orris," Henry rasped. His hair was in disarray—Orris hadn't noticed that at first—and there was a pillow crease on his cheek. He stood still under Orris's examination, except for his Adam's apple, which bobbed as he swallowed.

Orris still held his fist in the air; he let it fall. Heat pooled low in his belly and spread up his spine, then flashed through his brain in a sudden fever. He was delirious, incapable of rational thought. He grabbed Henry's bare shoulders and dragged him close for a rough and ravenous kiss.

The kiss was good. Henry's body against his, arms around him, was better. But not enough. Orris put his newly increased strength to use as he wrestled them both out of the doorway, back onto the bare bit of ground in front of the cabin. Henry was bigger and could certainly have resisted, but he didn't, and when Orris pushed him down, Henry let himself fall, pulling Orris down on top of him.

Orris nearly lost himself completely. He licked and nibbled at Henry's skin and rutted against him like an animal. He realized he was making a sound deep in his throat, a needy moan, but didn't care.

"Orris. Orris, wait." Henry grabbed Orris's shoulders and held him still. A flush covered Henry's chest and face, and his hair was wild beneath him.

Orris blinked a few times and tried to regain some control. "You don't want—"

"God, yes. I want. But this is… a dangerous time to do this."

"I don't care. It's always been a dangerous time for me."

Henry considered this a moment. "I guess so." The corners of his mouth lifted. "I want to see you and taste you too. Please."

Orris found it physically painful to pull away from Henry, as if he were tearing off a limb, but he complied. He rose to his feet and undressed, while Henry propped himself up on his elbows to watch, his legs splayed invitingly. Orris's impatience caused him to fumble with buttons and laces, and soon he was as naked as Henry. Under other circumstances, he might have felt chilled—the morning was not warm—but a raging fire still flamed through his veins, heating him from the inside out.

Henry must have liked what he saw, because he smiled broadly, and the rosy head of his cock bobbed against his belly.

Orris fell on top of him, hard enough to make Henry *oof.* But Henry wrapped his arms tightly around him and nuzzled at his neck. "Delicious. So good, Orris."

"Mmm," Orris replied, reveling in the sensation of skin against skin.

"This is… this is new to me. Better than I dreamed of."

Orris reared up slightly so he could see Henry's face. "You've never been with a man?"

"I've never been with *anyone.*"

"You're a virgin?" That possibility had never crossed Orris's mind.

"I ain't from New York City. Not too many opportunities in these parts."

Glancing briefly at the trees that ringed them, Orris nodded. "I understand. Are you quite sure you—"

"Ain't never been more sure of anything," Henry answered with a grin. "Just wanted to warn you. I probably ain't gonna be very good at it."

An unexpected laugh bubbled up from Orris's throat. "I promise I won't grade your performance if you don't grade mine. I'm not so very practiced myself."

"You had a lover."

"I did. But we were together only a few times, really. We rarely had much opportunity."

"And before him?"

"A few… clumsy fumbles with other boys. Nothing like this." He stroked Henry's smooth cheek, then his chest. "Never anything like this."

Henry rumbled an approval and squeezed Orris's buttocks. "I ain't met that many people, Orris. But you're the first one I ever ached for. Ever since I first saw you."

If Henry was going to be so honest and direct, Orris could hardly be closemouthed about his own feelings—even if he didn't understand them, even if they didn't make sense. "It's the same for me. Daniel was… he was nice. I liked him. But there's something about you that draws me like no other man has. Something… I don't even have the words for it."

Although Henry smiled, his eyes were serious. "I'm different, Orris. You need to know that. I ain't…. There's nothing like me in New York City."

"I know."

And truly those were enough words for now. Orris wanted to use his mouth for other things. And so he did—tasting Henry and being tasted. He shuddered helplessly as Henry explored his body, mapping a new frontier; and he reveled in making Henry whimper and shout. The noises they made together echoed across the clearing, and that was wonderful in itself. Before, Orris had always needed to remain quiet.

But when Orris entered Henry's body—his way eased slightly by spit and by the eager droplets their desperate cocks had produced—they both froze to stare at one another, wide-eyed.

"I've been waiting for you my whole life," Henry whispered. "Didn't think I'd ever find you."

"I was thinking the same thing."

"How much will you give up for me?"

Orris didn't even need to think about the answer. "Anything. Everything."

He had to move then, and he did, and Henry arched and writhed underneath him. When they pulsed their completions in unison, they yelled loudly enough to startle birds into flight.

After, they lay entwined on the ground, sweat sticking dirt to their skin. Henry snuffled deeply into Orris's hair. "Thank you."

"Believe me, it was my pleasure." Orris wiggled slightly against him. Given a few minutes to recover, he was reasonably certain he'd be up for a second round. Outdoor nudity was unexpectedly stimulating.

"Didn't think I'd be able to… to keep control. I couldn't have if I'd been inside you."

Orris shivered slightly at the thought of Henry inside him. He would like that very much. "There's no need for you to maintain control. I'm not delicate. You won't hurt me."

There was no humor in Henry's answering laugh. "I would. And not because you're fragile, Orris—you ain't. It's only…. God, I want to change you. To make you like me. And that ain't fair to you."

Orris sat up. He rubbed his fingers through his hair, dislodging a few pine needles that tickled when they fell down his back. "There's nothing wrong with being like you. You're the most remarkable person I've ever met."

"If you were like me, you couldn't ever go back to New York."

"I can't anyway. And frankly, I don't want to. There's nothing for me there."

"But there's something for you here." Henry sat too, and he settled his hand on Orris's shoulder. "You got family here. I know your brother a little bit. He's a good man. Are you willing to lose him for me?"

"I...." Orris looked down at his lap. His spent cock was damp. A storm of emotions churned inside him. "I can't have both?" he finally asked, looking up again. But he knew the answer.

Henry shook his head sadly. "I'm sorry." He stood and then held out a hand to Orris, who used it to leverage himself up.

Now Orris was cold. He wrapped his arms around himself, wishing for Henry's embrace instead. "It's a terrible decision."

"Then think about it awhile longer. Be sure. Because if you choose me, you can't go back."

"Thank you for being patient with me."

Henry's smile was a little bit crooked, which made it all the more endearing. "I don't want to be patient. I want to grab you right now."

"And I want to be grabbed." Orris smiled at him before retrieving his clothing. Henry watched silently while Orris dressed. They walked together to the edge of the clearing, Henry uncaring of the uneven ground despite his bare feet.

Just under the canopy of the firs, Henry cradled Orris's face in his palms. "I'm glad you came here today. But for the good of us both, don't return unless you decide to stay. And for God's sake, stay indoors the next few nights. Please."

Carefully not making any promises—nor thinking too carefully about the last part of Henry's request—Orris caressed him back. "I'm glad I came here too. Whatever happens, I may have regrets. But I won't regret the time we spent together today."

They kissed again, a soft contact that was more about affection than passion. And then Orris headed back downhill, toward the farm.

Chapter Nine

WHEN ORRIS returned from his visit to Henry's cabin, Samuel was repairing a fence post alongside the sheep paddock. Samuel gave him a very long look—perhaps taking in his disheveled clothing and messy hair—but only grunted at him before returning to his task. Orris walked past silently.

After dinner the family gathered in the parlor. The baby was uncharacteristically content, sucking on his fingers and watching everyone with his wide brown eyes. Lucy rocked him slowly in her arms and discussed plans with Samuel. They were trying to decide whether to buy a few dairy cows the following year. None of their closest neighbors kept cattle, and Samuel and Lucy might be able to sell them milk. The girls sat on the rug and played cat's cradle with some lengths of gray yarn.

Orris reclined on the sofa—it was much better for sitting than sleeping—and watched them all.

"What do you think, Orr?" asked Samuel, turning in his direction. "If we're going to get cows, we'll have to clear the trees from the south end of the property to make a pasture. Chopping them down is hard enough, but pulling the stumps—that's *really* work. But we could sell the lumber for a decent price. Maybe even get enough to pay for the cows. Would you mind playing lumberjack for a while?"

"I'll help however you need me," Orris said. But he was picturing all the hills denuded of forest, reduced first to farmland and then to crowded, stinking cities. He pictured all the creatures of the forest—the birds, the deer, the coyotes, the wolves—confined to smaller islands of wilderness until those were gone too. But he also imagined Samuel, Lucy, and their children comfortable and content. Not ostentatiously wealthy, but prosperous. Never having to worry about whether there would be food on the table or a good roof over their heads.

Not too long after that, Orris begged exhaustion and went to his room.

Usually he cleaned himself before he went to bed, using the basin, towel, and soap on the bedroom's small washstand. But not tonight. Instead he fell asleep with Henry's scent still thick on his skin. He slept fitfully, waking several times with the conviction that someone waited for him just outside. And once he thought he heard a wolf's lonely howl.

MORNING DAWNED gray and damp. Orris made sure the animals had fresh water. He fed Beau, but the horse whinnied and shied away from him, so Orris made quick work of it and then moved on. He spent a fairly miserable few hours bent over, pulling weeds. But he didn't complain. After all, the work needed to be done.

Lunch was large and filling. The girls sat on either side of Orris as he ate, and he helped them with their sums. He'd always been good with numbers—the only thing about him that his father had ever praised.

Orris donned his outerwear in the anteroom and prepared to tackle more weeds. But Samuel stopped him just as he was going out the door. "Want to ride into town with me? I need a few things at the store."

"But the weeding—"

"There's always chores. But sometimes even a farmer needs a little break. Come with me. The weeds will wait for you."

They didn't speak for the first mile or two of the rattling ride. But when they turned onto the larger road that led directly to town, Samuel cleared his throat. "You sure you don't want to go into Portland for a few days, Orr? You could pick up some wallpaper samples for Lucy while you're there."

"No. Thank you. But if you want to go, I can help keep things going on the farm."

"Nah. It'll wait. I just thought...." He settled his hat farther forward on his head. "Never mind."

"Thanks, Samuel. For everything, I mean. I'd have been lost without you."

After a brief silence, Samuel said, "If you're not careful, Orr, you could get lost again. We ain't all that civilized here yet. Sometimes men walk into the forest and they never come back."

Orris nodded but didn't meet Samuel's eyes. He turned his head to the side, as if the field they were passing fascinated him. "I want you to know, Samuel. I won't... I won't disgrace you. Or let any other harm come to your family."

"I know."

Orris listened to the creaking of Beau's harness and the slightly squashy clops of his hooves on the muddy road, and he thought back to a time shortly before he and Daniel were discovered in bed together. They'd attended an art show displaying works by some radical new painters, most of them French. Impressionists, they were called. Daniel hadn't cared for the exhibit at all, but Orris had been quite intrigued. The landscape he passed through now resembled something from one of those Impressionist paintings, all watery swatches of color without sharp detail. He would never see artwork like that again—he knew that—but was it such a great loss when he had the real landscapes before him?

"Do you remember Mary Delaney, Orris?"

Disturbed from his brief reverie, Orris turned to his brother and blinked. "Who?"

"Mary Delaney. She was one of our servants. You used to call her May-May."

"I don't…. Perhaps." Orris had a vague impression of a kind girl who smelled of soap and who comforted him when he suffered small injuries. His mother had died giving birth to him, and he supposed that when he was very young, he'd welcomed whatever affection he could get.

"She was very pretty. The first girl I lost my heart to." Samuel smiled. "I was eleven or twelve and she… oh, she must have been almost twenty. Ancient."

"She used to sing to me at bedtime, I think. Once in a while."

"Probably. She liked you. She used to say that you were special because you were the seventh son of a seventh son."

Orris snorted. "Special? Right."

"No, she was sure of it. She told everyone it meant you'd be magic. A healer, maybe."

"You're the one who was going to be a doctor. I get woozy at the sight of blood."

"Well, Mary was insistent about it. She even used to argue about you with Cook, who claimed that seventh sons of seventh sons were actually werewolves."

Orris ignored the way his skin stood up in goose bumps. "Cook never did like me."

"Cook never liked anyone. I'm surprised she didn't poison us all."

They chuckled softly together. After a few moments, Orris asked, "What happened to May-May?" Again a shadowy memory of searching for her but not finding her, and nobody to hug him when he cried.

"Father sent her away when she got pregnant. She was unmarried."

"Who was the father?"

"I don't know." Samuel gave him a long, grim look. "But I have my suspicions."

"Would Father have—"

"He'd turn out his own son, Orris. Just for loving someone. You don't think he'd give a hoot about a servant girl, do you?"

"No," Orris sighed. "I don't think he would."

Allen's general store was busy this afternoon. Allen, his wife, and his half-grown son were all helping customers, while other people milled patiently among the bins and display cases. A few men gathered around the stove, talking loudly. Orris winced slightly when he saw that one of them was Dunning.

"Spencer," Dunning said, addressing Samuel and ignoring Orris as usual.

"Hello, Dunning." Samuel greeted the other men as well, and they nodded back.

Orris pretended to examine a display of spices in metal tins while the other men discussed plans to incorporate Beaverton into an official town. From what Orris could tell, those who lived in the town itself and had businesses there favored the notion, feeling it would bring progress and prosperity, while the farmers opposed it. Orris couldn't see what possible difference incorporation would make, one way or the other, but he didn't share his views.

After two of the men moved to the front of the store to talk to the shopkeepers, Dunning turned to Samuel. "You lost any more livestock?"

"A few of the sheep had the scours, but—"

"I mean to the wolf."

"Oh. No, we haven't had any sign of that."

"Me neither. Bastard must've died after I shot it."

Orris felt his stomach tighten and his hands clench into fists. He turned around to glare at Dunning. "You didn't have to kill it. You could have just scared it away."

At first Dunning looked slightly startled and confused, as if he hadn't realized Orris was capable of speech. Then Dunning's lip curled into a sneer. "Soft," he spat.

"I'm not soft. I'm just opposed to killing when it's not necessary. Wolves just want to eat. This used to be their territory before you came here."

Dunning stomped closer and jabbed his fat finger toward Orris's chest, but Orris didn't back away. "If it was up to me," Dunning snarled, "I'd gut and skin every one of 'em. I used to hunt 'em for the bounty.

They're thieving filth, and anyone who don't see that... well, that man's got a problem."

Orris raised his chin and looked Dunning in the eyes. "Maybe I have a problem with you, Mr. Dunning."

The last time Orris had been in a fight was when his next-oldest brother tried to steal one of Orris's tin soldiers. Orris had been seven or eight at the time, and his brother had beaten him soundly—and ended up with the toy too. Orris didn't know how a skirmish with Dunning would end. And he never got a chance to find out because Samuel grabbed Orris's arm and dragged him outside, then shoved him roughly into the side of the wagon.

"What the hell do you think you're doing?" Samuel yelled.

"I don't like him."

"He ain't my favorite person either, Orr, but that doesn't mean I'm gonna pick a fight with him over something stupid."

It wasn't stupid, Orris thought. He crossed his arms and glared sullenly.

With a quiet sigh, Samuel took a step closer. "Look. I know he's treated you poorly from the beginning. He's an ignorant jackass. But he's also our neighbor, and fighting him isn't going to turn him into a nice man."

"I know. I'm sorry."

Samuel clapped him on the shoulder. "Wait out here, all right? I'll be out soon."

Orris nodded before climbing onto the wagon seat.

THE FAMILY spent another peaceful evening in the parlor. Samuel didn't mention the incident with Dunning, although he occasionally shot Orris a slightly worried look. His older daughter was teaching the younger one to knit, which was entertaining. This time Orris waited until everyone else was ready to retire before he too stood.

"Good night," he said, and he received a chorus of return good wishes.

He didn't undress when he got to his room, though. He paced. There was very little room for it—just a few steps in each direction—and he kept jostling the washstand. But he couldn't stay still.

For the first time in his life, he wished he were a religious man. He would have prayed for guidance. As it was, all he could do was walk back and forth, back and forth, his face often buried in his hands.

He didn't know how he reached a decision, but he definitely knew when. A certainty settled in his mind as if it had landed there from above. He grabbed a piece of paper from a shelf and his pen and ink. But then he replaced them, unused. Walking quietly so as not to wake anyone, he left his room and went to the anteroom, where he grabbed his coat and hat. He quickly laced up his boots.

The clouds had parted enough for the full moon to shine through, clearly illuminating his way. But when he reached the forest, the trees blocked most of the light. He stumbled and tripped his way uphill, swearing softly under his breath the entire time. He didn't lose his way.

The clearing glowed like a theatre, with the cabin set center stage. The entire scene was timeless—nothing about it suggested the end of the nineteenth century. A medieval hermit could have lived in that cabin, or a prehistoric Druid. Civilization might as well be hundreds of years in the future.

Orris took off his boots and stripped out of his clothing, which he left in an untidy heap at the edge of the clearing. He began to shiver, but he didn't mind. He didn't think he'd feel cold for long. He strode to the middle of the clearing—to the spot where he and Henry had made love—and stopped.

And then he shouted as loud as he could: "I'm here! I've decided! I'm ready!"

He didn't hear anything behind him. But he felt the gaze of glowing eyes. He turned around slowly.

The wolf was six feet away. Droplets of moisture glistened on his fur, and blood stained his muzzle.

"I'm here," Orris repeated, this time in a whisper. He fell to his knees, spread his arms, and tilted his head to better expose his neck. But he did not close his eyes.

The wolf looked at him for the space of several heartbeats, then threw back his head and howled—an ancient cry of grief and triumph. The entire world echoed with the sound. Only when the last reverberations died away did he shift his weight slightly backward. He leapt.

And then the wolf bit.

Epilogue

THE WOLF stood on a small outcropping of rock. If he peered carefully through the trees with his keen eyesight, he could make out the small farmhouse below. A warm light glowed in several of its windows. When he cocked his ears forward, the light breeze brought him hints of human laughter. It was a good sound.

Not far from the house, a few cows dozed in a pasture, and near to them was a paddock with sheep. He liked the taste of sheep, but he wouldn't hunt these. His mate would be displeased if he approached the farm, and besides, he'd eaten already that evening. He and his mate had brought down a wounded elk and feasted grandly. His belly felt nicely full now, and when he licked his muzzle, he could still taste blood.

His mate—a larger, lighter-colored wolf—hopped lightly onto the rock beside him and made a small chuffing sound. The smaller wolf gently bashed the side of his head into his mate's shoulder. The larger wolf responded with another chuff and then a playful nip at the scruff of his neck.

Although nights were short this time of year, many hours remained before daylight. There was still plenty of time to run side by side through the forest, breathing in the scents of endless numbers of living things. Still time to chase one another, to engage in mock battles, to howl together over the joy of companionship, the sheer joy of life. And when dawn broke, they would still have energy to fall into bed together and find completion in each other's bodies.

The larger wolf chuffed for a third time, mouthed at his mate's muzzle, and then turned to run off into the moon-dappled woods. The smaller wolf followed without a backward glance.

KIM FIELDING is very pleased every time someone calls her eclectic. Her books have won Rainbow Awards and span a variety of genres. She has migrated back and forth across the western two-thirds of the United States and currently lives in California, where she long ago ran out of bookshelf space. She's a university professor who dreams of being able to travel and write full time. She also dreams of having two perfectly behaved children, a husband who isn't obsessed with football, and a house that cleans itself. Some dreams are more easily obtained than others.

Blogs: http://kfieldingwrites.com/ and
http://www.goodreads.com/author/show/4105707.Kim_Fielding/blog
Facebook: https://www.facebook.com/KFieldingWrites.
E-mail: kim@kfieldingwrites.com
Twitter:@KFieldingWrites

By KIM FIELDING

Alaska
Animal Magnetism (Dreamspinner Anthology)
The Border
Brute
Don't Try This at Home (Dreamspinner Anthology)
A Great Miracle Happened There
Grown-up
Housekeeping
Men of Steel (Dreamspinner Anthology)
Motel. Pool.
Night Shift
Pilgrimage
The Pillar
Saint Martin's Day
Snow on the Roof (Dreamspinner Anthology)
Speechless • The Gig
Steamed Up (Dreamspinner Anthology)
The Tin Box
Venetian Masks
Violet's Present

BONES
Good Bones
Buried Bones
The Gig
Bone Dry

GOTHIKA
Stitch (Multiple Author Anthology)
Bones (Multiple Author Anthology)
Claw (Multiple Author Anthology)

Published by DREAMSPINNER PRESS
http://www.dreamspinnerpress.com

The Black Dog

Eli Easton

Thanks to my beta readers Jamie Fessenden and Jay Northcote—especially Jay for her Brit pick!

~1~

"I'M TELLIN' ye, it was the Black Dog. Now what the hell are ye gonna do about it, Hayden MacLairty?"

The dead sheep, all four of them, made a grisly spectacle on what remained of the green summer grass. All of them had their throats crushed and bloodied, and two had their stomachs torn open, too, inviting flies to the feast. Hayden couldn't quite wrap his head around it.

There were no bears or wolves in Scotland. A vicious pet or zoo animal might have gotten loose. Or perhaps it was a pack of stray dogs that had gone rogue. But what would kill four sheep and not feed? The animals were not so much eaten as *displayed*.

Hayden knelt down by one of the disemboweled sheep, trying to get a closer look at its wound. It looked torn, as from claws or teeth, not cut with a knife.

"I'll take 'em to the vet in Ullapool. See if he can tell me anythin' about what done this."

"I told ye what done this! It was the Black Dog!"

Hayden straightened up to his full height, not averse to using his size to shut up Dylan Mitchell. Dylan was one of many colorful characters in Hayden's precinct. He drank, and he saw things, and normally Hayden could ignore his wild stories. But not today, not with four dead sheep.

"Now you listen here, Dylan. There ain't no such thing as the Black Dog."

"I seen it! Why, just two nights ago—"

"And whatever killed your sheep is real, not some supernatural phantom, and that means I've gotta catch it. I'm not likely to catch it if I'm wastin' my time lookin' for spooks."

Dylan's face clouded with anger. "Ye don't never listen to me, Hayden. But I know what I saw. Seen that thing five times now, the first time when I was nigh on ten year old, and there weren't no liquor involved then. And I drink plenty without seein' the damn thing. When I see it, it's because it's there. So what're ye gonna do about it, hey? I can't afford to lose four head."

"I'll post watch for a couple of nights," Hayden agreed reluctantly. "I'm not arguin' with you. We gotta find this thing." *And if you didn't get drunk as a lord every night, you could watch your land your own damn self.*

"'Course we do! My sheep one night, maybe my wife the next! I wanna know what yer gonna do about that monster."

"Now, Dyl, it won' do a lick of good to berate the man." Laith Mitchell spoke up, thank heaven. She was a good woman with a heck of a lot more sense than her husband.

"How 'bout you?" Hayden asked her. "You seen any animal in these parts that might have done this?"

She shook her head regretfully. "No, Hayden. The O'Ryan's lab goes wanderin' from time to time, but he's gentle as a kitten. Ain't seen nothin' else."

Dylan glowered harder.

"Right, then. I'll just load 'em up." Not for the first time, Hayden wished he had a subordinate to give such menial work to. He spread out plastic bags in the back of his Land Rover that was marked with the cheery yellow and blue check of the Scottish police. Then he hauled the heavy, bloody sheep into the boot. He had to drive them over an hour each way to Ullapool. But anything that ever had to be done, Hayden did himself. He was the only constable in the small hamlet of Laide and its surrounds. He covered a territory of nearly a hundred miles square, and he himself was the entire breadth and width of the law here. He might call in help if there was real trouble, but not for sheep. And decidedly not for a phantom black dog.

IT WAS nearly dark when Hayden got back to Laide. He passed the Black Dog pub. There was a strange car in the lot, a rental, so apparently Angus had tourists in. Hopefully, they were there for the night and not just a meal. It was a good day when Angus could let out one of his upstairs rooms.

Maybe Dylan would show up at the pub tonight and spout off about the Black Dog. Nothing like a little local color to give the monster-hunters that chill up the spine. The wild northern end of Scotland was popular with long-distance cyclists and the occasional hardy hiker. But the few who stopped in the tiny hamlet of Laide had the legend in mind.

Hayden sighed. How he'd love to put up his tired feet at the pub and have a pint. But he had other obligations.

AT HOME, Hayden let himself in quietly. As always the house smelled sourly of camphor and rose water and cabbage.

"Hullo," he said to Ruth as he entered the kitchen. "And hullo, Mom." He kissed his mother on the top of her head, assessing her condition automatically. Her crazy thick black hair, shot through with gray, was freshly washed, a task Ruth only managed a few times a week. She was wearing a thick purple cardigan. It was a bit too small on her large frame, but it was clean. And she had on real trousers today—some old khakis—not PJ bottoms.

His mother looked up at him and smiled. "Hayden! Ruth made us supper. Isn't that nice?"

It was a good day then. Deep inside, where fear gripped his stomach in greedy handfuls, the tension eased.

"That's lovely, Mom. What're we havin', then?"

"Pot roast! Can't you smell it? I'm surprised the whole town isn't outside the door wantin' to be let in. Smells delicious!"

Hayden swallowed and looked at Ruth. She shook her head a little. "I've got some baked chicken in the oven," she said quietly.

His mom ignored Ruth, going on and on about the pot roast. He sighed. A year ago he would have chased that phantom. But he'd learned better. Even if he went out and got a pot roast now, and they cooked it right away, by the time it was done, his mother would have forgotten all about it. She'd pick at her food like she always did, taking a few bites, and then claiming she was stuffed and couldn't manage another morsel. He had no idea why she wasn't a skeleton by now.

"I'm sure it'll be wonderful," he said. "I'm starving. I'll just go wash my hands, shall I?"

AFTER DINNER, his mother settled in to watch her programs on TV while Hayden helped Ruth with the dishes.

"What is it, Hayden?" Ruth asked, giving him a leery expression. "I know that face."

He sighed. "Ah, Christ. I hate this."

"Go on. Hemming and hawing won' make it any easier."

He bit his lip. "Dylan Mitchell lost four sheep last night. I'm thinking it's a pack of dogs. Told him I'd watch out tonight. Our farmers can't afford to be losin' livestock."

Ruth rinsed the dish soap from her hands and turned to face him. "Hayden, of course I'll stay, but this is what I've been tellin' ye. You can't manage. You can be called out any time day or night with that job o' yours. And she shouldna be left alone."

The anxiety in Hayden's stomach returned with a vengeance. Dear God, he'd be growing a family of ulcers in there. "I can't afford to hire a nurse, even if she'd take to one. What am I supposed to do?"

"Well, you know what I think! One of those fancy brothers o' yours should be helping out."

He didn't disagree with the general concept. It was the particulars that were the problem. Jamie and Loren were both taking graduate courses in London. Jackson, Levi, and Moby had jobs and families of their own to care for hundreds of miles from here. And Sam was on a ship somewhere with Her Majesty's Navy.

They'd all gotten away from Laide. And Hayden, the youngest, was left the loser in the MacLairty game of musical chairs. *Last one standing.* Then he felt guilty. He wasn't the one with dementia. He shouldn't be whinging about his own troubles. Besides, he honestly had no desire to leave Laide.

"You know that's not gonna happen," Hayden said tightly. "And you know how she is. Last time that social welfare lady stopped by, Mom screamed bloody murder, and she didn't calm down for days. She won't abide a stranger."

"I know," Ruth said quietly. "Which is why I told my niece and her husband they could have my cottage for the summer. And why I'm gonna be bossy and tell you I'm movin' into the spare room."

It was so welcome and yet too much at the same time. Hayden leaned against the counter, light-headed with relief. "I canna ask you to do that. I can't pay you for more hours, and it's not fair to you. You have a life."

Ruth gripped his hand. She had a lot of strength for an old lass. And the light in her fierce eyes made it clear there was no faltering in her faculties either. "I've had a life, and, God willing, I will have one again. But right now Becca needs me. And you need me. And she's been my best friend since we were six year old, and that doesn't stop because she can't remember what year it is. Of course, I don't want any more of your money, Hayden MacLairty."

Hayden swallowed. "That's… I don't know how to thank you."

Ruth smiled, but she still looked worried. "It'll be a relief to be able to keep me eye on her, to tell you the truth. You're a right bonny son, and no mother could ask more. But if you ain't workin' nights, you sleep like the dead, and don't think I don't know it."

"Hayden!" His mom called from the other room.

"Thank you, Ruth. Really." His throat felt thick with gratitude.

Ruth snorted. "Yes. I'm sure any healthy young man would be itchin' to live with *two* old crones. Go on, then. See what she wants."

Hayden went into the living room. His mother waved frantically at the TV screen.

"Hayden, look at that dog! Isn't he the cutest thing!"

Hayden sat on the arm of his mother's recliner and took her hand. "He's sweet, isn't he?"

"You've asked and asked for a dog, but you know how your father feels about it. Maybe this Christmas, if you get that A in Maths. Do you think you could do that, lad?"

"Sure, Ma. I can do that." His father had been gone for ten years, and Hayden had been out of school far longer. He often wondered how his mother could look at him and see a teenager instead of a man just turned thirty-two. But her misfiring brain had its own rhyme and reason.

Becca frowned. "I had a dog once. His name was Bandi. Did I ever tell you?"

Hayden rubbed her cold hands. "No, Ma. Tell me about Bandi."

"He was a German shepherd. Used to sleep right by my bed. And he'd follow me to school. And I'd say 'Thank you, Bandi! Now go on home!' when we got there."

"Uh-huh."

"And do you know what happened to that dog? He got into the neighbor's chicken coop and ate a chicken. Oh, did Pa gave him what for! Lord, Hayden. But Bandi, he'd got a taste for it, ye ken. And he wouldn't stop. So Pa took a rifle and put him down." There were no tears in her eyes, but her voice got soft. "Ma said Bandi ran away, but the neighbor's son told me the truth. Pa shot him."

"I'm sorry, Mom," Hayden said, like he always did.

"Oh, look! It's Bette Davis. Isn't she lovely!"

~2~

OH FOOKIN' hell, it was cold. It was downright Baltic.

Hayden was no stranger to wind. It was a constant companion here on the northern coast. But tonight it was a right bastard. His anorak did well enough from throat to hips, but his face was being slapped like the wind was an angry lover, and he might as well be wearing nothing at all on his legs. It didn't help that his winter-weight uniform trousers had shrunk up in the wash, *again*, leaving his ankles to fend for themselves. At least the constant battering kept him awake.

He uncapped his thermos and poured another cup of coffee, but even that was cold. He tossed it on the ground in disgust and was in the midst of screwing back on the lid when he spotted movement in the distance. His hackles rose in an instant.

The landscape around Dylan's farm was all sweeping hills with low, grubby vegetation and, in the distance, the sea. He'd chosen a high point close to Dylan's flock and the waxing moon was bright enough that he could see them—huddling puffballs in shades of gray on gray. Near them in the moody gloom, a figure moved. It was hooded and on two legs. Hayden knew at a glance it wasn't Dylan, nor anyone he knew. The jacket was sleek and sporty, like a well-heeled hiker might wear, and from a distance, the figure looked slight. *Stranger. Trouble.*

Hayden had had an uneasy feeling the past few months now, something not right, something threatening hidden just out of reach in the shadows of the rocks. Fanciful bollocks. But the dead sheep were not his imagination, nor was the stranger. His hand went to the strap of the shotgun slung over his back. He didn't normally carry a gun, but tonight he'd taken the weapon earmarked for vermin control from the locked safe in his office in case he came across any rogue dogs. He crept forward fast, stooping low.

The figure seemed to be wandering aimlessly, oblivious to Hayden's approach. Hayden was only twenty feet away when the figure turned and spotted him. The man startled, then ran.

There was nothing for it. Hayden dropped the shotgun from his back, broke into a run, and tackled the man. The pair of them sailed through the air before they hit the ground hard.

"Jesus Christ, I think you broke something!" the man gasped. He sounded winded—and American. Hayden felt a twinge of guilt for landing on him so hard, but the man was where he oughtn't be and when he oughtn't be there. Hayden pushed to his feet and grabbed the man's elbow to drag him upward.

"Who the hell are you? And what in God's name are you doin' out here?" he demanded, anger making him sharp.

The man straightened as much as he could whilst clutching his diaphragm. He looked up at Hayden with resentment and did a double take, his eyes getting round. "Dear God, you're big. I was... I was just taking a walk. I sincerely hope you don't intend to kill me."

"Well, I might do. This here is private property, ye ken. And it's a helluva cold night for walkies."

"You're telling me!" The man shivered. "Look, Dylan said I could come."

"What?"

The man sighed. "Fuck, it's colder than a snowman's ass out here. Look, Dylan was in the pub tonight, and we were talking about the Black Dog. He said he'd seen it out here. I asked if I could come look around and he said 'sure.' So I—"

So the man was a monster-hunter and Dylan had been shooting his mouth off again. Typical. "Aye? He was probably three sheets to the wind when he said it."

"Yes, but so was I, so it doesn't count," explained the American. He winced. "Christ, I think you broke a rib."

Hayden poked a hard finger at the guy's chest.

"Ow!"

"Don't feel cracked to me. But you best get back to the pub and check on it, me lad. Right now."

Even in the moonlight, Hayden could see the stubborn set of the man's chin. "Excuse me, but I was invited here by the landowner. I don't see how it's any of your business. Who are *you*, anyway?"

Keep calm, Hayden told himself. But in truth, his anger was fading, and he was starting to enjoy this. He got little enough challenge in this job. And the stranger was obviously not a threat and... interesting. He seemed intelligent and he was pleasant looking. Dark curls poked from under the hood of his jacket. His dark eyes were large and bright, and his face had a poetic paleness in the moonlight.

"Constable MacLairty," Hayden said gruffly. "And lemme explain. First, there's no such thing as the Black Dog. It's a *legend*. Second, it's not safe to go wanderin' out here at night. You'll snap your leg steppin' in a foxhole, or maybe you'll run into the stray dogs what killed Dylan's sheep last night. And seein' as how I'm the closest ambulance-taxi-police officer, I'm the one who'll have to pick up your bloody carcass when that happens. So I'd appreciate it very much, Mr....."

"Corto. Simon Corto." The man folded his arms over his chest.

"...Mr. Simon Corto, if you would get your arse back to your room in town. Now is that clear enough for ya?"

Hayden's firm tone didn't seem to impress the man. He looked Hayden up and down—and up and up. "MacLairty. I've heard mention of Mount MacLairty, but, silly me, I thought they were talking about an actual hill."

His tone was dry, and Hayden had a devil of a time keeping the smile from his lips. He'd never been called "Mount MacLairty" before, but, he had to admit, it was cleverer than most cracks about his size.

"There is, indeed, a Mount *McLarty* some hundred miles west o' here," Hayden remarked drolly. "Perhaps you should go visit."

"I did promise myself some mountain climbing while I was here."

There was a flirty edge to Simon's words. Hayden held fast to his glower, but his heart tripped a little faster.

"Sorry. That was... right. It's too fucking cold out here anyway. I'll gladly leave. But if you're the local constable, I'll want to talk to you. I'm an author—Simon Corto." The man repeated his name as if it should mean something. It didn't. He held out his hand and Hayden reluctantly shook it. His own hand, fitted with a woolen glove, outsized Simon's by a mile, but there was energy and strength in the man's grip. "I'm planning a book around the Black Dog—the Black Dog *legend*," he added meaningfully. "Is there someplace in town I can reach you?"

"That would be the building with the post office."

"Right. Well, good night, Constable."

With an apologetic look, Simon Corto turned and started walking against the wind to the road and presumably his car. Hayden had a strange urge to follow him, make sure he made it safely. After all, if Mr. Corto was not the threat Hayden was out here to find, that meant he was in danger too.

But that was stupid. The damn tourist had got himself out here. He could get himself back to town. Hayden made himself turn around and return to his lookout point.

HAYDEN HAD been around the block a few times, and he'd heard more than one person brag about "writing a book," especially about the Black Dog. Most of these people were full of more hot air than a summer storm.

So he was surprised to find that Simon Corto was exactly what he'd said he was. The man's website showed he was with a major publisher. He'd even had a few *New York Times* bestsellers. Digging into some of the descriptions of his previous books, Hayden noticed a theme. Simon wrote fiction based around true-life legends—the spirit of a witch in New England and something called the chupacabra in Mexico were his most recent.

Simon Corto also looked much more intimidating in the black-and-white photo than he had in the middle of the night in a hooded wind coat. He was slender, soulful, handsome, and more than a wee bit posh.

Hayden sighed at the computer screen in his tiny office.

Maybe he should have been nicer to Mr. Corto. Maybe he shouldn't have tackled him and nearly broken the man in half like a big, blundering oaf.

Maybe he should go over to the pub right now and make sure their distinguished visitor wasn't going to sue.

HAYDEN STOPPED by the post office counter on his way out. Beverly was flipping idly through someone else's magazine.

"Anything good there?" Hayden asked her, peering over her shoulder.

"Johnny Depp has a new girlfriend."

"Och! Sorry for your loss." Hayden tsked. "But we might be havin' some news closer to home."

"Aye? And what might that be?"

"What if I told you a bestselling author might be writing a new book about the Black Dog? Would you be for it or agin?"

Beverly considered Hayden carefully, as if he might be pulling her leg. She was only a year younger than he was, and she'd inherited the position of postmistress from her mother. She'd always shown more interest in Hayden than he had in return, and he used the fact that she'd once dated his brother Liam as an excuse not to pursue things. In truth, he regarded her more like a sister.

"Well, Hayden, I'd say hallelujah and where do I sign up? Is it true? Could do a world of good for our tourist trade."

"That's what I was thinkin'." Hayden rubbed his chin thoughtfully.

"The last book's been sitting in that window there since I was a wee lass." She nodded to the dusty paperback for sale in the window. *Devil Dog* had a lurid cover from 1963 and was the last book written about the legend. "Who's the author, then? Will it really happen, d'ya think?"

"Assuming I haven't cocked it up," Hayden muttered, heading for the door.

"Cocked what up? Whaddya mean? Is the author already here, then? Is it a man?" She sounded hopeful and increasingly urgent.

Hayden touched his finger to his nose in a *keep it quiet* signal. "No point gettin' people's hopes up 'til we're sure. Aye?" It was a lost cause. The story would be all over town by noon as he well knew. He opened the door.

"Hayden MacLairty! Don't you dare leave me hanging!"

The bell jingled cheerfully as he shut the door.

IT HAD been a good morning. Simon woke up at the first light of dawn, his skin slick with the remnants of a nightmare. He'd gotten up at once and spent three hours at the little desk in his room above the pub, hair uncombed, teeth unbrushed, in his pajamas, typing out a scene on his laptop.

A scene in which his hero was stalked on the open hills of northern Scotland by the Black Dog.

It was visceral and real. And, strangely, there had been an erotic element to his dream, a sense of anticipation that had made him wake up full and throbbing. Curious. His brain must be mixing up his run-in with that constable last night and the Black Dog legend. Admittedly, being tackled by a man who had to weigh well over two hundred pounds had not exactly been a sensual experience. He had nonetheless found MacLairty absurdly attractive. At least Simon had thought so after he'd remembered how to breathe. *Mount MacLairty.* Tall, broad, big all over, with a handsome, ruddy face and hair that was most likely brown, but in the dark Simon was willing to pretend it was red. And who knew a thick Scottish brogue could be so hot? Especially considering the bitterness of the wind last night.

Christ, the wind! Chicago had nothing on the northern coast of Scotland.

Simon wrote his scene, and it was damned good, if he did say so himself. He felt inspired. He was almost grateful to James, that asshole, for pushing him to get on that plane out of a sheer desire to avoid the man.

Six months. Six months of thinking they were monogamous. It had been the first real relationship he'd attempted since Billy, and it had been a joke. At least it had been to James, apparently.

It was good to get away from Manhattan, away from that entire scene. It was nice to remember there was another world out there, one fresh and basic. Maybe he'd even stay awhile.

DOWN IN the pub, Simon ordered a full English breakfast. He was unusually hungry. Angus had just delivered the plate with his cheerful wishes for good digestion when someone strolled into the pub. It was MacLairty. Simon would know him anywhere. No one else could be that huge and that... vital. His black uniform also was unmistakable. His expression, however, was quite different than Simon remembered. His eyes met Simon's, and he looked abashed. Simon had the idle thought that he preferred MacLairty rude.

MacLairty came right up to his table. "Good morning to you, Mr. Corto."

"Well if it isn't the man I have to thank for a pretty array of bruises this morning," Simon said mildly.

MacLairty blushed. Now that Simon could see him in daylight, he decided the man's hair was light brown, or what he could see of it under the constable's cap. But his complexion was pure ginger—fair and freckled with a ready blush.

"About that—" *Aboot tha'*. Damn. So sexy. "I wanted to apologize for tackling you last night, sir. But you shouldna have run."

"I supposed I shouldn't. But you scared the life out of me, charging at me like that. In the dark. You're quite seriously large."

"Aye, sir." MacLairty reddened further.

Simon decided to let him off the hook. "Actually, I should thank you for providing me with some juicy emotional fodder for my book. And I didn't even have to suffer any permanent damage to get it. I woke up this morning inspired to write. That makes it more than worth it to me."

Hayden opened his mouth. Shut it.

"Not that I would care to be tackled again. A simple greeting would do next time. If you promise you didn't come here to harass me, I'll invite you to sit and have a cup of coffee with me, Constable MacLairty."

MacLairty gave a brisk nod, pulled out a chair, and sat. He seemed nervous and only managed perfunctory utterances as Angus came over and served him a cup of coffee.

Simon watched his discomfort with interest. MacLairty had certainly had a change in attitude. Probably, he'd looked Simon up online. So was his nervousness now because he was intimidated by Simon's background? Trying to impress him? Or....

He'd like to believe there was attraction in the mix somewhere. But that was tilting at windmills. MacLairty was probably married with four or five "bairns." Simon glanced at his hand, but didn't see a ring.

MacLairty took a sip of his coffee and pasted on a confident smile. "Now, then. You must call me Hayden. I have no intention of harrassin' you, Mr. Corto. In fact, I'm at your disposal for any wee thing you might be needin'. And may I say, welcome to Laide."

Simon raised an eyebrow at him, but he held out his hand. "Thank you, Hayden. Call me Simon. And you should be careful what you offer. I have a list of places associated with the Black Dog that I'd like to see and no idea where they are."

"I'd be happy to take you around, sir—"

"Simon."

"—Simon. There's no place 'round here I don't know the back of."

"If you're serious, I would very much appreciate that, Constable."

"Hayden."

Simon felt a trickle of amusement. His smile widened. "*Hayden.* Maybe if we say it to each other often enough, we'll both get the hang of it eventually. I'd love a tour. That way I can grill you on the local legend while we drive."

"Aye. We can go whene'er you like."

Simon hoped Hayden didn't plan to be *too* nice. He rather liked the rough edge of him. He decided to push. "Since you're being so accommodating, perhaps you'd care to fill up my rental car tires too? The roads coming up here were murder."

"Now that, Simon, would be pushin' it," Hayden said cheerfully.

Simon laughed. "Well, it was worth a shot. Are you free after lunch? I'd like to get a bit more writing in this morning."

"Pick you up here at one, then?"

"It's a date."

Hayden blinked hard, but he managed not to lose his smile.

~3~

"THAT THERE'S the Peaks." Hayden pointed out the ragged cluster of rocks that stuck out from the cliffs above the sea. He'd always thought they looked like a small, roughly hewn castle, one a troll might inhabit perhaps. It had taken them ten minutes to hike to the landmark, which was a fair enough way to use a bonny afternoon in October. It certainly beat doing paperwork at his desk.

Simon began clicking away with his camera. "Interesting." He peered over the cliff at the twenty-foot drop to the beach. "From the stories, I thought it would be higher."

"Aye. We Scots do have a talent for exaggeration."

Simon gave him a funny look. "Do you know the tales about the Black Dog and this place?"

"The Black Dog was seen here, they say."

"In 1940 by a boatload of smugglers."

"Was it now?" Hayden wasn't all that interested, but he'd pretend to be if that's what it took to get Simon's book written.

"Yes. Picture a small boat paddling in to shore from a ship anchored out there. There were five men aboard, all of them hardened smugglers. And they look up and see this huge hound standing atop these rocks, silhouetted against the sunrise. It was growling and slavering at them. It was so menacing, so terrifying, they turned that boat around and sailed on up the coastline for half a day before they dared land."

Hayden was impressed. "Is that the right way o' it?"

Simon nodded. "Left enough of an impression for one of the sailors to write about it, at length, in his journal."

Hayden couldn't help himself. "And you don't think it might have been a local farmer's dog what scared them off?"

Simon drew out his notebook and flipped to a page. "I've dismissed a lot of stories like that, but not this one, no. The key is the date, 1940. England entered World War II in 1939."

"Aye."

"Well, you see, the Black Dog—the *true* Black Dog—always appears at times of national crisis."

"Can't say as I've heard that before."

Simon considered him. "I tell you what. Let me finish up here and then how about grabbing tea somewhere? I have some questions I'd like to ask you."

"SO YOU'RE really doin' a book, then? You're not just here on... consideration?" Hayden asked as they settled in to tea at the small hotel on Gruinard Bay. The little tearoom was only slightly bigger than Hayden's office, and it was crammed with gingham checks. He felt especially oversized sitting at the round luncheon table. But it was the closest place that served tea and the owners were good people.

"I had some personal reasons for deciding to come right now, but yes. I'm quite serious about doing the book. I've done a considerable amount of research already. And now that I'm here, I'm even more convinced. This place has an amazingly bleak, isolated vibe that's incredibly exciting. There will definitely be a book. In fact, I've already started it."

Hayden felt relief, though he wasn't sure he agreed with either "bleak" or "exciting." Then again this was just home to him. "Well, I wish you all the luck w' it, then."

"Thanks. But I'd like to hear your perspective. Tell me what you know about the Black Dog."

Hayden shrugged. "It's a mythical monster, like the Loch Ness, only not a tenth as famous."

"And?"

"It's larger than a regular dog. The size of a cow, some say. Vicious. Stalks its prey. We were told spooky stories about it when we were bairns. Guess it serves to keep the younguns from wandering off at night."

"And as a constable?"

"Honestly, hadn't heard much of it 'til just recently. There were some tourists what came into Angus's pub a month or so back, pale as death and goin' on about seeing an 'enormous black hound with red eyes' near the road. I took their statements down. Not sure what it was they saw, to be honest. Then Dylan started saying he was seein' it agin too. Then the business with his sheep. You have to understand—Dylan, he's not what I would call the most reliable witness." *Especially not when he's in his cups telling his tall tales to anyone who'll listen.*

"And yet his sheep are dead."

"There is that," Hayden admitted cheerfully.

"And you've never seen it yourself?"

"Och, no." Hayden supposed it was a question to be expected, though this whole thing felt a little ridiculous. He wondered how much Simon bought into all of this, and if he were maybe a wee bit addled. Which would be a shame because he was a handsome and otherwise intelligent man. And he didn't put on airs, either. That might be what Hayden liked about him the most.

Simon pulled out his notebook and opened it. "You're rather a wet blanket, aren't you, Hayden MacLairty? Don't worry, I won't hold it against you."

The man was teasing, Hayden was pretty sure. Simon shifted closer to share the notebook and his thigh pressed against Hayden's. Simon didn't move it with an apology, as another man would have done, and he didn't acknowledge it either. Something warm flipped over in Hayden's stomach. He felt frozen in place.

"Do you know the origin story?"

"Er... some ancient laird, it was. During that wee spot o' trouble with the Vikings."

Simon laughed. "That's right. It started during the Viking invasion at the end of the 9th century. A local lord of the Picts, name of Fergus mac Causantin, supposedly prayed for the strength to repel the invaders. Whether to God or to the Devil depends on who's telling the story. Since the Vikings had berserkers, warriors who took on animal-like ferocity, he prayed for the same. According to legend, he was granted the power to turn into an enormous black hound that was so terrifying, it frightened even the Vikings."

This was ringing a bell. Hayden had learned as much in school long ago, but he'd forgotten the fine print. "MacCausantin. I know the name. There're some ruins near here called that."

"Oh, I'll definitely want to see those! Anyway, if you look at the history of the Black Dog sightings, they tend to be around times when this area was under threat, like during the War for Scottish Independence. There's an English regiment that swear they were practically decimated by the Black Dog. And then multiple sightings during World War II."

"But...." Hayden frowned.

"But why is it back now when there is no threat?" Simon prompted.

"Well, that question assumes there truly *is* a Black Dog and that it *is* back. Do you honestly believe tha'?" Hayden tried to keep the doubt from his voice. God knew, he didn't want to chase off Simon Corto and his potentially business-booming book. But he wasn't going to pretend to be a half-wit either.

Simon leaned in closer, speaking intimately. "Look, it doesn't matter to me if the Dog is real or not. I'm a fiction writer. My story flies either way. It only matters that it's an interesting legend with enough meat to work with, and it is that."

Hayden nodded, relieved.

"But honestly, the historical accounts are pretty convincing. What I didn't expect was that there'd be sightings *now*. I was as surprised as anything when Dylan Mitchell started talking about it the other night at the pub. And according to you, he's not the only one who's seen it. And then there're the sheep."

Hayden finished off his tea, wishing it was a pint instead. He rubbed his chin. "You got me thinkin'. Never put much stock in it before, but some of the old ones, they call it *Coimheadair.*"

"What's that?"

"It's Gaelic for like… guardian, protector."

"Is it? Interesting." Simon glowed with pleasure, and Hayden watched him mentally tuck that tidbit away. "So… there's been no trouble around here lately? Theft? Vandalism?"

"Not to speak of."

Simon got a faraway look. "Because I was thinking, for my story, I might have the plot involve a serial killer in the area that's threatening people. And that brings out the Black Dog."

"Now there's a cozy tale to bring in the tourists," Hayden said dryly.

Simon blinked back to focus and grinned at him. "You'd be surprised. The grislier the better, in my experience. There's a reason the Tower of London and the London Dungeon are two of the city's biggest attractions."

"You may have the right o' it. But sadly, I can't produce a serial killer for you. It's a busy day when I can issue a speeding ticket 'round here."

"Ah, well."

They both reached for the last biscuit on the plate and their fingers touched. Hayden drew his hand back fast, shocked at the bolt of sensation the brush of skin sent through him. "Sorry, lad. You take it." He became aware, again, of Simon's thigh still pressed against his. A heavy wave of warmth swept through him.

Hayden looked around the room—anywhere but at Simon Corto. He didn't move his leg, though, and the sensation didn't stop.

Simon left the biscuit on the plate and cleared his throat. "So, Hayden. Are you married?"

That question was no coincidence. Simon had to feel it, too, this strange spark. Now Hayden did move his leg, pushing his chair back a bit to break contact, unnerved. "No, not I. My mother is ill, ye ken. I've not the leisure for much of a private life at the moment."

"I'm sorry to hear that."

"'N you?" Hayden couldn't help asking.

Simon smiled bitterly. "I was in a long-term relationship, but that ended a few years ago. Since then, I've not had much luck."

"Now it's my condolences you'll be havin'."

Simon's eyes met his, and there was something in them that reached right down inside Hayden, almost painfully intimate. "Thanks, but I'm not sorry at all."

"Ah. Well." Hayden cleared his throat. "If there's more you're wantin' to see, I can take you tomorrow. Best I get back to the office."

"No problem, Hayden. And thanks for today. I couldn't want a better guide."

"Glad to be of service."

HAYDEN DROPPED Simon off and went into his office. There were no messages and nothing urgent that needed his attention. No surprise there. He had paperwork that needed done. Monthly reports. And there was his routine road patrol that he wanted to get in before dark. But he was too restless to buckle down to anything. Finally he gave in and searched the web for more information on Simon Corto.

Three Google pages in, he found some older photographs of Simon and another man, dark haired, good-looking. They had their arms around each other. The byline said *Author Simon Corto and boyfriend Billy Stephanski*.

Hayden leaned back in his chair with a shaky sigh. There was that question answered. Simon was gay. And unless Hayden was very much mistaken, Simon was attracted to him. And what did he make of that?

He pondered it. If he was honest, he was attracted to Simon right back. And wasn't that a surprise? But the hot, tingling nausea he felt when he thought of the man, the itchy desire to impress and please him, the way

Hayden's body reacted when they had contact... well. It was hard to deny you have a cold when you were sneezing your head off, wasn't it now?

Hayden had never been the lover boy type. He hadn't had an interest in it the way his older brothers all did—girl crazy, the lot of 'em. He'd had his way with more than a few women, women aggressive enough to throw themselves at him. He'd even tried it on with a lad once or twice, to see if it might be more to his taste. It was fair enough, but not so brilliant he'd repeated it. Sexual contact had never been a thing he needed, a thing he sought out. He knew himself to be strange that way, a "cold fish." But then he was unusual in plenty of ways—his size for one, and the fact that he'd never had a desire to leave Laide.

What was he going to do about Simon Corto? That was the question. He'd never felt such a physical reaction to an individual before. If Hayden had lived in a different town, a big city somewhere, he might dare try it on for size. But here, in Laide, such an indiscretion would be stuck to him forever. He couldn't have that.

No, he was happy to play host to Simon Corto, but he couldn't risk anything more.

HAYDEN PICKED up a few items from the town's only market on his way home. He could tell the moment he entered it was a bad night. His mother was in a nightgown—already or still. She was pacing around the house with an angry expression, her hair wild.

"No, it's not. No, it's not. No, it's not," she said over and over.

Ruth saw him at the door and turned to him with exhausted relief. "Oh, Hayden. Thank the lord you're home."

Hayden took off his jacket. "How long's she been like this?"

"Nearly all day. I just—she's been so agitated, and I've only been able to distract her for brief spurts here and there."

"What can I do?"

"If you'll watch her, I'll make some pasta up right quick. Might be good for her if we all sat down at the table like usual."

Ruth obviously needed a break herself. "I've got 'er. Go ahead to the kitchen and take your time."

Hayden failed at getting his mother interested in TV, but she did sit down to look at a photo album with him. She slowly settled as he turned the pages and talked low and quiet about each photo. He had to show her the old ones. She didn't recognize the newer photos, and that always made her upset and confused.

"Oh, look," she said, putting a finger on the page. "That's my brother, Bobbie. And look, Hayden! There's Bandi in the back! Did I ever tell you 'bout my dog, Bandi?"

"Tell me, Ma."

"He was a German shepherd. Used to sleep right by my bed! And he'd follow me to school! And I'd say 'Thank you, Bandi! Now go on home!' when we got there."

"Uh-huh."

Hayden listened to the story about the unfortunate Bandi again, and about how his grandfather had shot him. Every time his mother told it, she used the same words, even the same inflections. The human brain was a curious thing. His mother's had worn grooves in places where things repeated so well, they might have been prerecorded. And other places, like her memories of her grandchildren, were wiped smooth.

"I'm sorry, Ma. I know you loved that dog."

His mother said nothing, only turned the page.

BY THE time they'd finished dinner, his mother's agitation had blown over and she looked tired. She settled in to watch her evening telly with her mug of tea and the afghan tucked around her legs.

Ruth cornered Hayden in the kitchen. "Rumor is there's a writer in town. Rumor is he wants to write a book about the Black Dog, and you're helpin' him." She sounded upset.

"Aye. And how is that a bad thing?"

"We don't need strangers pokin' into our business, Hayden!"

"Are you daft? This town is so dried up it might just blow away at any second. We need money! And since there ain't no grand factory lookin' to move to Laide anytime soon, that means we need tourists. Anything that might help bring some interest in, I'm all for it."

"But… pokin' around. Diggin' into things. It can't be good," Ruth insisted.

"Why? We've no secrets."

"Everyone has secrets, Hayden!"

"Well, you may have. But I don't." Even as he said it, Hayden thought of the way he'd felt when his leg had been pressed against Simon's. Maybe he did have a secret or two at that.

"Och!" Ruth started cleaning up the table angrily. "You dinnae ken. But I'm tellin' ye, it's trouble. And if you insist on helpin' this man out, I don't know what you're thinkin', Hayden MacLairty."

Hayden had never known Ruth to be so unfriendly about visitors. He wondered what she was afraid of. And he wondered, too, if it was her worry that had set his mother off today. She was sensitive to those things. But Ruth did the best she could, God bless her. He could hardly call her to task for it.

And suddenly, he was exhausted. He had been up most of the night before, after all, and then all that tromping around this afternoon with Simon.

"Thank you for today," he told Ruth gently. "Now why don't you go on home and relax. I'll put Ma to bed."

Ruth gave him a hug—apology? comfort? "If you need me tonight, call. I'll be ready to move into the spare room on Saturday."

"Ta, Ruth." Hayden gave her a tired smile, and she left without saying another word.

~4~

HE WAS standing on the cliffs overlooking the sea. He looked down at the crashing waves and saw it was even higher than he thought. Such a fall….

A hand touched his back. He didn't startle, but settled into it, warm and sure.

"Let's run," Simon said. A challenge. His eyes were dancing, mesmerizing.

They ran. Over the cliffs, up and down, and somehow the dips and rises were easy, and Hayden felt his thighs pumping hard. Simon was ahead of him, dressed in that anorak, and he ran so fast his dark curls blew in the wind.

The more they ran, the more Hayden had to catch him. *Wanted* to catch him.

He was hard and aching when he tackled Simon and threw him to the ground. Simon was on his back looking up into Hayden's eyes. And then there were no clothes between them.

The wind whipped around them, licking the skin of Hayden's bare calves and back and arse. And beneath them was soft moss over granite stone, velvety and cool. It was delicious, as if the land were making love with them, an active third party, soothing and spurring on their arousal.

And he was aroused. Dear God. He'd never felt arousal like this, as if his entire body was sensitive, swollen, and throbbing with pleasure. He was grinding into Simon. He could feel every inch of his warm flesh, the sharp plane of his bones, and the hard line of his cock as it spread moisture on Hayden's belly. He thrust, his fingers firm around Simon's face, their eyes locked.

"Hurry," Simon was saying, eyes filled with lust. "Hurry. Hurry."

The clifftop they were on was crumbling, Hayden realized. That's the warning Simon meant. But Hayden couldn't stop. Just a wee bit more and he would come. He would make Simon come. God, it felt *so good,* and he didn't even care about the danger. It was exciting, made the pleasure more acute. They were flying. And only a few thrusts more—

Hayden awoke with a thump, his body landing on the floor next to his bed, his cock pulsing in orgasm. It was an equally rude and wonderful awakening, and he lay there for a moment, rubbing his hand over his cock, trying to hold on to the powerful sensations as long as possible. Dear God, he hadn't had an orgasm that felt that good in years, if he ever had done. And a wet dream yet! When had he ever had one of those?

Very strange.

There was a knock on his door. "Hayden? Everything all right in there?" It was Ruth.

Hayden looked at the clock on his bedside table. 7:00 a.m. She was here early. "Ta! I'll, uh… I'll be out in a shake."

HAYDEN DECIDED to do a routine patrol before going into the office. He'd bypassed a few of the hamlets on his rounds while showing Simon the area. He wanted to do a drive-through to make sure all was well before he got sidetracked again today. And besides, the weather was fine and warm for October.

He was on a track that ran through the Loch Dale woods when he saw a walker on the side of the road. It was a woman dressed in outdoor gear. Her back was to him, and there was something off about her walk—stumbling and stilted.

Hayden slowed down and lowered his window, prepared to check on her. But when he saw her face, he knew at once something was very wrong.

He pulled ahead of her and parked the Land Rover on the grassy shoulder. He jumped out and headed for her, before reminding himself to *slow down, be gentle*. It was no use scaring her. The woman had stopped moving and was staring at him, blank-faced and unresponsive.

"Miss? Are you all right?"

Hayden approached her warily, taking in the details with a policeman's eye. She looked to be in her thirties. Her jacket was covered with sweeps of mud. Her hair, dyed black, hung limp and tangled around her face as if it had been wet. One twig wrapped around strands of hair on the left side. Dried blood streaked her face and her hands, which were down by her sides and visibly shaking. She had on thermal leggings and no shoes. Her bare feet were white with cold, dirty, and bloody. Her eyes… she was in shock.

Hayden stopped a few feet away, his hands held up placatingly. "Miss? Can you tell me your name? Are ya hurt?"

Nothing.

"Miss?" Louder.

The woman blinked, focusing on Hayden as if seeing him for the first time. Then she opened up her mouth and screamed.

HAYDEN PULLED into the small car park at the Black Dog, driving fast. He'd spoken to Angus on the phone, and Angus was waiting.

The story he'd managed to get out of the woman—Anne Brauber—on the drive, halting and repetitive in turn, was hard to swallow. And yet, the woman's shock and fear left little room for skepticism. Clearly, she and her husband had been attacked by *something* while camping. And just as clearly, Ben Brauber was still out there, dead or alive.

Hayden went around to the passenger side and opened the door, helped Anne stand. She was stiff and in pain, though he didn't think anything was broken. Her skin was still deathly pale and her body wracked with shivers, even though he'd wrapped an orange insulating shock blanket around her.

"Anne, this is Angus. He's a good friend. He's going to drive you to hospital while I go check on... on your husband. All right?"

"Ben?" She looked at Hayden, horror lurking in her eyes. "Ben?"

"It'll be all right. Let Angus help you now."

She made no protest as Hayden half carried her to Angus's car and put her in.

"Thanks," he told Angus. The landlord was a slight man, gray-haired but still wiry and strong. He was the most reliable man Hayden knew in the area. "Sorry to have to ask, but...."

"No trouble a'tall. Margie's watchin' the pub."

Hayden sighed. "She says her name is Anne Brauber. She and her husband are here from London. They were camping out by Loch Dale. I didn't go through her pockets, but if I find anything at the campsite, I'll call the hospital with it."

"And her husband?" Angus whispered.

Hayden shook his head.

Anne watched Hayden through the front windshield as Angus pulled out. He gave her what he hoped was an encouraging wave. When Hayden got back into the Rover, he was startled to see Simon sitting in the passenger seat.

"No," he said, angry.

"You should have backup," Simon insisted. "I heard some of it when Angus was talking to Margie. You shouldn't go out to that campsite alone. At the very least, it would be good to have a witness."

"It's not safe. And this is police business. I canna have a civilian in the car."

Simon shrugged, though he didn't look as calm as he was pretending to be. "I'll follow you, then." He opened the door.

"Simon—"

"You're not liable for my dumb-ass decisions. All right? I'm coming."

Hayden gave up and started the Rover.

THEY MADE a stop at the post office—apparently to get Hayden's shotgun. When they reached the trailhead, Hayden parked next to an older black Saab that was already there. Simon pulled in next to him in his rental car. He figured the Saab belonged to the unfortunate woman and her husband. He waited inside his car while Hayden checked it out. The Saab appeared to be locked and undisturbed, and Hayden made a call to whomever it was he was keeping apprised of the situation.

Simon got out and wandered a few steps away. He noticed he had a bar on his cell phone and contemplated posting something about where he was on his blog. After all, it was possible he was walking into very real danger. Shouldn't someone know?

But he didn't post anything. It felt like that would be taking advantage of the situation to intrigue his fans. And it felt like a betrayal of Hayden too.

Hayden hung up and got the shotgun from his Rover, slung it over his back. He walked over to Simon, his face grim. "You stay here. Inside your car."

Like that's going to happen. "Ah, no. I'm going with you. This is a public trail as far as I can see."

Hayden narrowed his eyes, his jaw set. His eyes sparked with that same fire Simon had seen out on the hills that first night—and it made him shiver. "I canna guarantee your safety. We don' know what's out there."

"But I'll be with Mount MacLairty. And you have a shotgun," Simon pointed out. "I'm not afraid. And as I said before—you need backup and a witness."

"There's a dangerous animal out there!"

"Yes. And do you really think I'm such a coward I'd let you go alone? That's not going to happen, Hayden. Would *you* let *me* if the situation were reversed?"

Hayden opened his mouth to protest. Closed it.

"Unless you're dying to handcuff me to a steering wheel?" Simon suggested—suggestively. "Because that's the only way I'm staying here."

Hayden mumbled something that was so thick with brogue Simon could in no way decipher it, but it probably involved dubious statements about his parentage. The constable turned and headed into the wood. "If you must go agin my advice, stick close."

Simon followed fast on his heels. Yes, he would definitely stick close. The truth was, he was nervous. From what he'd heard Hayden tell Angus, and from the way the woman had looked in the pub parking lot, Anne and her husband were attacked out here. But he didn't want to miss out on what could be important information on the Black Dog for his book. Besides, he seriously would never be able to live with himself if something happened to Hayden while he, Simon, was sitting safe in the car. He'd been in dodgy situations before doing research for his books, and he was confident he could be of help to Hayden if it came down to it. That was a win-win, right? He realized his gut-level concern for Hayden's welfare pointed to a worse crush on the man than he'd already supposed. But there would be time to think about that when they were somewhere with walls and locks.

THE FOOTPATH wove between field and forest. The autumn day was heating up more than Hayden liked, and he could feel sweat trickle down his back inside his shirt. The shoulders were tight again, the godforsaken thing, always shrinking in the wash. And it felt damn constrictive as he walked. They were silent, saving their breath for the exertion. Hayden kept a fast pace and Simon stayed close behind as if worried about being left. The erotic dream Hayden had had the night before was gone now as if it had never been, as if he'd dreamed of a dream. At the moment, all he could feel was a sharp-edged worry for Simon's safety, and for what might have befallen Ben Brauber on Hayden's home turf.

Please, God, don't let it be like the sheep.

The path finally opened up at the small loch. Hayden saw the tent right away. It was a bright goldenrod in color and collapsed like a balloon with the air let out. One aluminum pole stuck up like a protruding broken bone, and gold nylon moved gently against it in the breeze off the loch. It was deathly still.

Hayden held out a palm to stop Simon from going any closer. He slipped the shotgun off his shoulder and held it ready in his hands. "Stay here."

"Be careful." Simon's voice was steadier than Hayden felt.

He slowly approached the tent, taking care to watch where he was stepping, not wanting to cover up any evidence. As he eyed the soft dirt ground, he saw prints—animal prints, large ones. His heart beat faster. He hadn't believed Anne, not completely. Or maybe he'd just been praying she was wrong.

At the tent he found Ben's body, partially covered by the gold nylon. He was on his stomach, his elbows cocked like maybe he'd been trying to crawl away. His head was turned to the side, eyes open and dull with death. Blood soaked the ground around his head. So much blood. Hayden looked around, gun in his hand, but he neither saw nor heard anything in the area. After a long moment of listening, and another visual check to make sure Simon was okay, Hayden slung the shotgun back into its holster and pulled some latex gloves from a pocket. He put them on—damned small things. Then he carefully leaned closer to the corpse and pulled the shirt back so he could see.

Fooking Christ. Ben Brauber's throat had been ripped out. It wasn't a knife cut, but a wide and vicious wound. Nearly all the skin of the throat was gone, the tissue underneath savaged. Hayden wasn't an expert in animal bites, but it certainly looked like the work of angry fangs to him. That was consistent with the general damage to the campsite—and the prints in the muddy earth.

One of the animal prints was fresh and clear by Ben's head. Hayden took out his phone and snapped a photo, then took one with his hand next to the print for comparison too. The paw print was enormous. There was no way that was any ordinary stray dog, vicious or no. He photographed Ben, taking close-ups of the neck wound, and took images of the scene.

At last he stood, feeling sick in his stomach and dizzy in the head with a sense of unreality. He tucked away his gloves and phone, and walked back to Simon.

"He's dead?" Simon asked, anxious.

Hayden nodded, feeling like his entire body was clenched tight.

"Is it...? Do you mind if I...." Simon was looking toward the body, but he hadn't moved one inch.

"Sorry, but I canna let you get closer. It's a crime scene." Like a consolation prize, Hayden added. "I... did find paw prints."

Simon swallowed hard. He nodded. "All right. Now what do we do?"

"We hike back to the cars. I'll call it in, but I want to get us both safe first."

"Okay." Simon paused for a moment, looking around as if trying to memorize the scene. Hayden followed his gaze and saw the setting as a stranger might. The small loch was a deep gray-blue and peaceful looking. It was surrounded by trees and this small clearing. The sky was a crisp, brilliant blue with fluffy white clouds, and some of the trees around the loch were a brilliant red. The metal grate of an old fire pit was built to one side for campers. The scene looked so ordinary and welcoming. Beautiful even.

Hayden felt a burn of fury that someone, or something, was threatening his home.

"Let's go," Hayden said brusquely.

THE WALK back to the Rover was brutal. They walked even faster than before, both spurred on by what they'd found. Hayden was well enough able to picture having a run-in with the beast—*that thing*, whatever it was. He told himself the creature had attacked at night twice now; it was unlikely to attack during the day. It was probably holed up somewhere, asleep. But that didn't make it any easier to be hiking through the woods, knowing it was out there, knowing what it was capable of, knowing Simon was with him and vulnerable. What if Hayden couldn't protect him?

Simon said nothing, but they walked as close together as they could without tripping over each other's feet. Hayden placed Simon in front, knowing what it was like to be looking over your shoulder. He touched Simon's back regularly to assure the man he was there. *Keep moving.*

There had never been a more welcome sight in the world than that of the car park when they finally reached it. Hayden opened the Rover's door for Simon and made sure he was safely inside before getting out his phone. With a breath of relief, he placed the call. Inverness told him they'd send backup—a proper detective. He was told to wait there. He uploaded the photos he'd taken. Then there was nothing to do but wait.

He got in the car, wishing he had something hard to ease the chill. He poured a cup of coffee from his thermos and handed it to Simon. "It's just barely warm, more's the pity."

Simon took it gratefully. "Did she see it? The woman? Anne, you said?"

"Aye. She saw it." Hayden found an extra Styrofoam cup in the backseat and poured a cup for himself.

142 142 | ELI EASTON

"And? What did she say?"

"They were asleep, and they heard somethin' movin' around outside." He took a deep breath. "Her husband shouted at it, tried to scare it off. And when that didna work, he grabbed an electric lantern. The thing was rippin' at the tent by then, and he went out the front to try to scare it off with the light. Anne heard the attack. She got out of the tent and ran. Said she heard him die."

"Oh my God, Hayden."

For a moment Simon said nothing. The bright day outside seemed a strange time to tell such a dire tale.

"What did she say it was?" Simon asked quietly.

"She thought it was a bear at first. It was big and black. But when she looked back to see what was happening to Ben, it raised its head…."

Simon waited.

"She said it was an enormous black dog."

~5~

THE NEXT three days were relentless. Inspector Deagan from Inverness came, and Hayden had to play host, shuttle him around, and arrange interviews. Deagan interviewed Anne Brauber, Dylan Mitchell, Angus, Simon, and even called up the couple who'd filed the report about seeing the dog on the road.

On the morning of the third day, Deagan walked into Hayden's office with his suitcase. "I'm headin' back this mornin', Constable. The case is being handed over to the NDWA. I assume you'll be available to offer them every assistance."

Hayden was genuinely surprised. This seemed like an extreme case for the National Dog Warden Association. "The NDWA? But a man is dead."

"Aye, it's a terrible thing to be sure. But even though the victim is human, the killer is not," Deagan gave Hayden a tight smile. "Bit out of our territory, ye ken? You've got a rabid beastie on your hands. They'll be sending on people to track it down."

"What about the coroner's report? Do they know what type of animal it was?"

Deagan seesawed a hand in the air. "Canine, they think. A very big canine, 'cording to the teeth marks. Now listen up, Constable MacLairty. A word to the wise. This thing might be wild, but it might not be. While the NDWA is searchin' for it, you might dig around 'n see if you can find anyone in the area what has a dog that size. It's only attacked twice now. Maybe it got loose." Deagan put a finger to his nose and winked, as if he'd just handed Hayden the biggest bloody tip since his Pa had told him about condoms.

"Will do, sir," Hayden said stiffly. He shook hands with Deagan, and the man was gone.

HAYDEN PUT up closure notices at all the campgrounds and walking paths in the area, advising people to stay clear for the time being. Local businesses weren't happy, but the story had been a boon to the local press.

He spent the rest of the day on the phone, talking to the NDWA and concerned citizens.

Barbara, the postmistress, was not above using her close proximity to try to get the inside word. "Some people're sayin' it's the Black Dog. How can that be, Hayden?" she asked, appearing in his doorway.

"It can't," Hayden said firmly. "'N I think you'd know better than to take gossip for true."

"But what if it is? Why would it kill a camper? Nothin' like that's ever happened before. It's hard enough 'round here without scarin' off the outdoor types."

She sounded genuinely worried, and she wasn't the first. Never mind what Simon had told him about gruesome being a draw. People might like to stay in haunted pubs where the worst to fear was a cold spot, but they didn't want to camp out where there were man-eating predators.

"It's most likely a stray dog. They'll find it, and that'll be the end of that. At the end of the day, it'll bring us some free press." It's what he'd been telling everyone who asked. He'd repeated it so often he almost believed it.

"I hope you've the right o' it," said Barbara with a shiver. "Be careful what you wish for, ye ken? And me always complainin' that nothin' excitin' ever happens here."

"Aye. I know jus' what you mean."

SIMON SENT Hayden a text about having new information, so Hayden closed up his office a bit early, posted a note that he was at the Black Dog, and called home. Ruth said his mother was still feeling under the weather and was resting. She was being "no trouble a'tall," and he should feel free to eat dinner out or work late.

With all this craziness, Hayden had been working long hours, and Ruth had moved into the spare room so Becca wasn't alone. He owed Ruth more than he could possibly repay. He was lucky his mother had such good friends. That *he* had such good friends. One thing about Laide—people took care of their own.

SIMON HAD gotten them a table. They both ordered pints of dark ale and the lamb special. Hayden found he wanted to talk about anything *but* the murder, or the Black Dog, so he asked Simon about his family.

"I grew up in Manhattan, and my parents both still live there. I have a love-hate relationship with the city. A kind of can't live with it, can't live without it schizophrenia. I love things about it, but I have to travel frequently or I'd go crazy. A place like this—someplace open and wild—is the other half of me. Somewhere in my DNA is an old man with wellies and tweed, and he can be an insistent bastard."

Hayden smiled and cocked his head, studying the urbane man in front of him who, nevertheless, seemed at home here. "I can almost see tha'."

"Yes, I call him Hal. So when I leave the city, I tell my friends I'm off to feed Hal."

Hayden laughed.

"I guess I don't believe anyplace can be perfect. Every place has its pros and cons. The same goes for relationships, actually. But this place... you live in a good place here, Hayden. It's bleak and it's beautiful. Hal is in pig heaven."

"I can't imagine leavin'," Hayden admitted. "This place... it's in my blood." He felt like he needed to say it out loud—to make sure Simon understood. And maybe to remind himself too.

Simon studied him with a strange expression. "I don't wonder. It suits you."

Hayden looked away, uncomfortable. "So you said you had new information."

"Right. I've been looking into the history of Fergus mac Causantin. He was quite the ladies' man. It's said he had over a dozen children, some legitimate, some bastards."

"So he didn't spend all his time fightin' Vikings, I take it?"

Simon smiled. "Apparently not. The mac Causantin name morphed into MacClausen. There are some still in the area, according to the phone book. And God only knows what families his female descendants married into. I suspect there's quite a bit of his DNA still living here."

Hayden felt a sense of unease. "MacClausen. I know them. They're a bad patch."

"How so?"

"Welfare family, father alcoholic, sons have been known to drive stoned, bash mailboxes, petty theft, that sort o' thing. Their older brother's in jail for aggravated assault. Nearly killed a man in a pub fight."

"Hmmm."

"I'll check up on 'em. But you're not suggestin' Fergus mac Causantin's descendants are still turning into dogs. Are you?"

Simon looked abashed. "Honestly? My logical brain says the camper was killed by a wild animal. But the part of me that writes stories and has read the history—that part isn't so sure."

Hayden felt about the same, though in his case it was his rational mind against the ingrained local superstition, which his MacLairty bones couldn't entirely dismiss, not now that he'd seen blood for himself. He leaned forward and spoke quietly. "Even if a man were to believe in the legend of the Black Dog, and that's a big if, wouldn't it be some kind of ghost? Not a… a berserker or shapeshifter or what have you, but a specter of the original Black Dog?"

"I've never heard of a spectral animal leaving paw prints and doing real, physical damage. Did they manage to find any hair or scat at the site?"

Hayden probably shouldn't be telling tales. But it was no longer a murder investigation, and Deagan had already blabbed most of it to the press anyway. So he told Simon the little he knew. They hadn't found scat, but they had hair samples and saliva.

"Canine, huh? Tell me the truth, Hayden. Do you think there's some extraordinarily large black dog or wolf loose in this area—this *particular area* that just happens to be known for a Black Dog legend? Doesn't that seem overly coincidental to you?"

Simon was sitting forward as close to the table as he could, leaning on it with his elbows. His knees made contact with Hayden's under the table.

Hayden had got little rest lately, and maybe he was in a vulnerable state of mind, but his attraction to Simon was back tonight, gaining in strength over the course of the dinner like a spreading infection. Sitting in the dimly lit pub, with a small candle on the table, Hayden was hard-pressed to keep the erotic dream he'd had from drifting into his thoughts. He could picture Simon's face below him, his hair wild, his eyes filled with lust.

Hayden swallowed. "I'm 95 percent sure it's just an ordinary dog."

Simon raised one eyebrow skeptically.

"Fine. I'm 90 percent sure," Hayden amended. "But given that I'm only 85 percent rational on my best days, that's quite high, ye ken?"

Simon laughed and looked at Hayden fondly. The warmth in his eyes made Hayden's blood grow thick and slow. He pushed aside his food half-eaten. He wasn't hungry. And Simon was watching him far too keenly.

"If you'd like, I can show you some of my research. It's on the computer. In my room," Simon offered.

"All right," Hayden said.

It was a bloody terrible idea. Him going up to Simon's room would be noted. Angus was already giving them sideways glances. And the way he was feeling, he might do something stupid. But with two pints in him, a sick mother at home, and a wild animal out there killing people, he found he didn't give two shits about something as mundane as public perception. In any case, he ought to look at the research. That was his job.

"All right," Simon echoed back. He looked down at his plate, carefully carving off another bite. His cheeks grew flushed, as if he might be blushing. But surely he wouldn't blush over Hayden MacLairty. Not a famous author and a man of the world. Hayden, on the other hand, felt the heat in his face and damned his fair complexion. He drained his beer.

SIMON WAS staying in the largest of the guest rooms upstairs. Hayden had been in it once before, but Angus had refreshed it since then with some yellow paint. The old brass bed was large and covered in cozy-looking quilts and eyelet pillows. A small window overlooked the main street, such as it was. There was an old wall heater painted white and a rosewood desk. The ceiling barely cleared Hayden's head, making the space feel even more intimate.

Simon shut the door behind them, and Hayden felt arousal and panic in equal measure. He tried to slow his breathing and act like it was all business. Which it was. Or it should be.

"What'd you want to show me, then?"

Simon licked his lips nervously and crossed to his computer. "I found an old photo said to be a print from the Black Dog. It was taken in 1940, around the time of that smuggler's account I mentioned."

"Aye?"

Hayden stepped closer, and Simon brought up the old black-and-white photo. A man's hand was placed next to the paw print, flat on the ground, presumably to provide a reasonable guide to size. The paw print was set in deep mud. It was wider than the man's hand, and nearly as long. It looked exactly like the print Hayden had seen near the dead camper, except this one might even be larger.

He was leaning in close, trying to see it. He looked up and found himself staring into Simon's eyes from mere inches away. He felt a strong pull. There was an unbearable desire to touch. Somehow the low current of dread he felt about the Black Dog was curled around this desire for Simon like coiled snakes of light and dark, or maybe fire and ice.

Simon was looking at him; want and doubt warred on his face. "Hayden, I think—"

No, no, don't bloody think.

Hayden couldn't bear the word at the moment. This was not something to be pondered over. It wasn't logical, it was instinct, like the Black Dog itself, wild and phantasmagorical, to be glimpsed and feared and run from, to surrender to, baring your throat to its jaws. In his mind, Hayden fell to his knees. But in the room with Simon, he grabbed the man by his shoulders and pushed him back, shoving him against the wall.

"Oh," Simon breathed. His eyes went dark and hot, dragging Hayden in. It turned out he needn't have spent that time worrying about what he'd do if Simon tried to kiss him, because it was Hayden, himself, who jumped over the cliff, and gladly too.

Oh.

It was different than kissing a woman. There was no slow coaxing of desire like a thread teased from cloth. This was spontaneous combustion, arousal as a nuclear bomb. And there was no mistaking it, not when Simon's tongue and teeth were doing desperate battle with his own, not when two burgeoning cocks pressed against each other through their clothes, and moans and stifled cries filled the air.

Simon wants me too.

SIMON THOUGHT he had to be as clueless as his friend Stephan always claimed when it came to men flirting with him. Because he was completely gobsmacked to find himself pressed against the wall by Hayden MacLairty— *all* of Hayden MacLairty, which was quite a lot of man.

It was true; he'd flirted with Hayden. It was difficult to completely contain his drooling in the face of that massive slab of strong, brogue-tongued beefcake. And Hayden was a sweetheart too, kind to wee orphans and shelter dogs, or at least he gave off that impression. But the impression he most certainly did not give off was that he was gay. Simon could swear the man had never so much as blinked in his direction, and in fact had blinked the other way when Simon's flirting had been obvious.

If there'd been any signaling at all, he'd missed it. And... oh, hell. Who cared?

Hayden was all hardness and heat and passion. Simon wrapped his arms around Hayden's neck so he could arch up against him and pull him tighter still. *Yes, please, more of this. Much, much more.* Their bodies fit together like tongue-and-groove—Simon's lean frame against Hayden's broad one. Their mouths were perfectly in sync. And their chemistry was so incendiary it shed particles like trailing sparks. Simon realized with shock that the weirdest part of this wasn't that Hayden MacLairty was kissing him—it was that it felt so singularly, heart-stoppingly good.

Simon ran one hand down Hayden's chest, feeling the warm solidity under his cotton shirt, past his stomach to his belt.

Hayden pushed back abruptly. Simon barely refrained from going after him, and the two of them stood there staring at each other. Hayden looked as shocked and lust-addled as Simon felt.

"Sorry. I'm…. God, what am I doin'?" Hayden muttered, abashed.

"I'm not sorry." Simon gave a shaky laugh. He touched his lips with his fingers, trying to convince himself it had really happened.

"I canna… I'm not…."

Simon pointedly looked down at the erection straining Hayden's uniform trousers. And hell, that was impressive in more ways than one. "Apparently you are, and you *can*."

Hayden groaned and squeezed his eyes shut. "No. You'll be leavin' and I'll be here and… and Angus is right downstairs and I canna."

Before Simon could get two brains cells together to figure out how to debate that, Hayden jerked the door open and left the room.

Simon's brain was still a few blocks behind in the race, but he had enough sense to realize Hayden's abrupt departure was a very bad sign.

If Hayden didn't want a repeat, that would be most unfortunate. Because now Simon knew what it felt like to kiss Hayden MacLairty. He knew how good it felt to want him that hard, and to be wanted that hard in return.

And how was he ever going to forget that?

~6~

HAYDEN PARKED as unobtrusively as possible on the lane near the MacClausen farm. They lived down a road to nowhere with not a neighbor in sight. Fortunately, there was a huge old oak just off the road that Hayden could hide the Rover behind. He got out and walked over to lean against the trunk, watching the house from the gloom of its branches.

The sons were home. Jamie's hanging-together-with-spit-and-prayer truck was in the driveway, and the soundtrack from some action movie blared from inside the house. Old Stan always did have a problem with his hearing.

Hayden settled in to watch. He'd felt uneasy about the MacClausens ever since Simon mentioned them in the pub. Something about them prickled the hair on the back of his neck and itched deep down inside, like an oncoming toothache. The family had been a thorn in his side for years. If there was a smashed-up mailbox or a home break-in, eggs thrown, or a camper's GPS device stolen, Jamie and Liam were the first place he looked. They were bitter and wild, stoned more often than not, and they had it in for the world.

But could they be... what? Shape-shifting black dogs? The idea was absurd. Maybe they were raising fighting dogs and one had escaped. Or could they be pulling a prank with some vicious breed they'd picked up at the shelter? Deliberately trying to imitate the Black Dog legend? Hayden saw no signs of an animal kept outside the house—no doghouse, no chains. He thought Mrs. MacClausen had a Scottie, but the wee thing probably never left her lap, and it certainly had never ripped out a man's throat.

He watched, not sure what he was waiting for, but on alert nonetheless. Dark fell hard and the TV went out, then the lights. And still he stood, the uneasiness only growing.

Simon. That kiss.

God, if he let his mind drift to that…. He twisted up with want and panic too. Why had no one else he'd ever kissed felt as good as that? Why Simon? Why did the man spark him like nobody ever had? Yes, he was attractive and intelligent. And sophisticated. And sensual. And he had the most engaging smile, but even so….

Oh bloody hell.

Think about the case. What if Simon was right? What if those historical eyewitness accounts of the Black Dog were to be believed? Could a man, in the depth of desperation, sell his soul to defend his homeland? Did the Devil, or God, even give a toss for a man's soul? And if Fergus mac Causantin could really do such a thing, turn into a beast to protect kith and kin, had it been passed down through his blood? Was there something here in this one bit of earth, some hidden truth behind the legend, that was as much a part of this place as the roots of the trees and the strata of the rocks? Is that why the old ones, the ones who could still recall World War II, looked at each other knowingly when there was talk of the Black Dog? Why they called it *Coimheadair*?

The notion was absurd, like a bad horror script. But then why did the idea have so much power over his mind?

Jamie's truck still loomed in the driveway. The house was still dark.

Hayden's mobile rang, making him jump. He fumbled trying to get it open. "Aye?"

"H-Hayden!" Simon's voice. Frantic.

"Simon? What's wrong?"

"It's… stalking me." He was whispering now. "Oh, God, Hayden. I'm a dead man." He sounded terrified.

"For God's sake, tell me where ye are!" Hayden was already getting into the Rover.

"Near the Peaks. It's here!"

For the love of God, what was Simon doing out at the Peaks alone in the dark?

"Listen to me! There's a place not far from there—northward—a small cave just below the cliff face. Try 'n reach it."

Simon said nothing, but Hayden heard a sound through the speaker that made his blood run cold. It was a deep, throaty, savage growl.

"I'm coming!" Hayden said. "Simon? Simon!"

There was a muffled thump as if the phone had been dropped on the other end, and then nothing more.

HAYDEN DROVE so fast on the dark roads that he nearly lost control of the car more than once. But sooner than he had any right to expect—and yet far too late—he screeched to a stop at the small car park for the Peaks. Simon's rental car was there. The man himself was nowhere to be seen.

"Dear Lord, please." Hayden ran toward the rock formation. *Please don't let him be dead.* He could picture finding Simon as he had that camper, his throat ripped out. *If you ever listened to a long-distant ancestor of mine, listen to me. All I want is for Simon not to be dead.*

His own breath was harsh in his ears, but as he neared the Peaks he heard it—the growls and scrabbling claws of a dog or wolf. Somewhere.

Oh God, don't let it be eating him.

He would kiss Simon in front of the bloody Queen, if only the man was all right.

"Simon!" he called, before he could think better of it. The sounds of the dog continued. It apparently was too focused to worry about an interloper.

Hayden swung his lantern around wildly. He didn't see man nor dog at the Peaks. Simon had run, then. They were both out there in the dark.

"Simon!" He shouted as loud as he could, cursing the blasted wind on the cliffs and how it caught up his words and flung them away.

"Hayden!"

The sound was faint, but it was there, up ahead.

Hayden ran forward, switching the lantern to his left hand so he could pull his gun with his right.

"Simon!" he called again.

He could hear the dog better now. The sound was baffled about by the wind, but he thought it was coming from the side of the cliff. Hayden shone the light down. The cliff here was a gentler grade than elsewhere, and below was a ledge that jutted out from the cliffs. On that ledge was—

An enormous black hound.

The dog was bigger than any dog Hayden had ever seen. It could well be as tall as a Highland cow, but its black hide was sleek and bulging with muscles, displayed by the moonlight only due to their constant movement and the sheen of its hair. Its waist was nipped high and tight, giving it a half-starved look. And it was scrabbling madly at the rocky opening of a small cave, one forepaw inserted. The rest of it was too big to fit.

Hayden was stunned and frozen in place until his mind supplied the reminder that Simon was likely in that cave.

"Simon!" Hayden yelled. "Are you a'right?"

"I'm... I'm alive." The voice came faintly from the rocks. He sounded hurt. Maybe badly.

Hayden swallowed and aimed the gun. He hesitated, taking another moment to look at the thing. It stopped what it was doing, drew back on its haunches, and stared up at him.

Its face was too dark to discern well, but he could see the glitter of white teeth, a mouth full of hideous incisors with jagged ends. And eyes. The thing had red eyes, and it stared up at him with something.... Fear? Recognition?

Hayden wasn't sure why he said it, why he didn't just pull the trigger. But there was something about the thing... like it was a part of this place. Like shooting it would be wrong. "Leave. Him. Be. And awa' wi' ye! Get!" He motioned with the gun.

The Black Dog stared at him for only a second longer, then it bounded up the cliff so fast he barely had time to pull back before it pushed violently past him and was gone into the night.

"WHERE ARE we?" Simon asked as they pulled up at a small cottage a short distance from the center of Laide. There was an exterior light over the door, but it otherwise looked deserted.

"This is Doc Gorden's bit. He's the closest doctor. Don' look like he's here, but he keeps a small infirmary open all hours for those that need it. Are ye sure you dinna want me to take you to hospital?"

"*No.* Please. Just some antibacterial cream and bandages. And maybe a stiff drink." Simon opened up the passenger side door to emphasize his point.

He was deeply shaken, but what he needed was light and comfort and company (and, yes, booze). He didn't think he could abide a long drive, an interminable wait, and the poking prods of strangers. He hadn't even been bitten, just scared half to death and a little clawed up.

If I had been bitten, would I have turned into the American wolf-dog in Scotland? It was a romantic notion, but probably not worth the flea meds and silver bullets in the end.

He was, perhaps, a wee bit hysterical, as Hayden might say.

Hayden didn't argue about the hospital. He let them into the infirmary and turned on the light. It was a small, comfortable room with plaid wallpaper and prints of hunting dogs on the wall. It smelled of disinfectant and on a counter was an array of tongue depressors, cotton balls, and other medical accoutrements displayed in thick glass jars that harkened back to the '40s. There was a desk and an old exam table topped with a green vinyl pad and a paper strip. The place was quiet, and Simon was just as glad the doctor wasn't there. He gingerly took off his ripped jacket, exposing bloodied arms, and sat up on the exam table.

"Lemme see," Hayden ordered sternly.

Simon held out his arms, and they both studied them. The cave had been too small for the dog but nearly too small for Simon as well. He'd gotten himself wedged in there, but the dog's claws had reached him.

He remembered vaguely something about Hayden looking at the cuts while they were still at the Peaks. He didn't remember walking to the car.

In the bright, flat light, the wounds looked bloody and dramatic. There were a lot of scratches, but none of them were deep enough to require stitches. Thank God his coat had been good and thick and had taken the brunt of the claws.

"Yer lucky," Hayden pronounced thickly.

"If you hadn't mentioned that cave, I'd be dead. It was stalking me. Watching me. When I started over the edge of the cliff there, it came melting out of the dark and stood there growling, like it was saying, *Go on, leave*. It didn't try to follow me. But when I crawled into the cave— it... it didn't like that. I think it wanted me *gone*. So it was trying to pull me o-out." His voice hitched. He stopped talking.

Hayden seemed familiar with the little emergency room. He ran hot water in the sink and helped Simon over there. He made Simon submerge his arms and lathered them good with blue antibacterial soap. It hurt, but honestly the hot water was worse than the soap and Simon was just grateful that he still *had* arms, so there was that.

"I'm lucky to be alive," he said, as Hayden rinsed him off. Then he realized Hayden had already said as much. "Sorry. Guess I'm still a bit wonky."

"'Course you are."

Hayden patted Simon's arms dry gently with paper towels, and guided him back to the table. Then he dug through some cupboards for cream and bandages and brought them over.

"Hayden," Simon said, putting his hand over Hayden's arm to stop his fussing.

Hayden met his gaze. His brown eyes were troubled and dark.

"That was... I mean, it's one thing to read about it in a gothic novel but... I've never been so terrified in my life. I never, *ever* want to be that terrified again." He was still shaking.

Hayden took both of Simon's hands and held them firm, as if to provide an anchor. "I'm sorry tha' happened to you here. *Here*, in my home, where you should ha' been safe."

"It's not your fault."

"As if that makes a lick o' difference. And what the fookin' *hell* were you doin' out there in the dark?" Hayden's eyes flashed with ire.

Simon had been looking for Hayden, actually, but he wasn't going to admit that. Unable to stomach another night alone in his room, he'd driven around the area, appreciating the glimpses of the moon over the sea and silver-tinged hills, and hoping he might see Hayden's Rover somewhere. By the time he'd driven by the Peaks, he'd admitted he wasn't going to find the man. He recalled a fairly straightforward path out to the rock formation and the sea. He wanted to experience what it looked like at night. And the Peaks wasn't particularly close to Dylan's farm or where the camper had been found.

God, he'd been an idiot. He just shrugged helplessly.

"I seem to recall you sayin' somethin' about me handcuffin' you once. If that's wha' it takes to keep you indoors, I'll be cuffin' you to your bedpost at sunset, and dinna think I won't!" Hayden was angry, but there was a hint of wet in his eyes. His emotion was running high—higher than could be justified for a mere police officer. Simon took that as a very promising sign.

Fuck it. Simon pulled Hayden into a hug. "Believe me, I'll handcuff myself before I ever do that again."

Hayden slowly put his arms around Simon's back. "You'll be hatin' this place now," he said over Simon's shoulder.

"No." Simon said it automatically, but he realized he meant it. He was more obsessed with this place than ever. And maybe that was predictable. He'd gone around the world looking for magic, making up stories to fill in for the lack of it. But this was the first time he'd found the real thing.

"The Black Dog really exists," he whispered.

"Aye." He heard Hayden swallow. "The Black Dog is as real as I am."

~7~

WHEN HAYDEN had stood on that cliff, looking down into the eyes of the Black Dog, he'd felt a knowing certainty. It was as if he recognized the thing, like it had always been there. His fear of the unknown had faded once he was looking at it, face-to-face. He'd only felt a burning anger that it was *hurting Simon. That just wasn't right.*

He should be shocked that the Black Dog really existed, that it was flesh and blood. But he felt nothing now except angry confusion. What bothered him was not that the creature existed. But that it was attacking people. Why? And why now? And who might it kill or seriously injure next?

"Here. Lemme finish this." Hayden pulled away from Simon's embrace and carefully dabbed the antibacterial ointment over his cuts. He wrapped soft gauze bandages over Simon's forearms, taping them well. He dug some paracetamol from the cupboard and handed Simon three of them with a glass of water.

"Drink all o' that," Hayden said. "You're in shock."

"I'm not in shock."

"Well, if you're not, I am. So do me a wee favor and—"

Simon put down the glass, pulled Hayden close, and kissed him.

It was soft at first, pulling him in for warmth and comfort and maybe a bit of a laugh in the face of death. It didn't stay that way. Hayden *whooshed* into flame like dry grass hit by a lightning strike and Simon sparked right back. Soon they were snogging as if they could reach heaven through each other's mouth. Hayden found himself standing between Simon's spread thighs, their bodies pressed tight, both of them hard.

He pulled away, with an internal groan. "Dear God. I dinna know why you make me feel this way. Or how." *But you're mine.*

It was frightening how sure he was of that. As sure as he was that the sea would still be here tomorrow and the day after that. He'd always imagined that sort of deep attraction to another human being to be a myth or at least something that happened to someone else. His mother told stories about meeting his father—knowing instantly he was "the one." That could never happen to cold fish Hayden. Yet he felt anything but cold now. He felt like the sun was rising inside his bones.

Simon put a hand on Hayden's jaw and smiled. "The first moment I saw you, I thought I was making you up. Too many Diana Gabaldon novels. I can't even believe *you're* real, much less the Black Dog."

Hayden laughed. "And here I was just thinkin' about the odds of someone like you walkin' into the tiny hamlet of Laide."

"Lucky for me I did. Where else could I have had a chance at having a torrid affair with a big, hunky Scotsman? Much less a big, hunky, ginger Scotsman."

"My hair is brown, lad. There's only so far you can push poetic license."

"You've freckles and red highlights in the sun. That's close enough for me."

But you're leaving, Hayden wanted to say. And he knew he, himself, would never go. Never. But he didn't want to sound like a weakhearted nelly, expecting assurance for the future when this thing hadn't even truly started yet. And besides... he didn't want to say anything to jeopardize their forward momentum, because if this didn't continue, right here, right now, he would die.

He found Simon's mouth again. He should be worried about the doc coming home, but he'd be able to hear the car, and besides, doc kept more than his share of the district's secrets. It was incredible to feel this kind of passion, a gift. He wasn't going to push it away this time.

So he let himself go.

He heard the ripping of cloth more than he was conscious of doing it himself. Then Simon's shirt was annoyingly bunched in his hands and he cast it away. The denims—they were a fucking insult to humanity and had to go. He unzipped them and ripped them off. Only afterward did he have a wee rational thought and remembered that Simon was hurt.

He blinked and Simon was naked on the exam table in front of him wearing nothing but the bandages on his arms. He was propped up on his elbows, his cock hard against his stomach, and his eyes huge. Hayden heard himself making a harsh panting sound. Christ, he was acting like an animal.

"I'm sorry—" he began, trying to get ahold of himself.

"Don't you fucking stop," Simon grit out fiercely. "Don't you even—"

It was encouragement enough for Hayden. He all but burst out of his own clothes, and then he was leaning over the table, devouring Simon. Hayden mouthed at Simon's chest, nipples, and stomach. He wanted to taste everywhere at once, and he couldn't stop taking deep inhales. The scent of Simon's skin was an aphrodisiac. It awoke some primitive part of

Hayden's brain and throbbed in his cock. Simon smelled of the earth in the spring, and there were faint traces of the stale sweat of fear he'd felt earlier and, over that, the heady musk of arousal.

"Oh my God," Simon groaned as Hayden reached his groin, taking in deep whiffs of the delicious smell at the root of him. "Hayden... fuck!"

Hayden rumbled his agreement and savored the taste of the slick of precome against his soft palate. It tasted of rutting things and of life, and he wanted more. He sucked Simon in deep, and at the same time, his hips had an irresistible urge to thrust. He wrapped his arms behind Simon's thighs, hands on his hips, and pulled him around toward the edge of the table. He was frustrated that he had to release the hard, delicious length in his mouth in order to get his hips where they needed to be. And then another trickle of reason broke through—Simon might not want him that way.

He straightened up and sought his lover's face. Simon didn't look afraid or reluctant. His lower lip quivered, and his expression was twisted with need. "Jesus Christ, you don't mess around."

"I want you," Hayden said without intending to. "I mean... I want to... but if you—"

"We're in a fucking first aid station," Simon snarled. "There's gotta be lube and condoms in here somewhere."

After that there was no more rational thought. There was only the instinct in Hayden to take, claim, and adore. For the first time in his life, he was a rough and greedy lover, gorging himself with abandon. He reveled in the sense of power beating through him, and in Simon's response to it, which was all *yes, yes, yes* and *more, more, more.*

When he finally penetrated his lover, he went slowly. Not only because he felt as giant as the heavens, and he was afraid he might split the man in two, but because he wanted to savor every moment of this claiming. Simon was on his back, but after a moment of Hayden fruitlessly trying to ease into him, Simon shook his head and pushed upright. He tugged Hayden to sit on the table, and straddled his lap. With one hand steadying Hayden's erection and the other around Hayden's shoulder, their faces were only inches apart. They both watched the emotions chasing across each other's faces as Simon slowly lowered himself, bit by bit, Hayden's hands supporting his hips.

"Oh, fuck," Simon breathed when he had all of Hayden inside him. "That's... that's a hell of a lot of man."

Hayden grunted and pulled Simon into a kiss. With his large palms splayed on Simon's lower back, he imagined he felt himself inside, a rod of steel burning deep in the accommodating body of his lover. It was the sexiest thing he'd ever felt and everything he'd never known to want.

"Can I?" he asked, his forehead braced on Simon's.

Simon wriggled a bit and gripped Hayden's shoulders with both hands. "Go. *Please.*"

Hayden did. He took Simon in that position, holding his hips hard and pounding up into him like a battering ram. The more Simon responded with enthusiasm to the wildness of it, the harder Hayden went. His body longed for more leverage, so he pushed Simon off and leaned him over the table, bracing a hand on Simon's back, and took him again. Simon yelled and cursed, apparently liking the angle.

Hayden was tingling from head to toe and on the verge of exploding when Simon rose up, pushing him off. He turned, and they stared at each other for a moment, both of their cocks red and ready to burst.

"I want to finish like this." Simon's voice was wrecked, but he seemed to know what he wanted. He climbed onto the exam table and lay on his stomach, tugging Hayden down flat on top of him.

In that position, with Hayden lying on Simon's back, and the two of them pressed as close as they could get, Hayden moved with long, deep thrusts. He laced their fingers on either side of Simon's head. Simon gripped his hands so hard it hurt. And when he cried out his release, grinding his hips down and painting wet stripes on the exam table, Hayden sucked the crook of Simon's shoulder and followed, bliss whiting out the room.

It took a long time to come down. The chemicals in his body realigned slowly along with the rotation of the Earth on its axis.

"What the hell was that?" he said when he could finally speak. He and Simon were spooned up together on the floor, he realized, probably because they both couldn't fit on the table side-by-side and standing was out of the question.

"I think it was sex," Simon said with a chuckle. "I've had it before, but apparently I was doing it wrong."

"I'll say." Hayden sat up gingerly, feeling a bit woozy. "Are your arms all right? I dinna hurt ye?"

"What arms?" Simon sat up carefully too. He looked at Hayden and grinned.

Hayden stared back and felt insane words lining up on his tongue. No. He wouldn't declare and he wouldn't beg, at least not now when he was awash in sentiment.

Simon seemed to read his mind. "Look, this isn't just sex for me. That is... I like you, Hayden. A lot."

Hayden nodded. "So you'll be here for a time yet?"

"Oh, I'll be here. Don't think I'll be going outside at night much, though."

Hayden cupped Simon's cheek with one large hand. "Good. Because you've given me enough heart attacks for one week. Stay indoors 'til we get this sorted. Ye ken?"

"Indoors. Right. Maybe you can join me there."

Hayden had a momentary flash of how luxurious it would be to make love to Simon in his comfortable bed at the pub. He wanted that. But it also crossed Hayden's mind that he should check on his mother, and there were plans to work out with the NDWA in the morning, too, plans that would probably involve more late nights.

He gave Simon a chaste kiss. "Well, I'll be doin' my best. Now we'd better get you to your rest, Mr. Corto."

HAYDEN DROPPED Simon off at the pub, making sure, once again, that he felt all right. By the time he got home it was 3:00 a.m. He was supposed to be on his first patrol by seven. He would normally have been irritated about that, but he felt too good to resent anything. He was floating on air. The future was unknown, but for now he would take the joy for all it was worth.

He let himself in as silently as he could, thinking only of getting undressed and horizontal as quickly as possible. But on the way to his bedroom, he slipped on the hallway floor.

There was something slick where it shouldn't be. He paused for a moment, considering it, then turned on the hallway light. The hardwood floor was dabbed with fresh mud. It went from his mother's room to the bathroom. It looked as though she'd walked there with muddy feet.

How had she got into mud? Had she gone out?

Hayden felt a sense of dread and horror that was all out of proportion with spots of mud, but this felt very wrong. He decided to check on Ruth first. He opened the door to the guest room, turning the handle slow and soft. The light from the hall cut into the room revealing the shape of Ruth in the bed. She was deep asleep, emitting soft snores. She'd had a cold the past few days, and her breathing was labored. A box of tissues and a bottle of cough syrup sat on the table.

If his mother had woken and wandered in the night, would Ruth have slept through it?

Hayden quietly closed the door.

He went to his mother's door next. He slowly opened the door.

The light from the hallway revealed mud on the floor of his mother's room, leading from the bed to the doorway. There was mud, too, on the light yellow comforter. The room was freezing cold. She was in the bed, covers to her neck, lying on her side away from him, her black hair spilling across the sheets. Despite the fact that she was there, his sense of unease coiled higher. Why was his heart pounding so hard?

He opened the door wide so the light from the hallway would shine in and entered the room on silent feet. Her window was open, explaining the frigid temperature. He went to close it and froze.

On the floor, beneath the window, were more muddy prints. Only these were not long and narrow, but wide and multipadded.

The print was that of a very large dog.

He felt the blood drain from his head as he stood there, rigid and still. His legs threatened to give way. He was terrified, but not because he expected to find the Black Dog in this room. He knew the truth already, even as he turned slowly to look at his mother.

She appeared to be deeply asleep, her hair wild, a smear of dirt on one cheek. The muddy animal prints went from the window to the bed. He crossed the few steps to her bedside without really being aware of it. He reached out a hand to grab the edge of the comforter. His hand was shaking.

He slowly pulled down the covers.

She was naked. He averted his eyes from her breasts. There was mud on the white sheets, big smears of it, and he followed them, pulling the covers down and down....

Her legs and feet were rank with dried mud. Her hands were covered in it, nails broken and several worn down so far they had bled.

He pulled the covers up, shut the window, locked it, and left the room. He was trembling, his heart encased in ice, as he poured himself two fingers of Scotch in the kitchen. He sat down heavily in a kitchen chair.

Jesus fucking Christ.

He drank the Scotch. One part of his brain insisted there was a rational explanation. It couldn't possibly be what it looked like. But it was a weak voice, and it couldn't outpace the scream of horror deep in his head.

He drank two more fingers of Scotch and went to summon Ruth out of bed.

RUTH CAME out to the kitchen in her robe. She took one look at him and went to the stove to make tea. When they were both seated with hot cups of the stuff, she met his eyes.

"I knew you'd find out. It was only a matter of time."

"For the love of God, Ruth!" He took a deep breath, trying to calm his anger and panic. "I hope to God you have something to say to me that makes sense. Because I dinna ken what to believe!"

Ruth clenched her jaw and looked at him grimly. "I think you do. Hayden, your mother is the *Coimheadair*. She has been since the last one died in 1981."

Hayden shook his head once, and wiped a hand over his face.

"She's wandered once or twice since…. That's why I wanted to be here. I locked her window tonight, and the front door. But she must have opened it before changing form. I'm… I'm so sorry."

"She fookin' killed a man!" Hayden said, the rage in him growing. "She killed that camper from London! And she nearly killed another tonight!"

Tears welled up in Ruth's eyes. "God forgive me. I thought I could contain her."

"Why the hell didn't you tell me?" he shouted.

"Shhh. You'll wake her."

He ground his teeth.

"I… I meant to tell you. But you've had enough on your plate. And it's not like we need the *Coimheadair* right now. I figured there'd be time enough once your mother passed. Let you be a free man for a little while longer."

"A free man?" he laughed bitterly. "What the fook are you talkin' about?"

Ruth paled as if he'd said something shocking. "Hayden… don't you realize? You'll be next, lad."

You'll be next.

As if the horror could get any worse, any worse than realizing that his own mother had somehow shapeshifted into the Black Dog and had killed a total stranger. And had nearly killed Simon too. *Simon*. But on top of all that to hear *he was next*?

He slammed his hand down onto the pine kitchen table. He hit it so hard there was a dull crack from underneath. "Have you lost your bloody mind?"

Ruth went even paler and trembled in fear. She held out one weak hand. "Hayden. Why... why do you think you've always been different? For God's sake, lad, you're thirty-three years old and you're still growin'! You've busted out of two uniforms this year alone. You're changing to be ready for it. It shows your mother's not long for this world."

He blinked and stared at her. He'd been denying the changes in his body, blaming it on the washing machine, blaming it on getting older. The hair on his chest had grown thicker in the past few years. His calves were bunched with muscles even though he spent most of his time in his car or behind the desk. *Lucky genes*, he'd thought.

Dear God.

"I think you'd better tell me everythin'," he said, barely a whisper.

Ruth nodded.

"IT WAS supposed to be me," Ruth said, her voice dull. "My father was the last *Coimheadair*. He told me when I turned sixteen. I'd always been a tomboy. Rough for a girl, ye ken? A bit violent. Och, but I had a terrible temper. Becca was my best friend. She helped calm me down when I got too fraught.

"When my da told me what I was to become, I couldn't bear it, Hayden." She looked at him with tearful eyes. "I was *sick about it.* I dinna want it. I wanted to die." She closed her eyes and took a deep breath. A cough wracked her, and she wiped her mouth. "Becca said 'why can't it take me? I don't mind.' And she didn't, Hayden. She loved this place, every blade of grass and every wild thing. She wanted to be a part of it that way. She spoke to my father. He said he dinna ken if he could change it, but if she really wanted it that much, maybe....

"Not long after that, I noticed that I was changin'. I began to slim down, even in my arms and shoulders. And Becca—she grew."

Hayden couldn't believe what he was hearing. "That makes not a lick o' bloody sense! Even if somehow the thing could be passed down—"

"I don't understand it meself, Hayden. But you know we're first cousins, Becca and me. My da was the seventh son in his family, and me in mine, and Becca in hers. Maybe it was close enough that it *could* choose her. She must have always had the potential for it. If I'd never been born or if somethin' had happened to me...."

"Why is there always *one*?"

Ruth frowned at him, as if he was being dim. "There must always be a Black Dog in the vale, Hayden. It's our birthright."

He rubbed his eyes. "Can she... can a *Coimheadair* change at will?"

"No." Ruth shook her head. "It only happens when it must. My da said some in the past had never changed a'tall, but there was just somethin' about 'em. People knew who they were. But *he* changed, during the war. Said when it came upon him the urge was so great, he couldna fight it. And he always knew, in his heart, that if he was changin' it was because we needed him. To him, it was a great honor. And to your mother too, ye ken."

Hayden considered that, his mind a mare's nest of protests and questions. "Then why is she doing this now?"

Ruth leaned forward and stared at him hard. "You know as well as I do. It's the same reason why she thinks you're still in school or that your da's just off to work. Her mind's not right. Maybe she dreams. Or maybe she believes we're in danger. Whatever is going on in her head, it's been enough to change her a few times now. And I... I don't know what more to do but lock her away. And ye ken, Hayden, if we do that, if anyone sees her change and finds out what she is, this place will ne're be the same again. We'll be overrun by scientists and the TV people and God knows all else. We canna let her go to jail or hospital. *We can not.*"

Hayden understood. Of course he did. And a further knowing set in, bitter as bile. *No one can know. Simon—he can't find out. He shouldna be here. He's a threat.*

And oh, that hurt. He felt ill.

"Hayden...." Ruth reached for his hand.

He yanked it away. "You should have told me years ago," he said angrily. "Or she should have."

Ruth nodded. "She was waitin' to be sure it was you. And then she wanted to let you enjoy your youth as long as you can. And then she was sick and I...."

Fuck you, Ruth, Hayden wanted to say. But what would be the point?

"I need to think," Hayden said, getting up abruptly.

He headed for the shower. There would be no sleep this night.

~8~

SIMON SLEPT late and woke up feeling so heavy he might have gained a hundred pounds. It was probably the result of amazing sex, the aftershock of horrendous fear, and his body's diverting resources to heal his arms. At the least, he couldn't blame it on booze. He'd had nothing to drink last night.

Except one *damned* fine Scotsman. Good Lord.

Coffee and breakfast down in the pub were his first priority. Angus made him a full English breakfast even though it was noon. Simon downed three cups of coffee before he felt fully awake. He kept finding a smile plastered on his face. He'd compose himself only to find it had sneakily returned.

He half expected Hayden to walk into the pub, but when he still hadn't appeared by the time Simon was ready to leave, he bit the bullet and asked Angus.

"Have you see Constable MacLairty today?" He tried to sound casual.

Angus gave him a funny look. "You mean Hayden? Last I heard you two were on a first name basis. No need to be formal on my account."

Simon swore he felt his cheeks heat. "Hayden, yes. Has he been by?"

"Hayden? Och, no. Then again, it used to be days and days before that man'd grace my door. Lately, though, he's been right underfoot. Must be your company, Mr. Corto."

Angus said it pleasantly enough, but Simon wasn't sure if he was implying *that*. And if he was, how Hayden would feel about it. Simon wasn't used to living in such a fishbowl.

He smiled stiffly. "Thanks for the breakfast, Angus."

THE EXCHANGE left Simon feeling a little unsettled. He decided he could use a walk. He walked down the main road through town to a little stone bridge and took a right onto a footpath that led back to the village. The day was overcast but not too cold, and the scenery was all hedgerows and rolling hills and quaint cottages that held a touch of mysterious gloom. It was spectacular. The landscape was moody with wisps of fog so slight they might have been his imagination. The trees were golden and dark red with the last of the fall foliage, and the grassy hills were browning. It was a lovely walk, even though the quiet did have him looking over his shoulder once or twice. *The Black Dog comes out at night, remember?* Still, he was relieved when he ended up back at the pub a quick forty minutes later.

The uneasiness from his walk only increased his desire to see Hayden. Maybe it was time he checked out the post office—and the tiny police station within it. He was expecting a package from his publisher, and though Angus had assured him it would be delivered to the pub, it couldn't hurt to check, could it?

THE WOMAN at the post office, Beverly, was very friendly. She didn't have Simon's package, but she did threaten to talk his ear off, wanting to hear about his books, about New York, about his Black Dog story, his marital status, and about the size of his shirts. Well, not really on the last one, but it felt that way. Finally, Simon got a word in edgewise.

"Is Constable MacLairty in today?"

"Oh, aye! I did hear him earlier. Go out the front, make a left on the path, and the door is just around the corner. You'll see the sign."

"Thanks."

Around the side of the small brick-and-plaster building was a dark wooden door, as old as time itself, with an antique-looking round glass bubble above it that read "Police Scotland." There was some Gaelic below that, *Seirbheis Phoilis na h-Alba.* On the door proper was a more modern logo on a white plaque. "Police Scotland" and, under that, "Keeping People Safe."

Man, that was a big responsibility, Simon thought. *Keeping people safe.* He wouldn't care for it, but it suited Hayden. He had a visceral memory of how he'd felt cowering in that cave, sure at any moment that dog would get enough purchase on his clothes to drag him out. And then—what it had meant to hear Hayden's voice.

The man had saved his life. Yeah. If anyone could live up to that motto, it was Hayden MacLairty. Simon opened the door and stepped inside.

The police office was tiny. It looked to be a single room with a door to what was likely a storage closet or small bathroom. Old metal filing cabinets lined one wall, a fax and various other equipment crouched under a window, and a desk filled what space was left. The desk was big, but it was dwarfed by Hayden MacLairty, who was sitting behind it. He was on the phone and his face looked haggard, tired, and unhappy. The quick look he threw Simon—a haunted, guilty look, just made Simon's uneasiness skyrocket.

"Aye. I'll be meetin' you there in an hour. Off out." Hayden hung up the phone.

"There hasn't been another attack?" Simon asked, worried by the drawn look on Hayden's face.

"No." The word was curt. Hayden stood and was at the coatrack by the door in two strides. This brought him, not coincidentally, close to Simon, but he avoided Simon's eyes and held himself stiffly. He might as well have had an invisible wall around him.

"Is something wrong?" Simon asked, his stomach twisting.

Hayden took a deep breath, still not meeting Simon's gaze. "Look. I'll be workin' with the wardens for the foreseeable future, until this thing's done." He hesitated. "I'll have no time for you. And anyway, it'd be best if you go on home. It's not safe here. And I don' want to be worryin' about you."

"Hayden... I know it was stupid for me to go out last night alone. But I won't do that again. I mean it. I don't have a death wish."

"Don't matter. Anythin' could happen at any time. Best you be gone as soon as you can arrange it." Hayden's coat was over those massive shoulders by now, and he pushed past Simon to reach the door. "I have to go. Think about what I said. Surely you have whatever you need for your work by now."

Finally, Hayden did look into Simon's eyes. He looked... regretful. Upset. But also determined and cold, like he'd steeled himself to do this and nothing was going to shake him.

There was no mistaking this. This was a brush-off. Simon felt hurt but mostly confused. The way Hayden had been last night—affectionate, passionate, warm. The bond between them had been surprisingly tangible and deep. This sudden turnaround—it was like Hayden was a different man.

"I... all right." Was all Simon could manage. Then they were both out the door. Hayden locked up and took off for his vehicle without a glance back or another word.

SIMON BROODED over it in the pub, slowly nursing pints of beer like they were his last meal on earth.

He kept puzzling it over in his mind. He felt stung, to be sure, but he had a hard time accepting it was real. What would make Hayden do a one-eighty like that? What *could* make him turn so abruptly? Obviously, Hayden wasn't out as a gay man, and he'd been nervous about starting gossip. But he seemed to have gotten past that last night in the infirmary.

Or maybe he just wanted to get off. Now that he has, he's ashamed and wants nothing more to do with you. Oldest story there is.

Simon considered it. That would make sense with another supposedly straight man. But Hayden honestly hadn't given Simon that impression last night. He hadn't closed off when the sex was done. And when he'd dropped Simon off at the pub, his eyes had still been warm and his kiss lingering.

I'll see you soon, he'd said. And he'd smiled wide. The things they'd admitted to one another, the way it had felt. It hadn't just been sex. And then today Hayden had been closed up tight as a fortress gate.

What had happened? Simon tried to untangle it the way he might a plot.

Hayden's mother was ill. Had she taken a turn for the worse? But why would that necessitate shutting Simon out? Unless she'd guessed about Hayden and Simon and had a fit about it, making Hayden feel guilty.

But why *would* she guess? And Hayden was a man in his thirties. He didn't strike Simon as the type to still be cowed by his mother's opinion.

Was it about the Black Dog, then? Simon turned the idea over in his mind. Hayden had asked Simon to leave. It wasn't really about Simon's safety, was it? What if it was because Hayden was afraid of what Simon was going to write?

The thought sent a hot, angry wave rushing through Simon's stomach. There was a sense of rightness about the idea, and dread. Maybe Hayden was pushing Simon to leave because he'd learned something he didn't want Simon to know, something that would make him, or the town, look bad. Simon was an outsider after all, and an author. Hayden obviously liked him, but Simon had no illusions that if it came down to choosing between his loyalty to the town and Simon, Hayden wouldn't blink twice.

Fuck.

"Yer face is as black as the Earl of Hell's Waistcoat," Angus commented as he brought over Simon's third beer. "You get some bad news, then?"

"You could say that."

"Well. 'Tis a dreich day inside 'n out. I'll light a fire in a bit. Might cheer you some."

"Thanks." Simon gave Angus a grateful smile.

"Care to talk it out?" Angus offered. He slung a tea towel over his shoulder as if prepared to linger for a while.

Simon wanted Angus's advice; he just didn't know what questions to ask. Hayden had said he was going straight home after he'd dropped Simon off. So he couldn't have learned much at that point. But earlier in the evening, he'd been watching the MacClausens's home. What if he'd seen something that he hadn't fully processed in the adrenaline rush of Simon's phone call, rescue, and then their hot session at the infirmary? What if later, after he'd dropped Simon off, he'd realized the significance of something he'd seen? Something he didn't want Simon to know?

"Do you know the MacClausens?" Simon asked Angus.

"Aye." Angus's face was careful. "The lads, Jamie and Liam, come in from time to time. Their da, Mac, used to sit at the bar near every night, but his hips ha' got such that he don' get out much."

"Would you say they're one of the oldest families in these parts?"

"Oh, aye, to be sure. 'Course, there's a lot of old families 'round here. But the MacClausens go way back. Mac knows near everyone and a lot of the old history too."

That got Simon's attention. "About the Black Dog?"

"Sure." Angus looked uneasy.

Simon fiddled with his glass. Maybe he'd just make things worse if he stuck his nose into it any further. But he wasn't prepared to give up and turn tail.

He wanted Hayden. He wanted this book. And he wanted to stay here, in Laide. He wanted that with a deeper conviction than he would have thought possible in so short an amount of time. He would fight for this if he had to. The decision made him feel good. He would fix this, show Hayden he could be trusted. It was certainly better than crying in his beer.

"Do you think Mac would be willing to see me?" Simon asked.

SIMON PARKED in the MacClausens's driveway and surveyed the house. It was way the hell out in the middle of nowhere, an old double-wide trailer that had seen far better days. The trailer was set back from the road, and the intermittent space was covered in tall dried grass, several car carcasses, and other bits of rusting and rotting junk. The only thing that looked new and in decent repair on the trailer was the satellite dish on the roof.

There was a menacing feeling to the place. Simon didn't like it, but he was determined to get information.

He forced himself to exit the car and knock on the warped plywood door. The man who answered it was almost wider than he was tall, with stringy greasy hair, a scruffy gray beard, and an odor like old onions. He looked Simon up and down.

"Mr. MacClausen? I'm Simon Corto."

MacClausen's eyes darted over Simon's shoulder. "Did you bring wha' I asked for?"

"Yes."

"Can I see it?"

Simon handed over the brown bag of Scotch he was carrying, and MacClausen eagerly peered inside. Then Simon pulled out his wallet and flashed the contents.

"I'll be havin' the cash now," MacClausen said firmly.

"Half now, and half when I leave," Simon bargained back.

MacClausen grunted, and Simon handed over two hundred pounds.

"Pull yer car round back," MacClausen ordered. "Don' need the whole world knowin' my business."

Simon couldn't imagine who on earth would drive by this desolate place, but he didn't argue. He moved the car, and then MacClausen let him in.

The inside of the trailer home was in better condition than the outside. It was clean, and though the sofa and recliner were old and worn, they had colorful quilts draped across the back. The windows were cracked open to let in fresh air, despite the coolness of the day, and there was a lingering odor of lemon cleaner.

Mrs. MacClausen, the woman no doubt responsible for the cleanliness, came forward to greet him. She held a tray with an old china teapot, cups, and a plate of store-bought biscuits. She looked to be in her sixties, with steel running through her red hair and a plump, unlined face.

"Here we are! Please make yerself at home, Mr. Corto."

She seemed nervous and eager about having a guest. Simon thanked her for the tea, and watched her anxious fluttering as she poured and served him and Mac.

"'Tis lovely, Ma. Now leave us so's we can talk," Mac ordered.

"Aye, love. Only don't—" Mrs. MacClausen looked at Simon warily.

"I know what I'm aboot, woman. Leave us," Mac repeated, more firmly this time.

Mrs. MacClausen all but wrung her hands, but she disappeared down the hall, and Simon heard a door quietly shut. Simon wondered what it was she was so worried about.

Without shame and any thought to germs, Mac dumped his cup of tea back into the little chipped teapot and proceeded to refill it with some of the good Scotch Simon had brought.

"Ye said on the phone ye had questions."

"Yes, well… I'm interested in folk legends, and I'm looking for stories about the *Coimheadair.*"

MacClausen studied him with a surprised, wary air. "The *Coimheadair*, ye say."

"Yes." Simon pressed on. "Dylan Mitchell was telling me he saw the *Coimheadair* when he was a boy. You must have been around age ten at the end of World War II. I wondered if you have any stories like that. If you ever saw the Black Dog with your own eyes."

Mac finished off his drink in a few gulps, and Simon immediately poured him more. Hopefully drink would turn Mac into a loose-tongued talker and not a belligerent drunk.

Mac frowned. "I seen more in my life than Dylan Mitchell 'ere has in his. 'N you can take tha' to the bank."

"Have you?" Simon leaned forward with an interested smile.

"Aye. Was five feet from the Dog once, wasn't I? Could smell its breath, I could."

Simon could say the same, but he pushed aside the fear that came with the memory of his own encounter with the Black Dog and kept his face calm. "Where did you see it? And what was it doing?"

"Me da and meself was out one night. Car broke down so's we set off for home on foot. 'N there we was, walkin' on the road, and the thing came right out o' the dark." Mac licked his lips nervously and finished his Scotch. Simon poured him another. "We froze, and it came right close to us, growlin'—that's a sound ye don' even wanna ken. It looked us over real good, and my da just stood there with his hand hard on my shoulder, warnin' me not to move. After a bit, the Dog decided we weren't a threat, and it melted back into the night and was gone."

Mac shook his head. "Never seen my dad afeared, before that day or since. But he was white as you please when we got home and babblin' to me ma. That was at the start o' the war, and we heard lots o' stories about the Dog then. It was watchin' out for us, ye ken?"

"I do," Simon said, feeling both thrilled and sort of horrified. He thought Mac's story had the ring of truth. That certainly implied that neither Mac nor his father were the Black Dog. "Did it ever kill anyone in those years?"

"They found a few bodies. Strangers. Spies, no doubt. And good riddance." Mac gave him a sideways glance. "'Course all this is mere legend, ye ken. A tall tale, like."

"Of course." Simon attempted a reassuring smile. He topped off Mac's cup.

Mac told a few more anecdotes about people who'd claimed to have seen the Black Dog, but there wasn't much new in it. Nevertheless, Simon wrote it all down dutifully. Mac's speech started to slur, and his eyes grew bleary.

"I've heard your family is one of the oldest in the area," Simon mentioned, when he judged Mac had had enough to drink.

"Aye, tis so." Mac was clearly proud about that.

"As old as the line of the *Coimheadair,* I bet."

Mac raised his chin. "Aboot so, I'd say."

"And is the *Coimheadair* generally a MacClausen?" Simon was braced for a reaction, but Mac's boisterous laughter was not the one he expected. "Mr. MacClausen?"

"Aye. Aye. Sorry, lad," Mac tried to contain his giggles. "Only the idea…! Aye, me auntie. We're nay the blood. Oh, no doubt there's a drop or two in the ol' family tree, but we ain't the high and mighty, ye ken. Nor would wish for it. Tis a curse, me da always said."

Simon felt a wave of frustration. Who else could it be? Angus? He didn't know the families in the area all that well, and while he'd read through lists of names while studying the records, they were a sea of letters to him at the moment.

"Now I'll be havin' the rest of my payment," Mac said confidently.

Simon clenched his jaw. "But you've told me very little. Who is the *Coimheadair*?"

Mac's eyes studied him far too keenly, suddenly not nearly drunk enough. "Sorry, Mr. Corto. Some secrets are nay for sale."

They were at a standstill, and Simon knew it. He tried to think of what else he could ask that would tell him something at least. "But you do know him? You know who he is?"

Mac smiled slyly. "Now there's yer first mistake, lad. It ain't always so, but our *Coimheadair*—tis a woman. She has the blood, and fierce she is, don' fool yerself otherwise." He held out his hand. "Now that's more than ye've a right to know, and I'll be havin' the rest o' it."

SIMON WAS lost in thought as he exited the MacClausen trailer. *A woman?*

He hadn't met too many women here. There was Dylan Mitchell's wife, Barbara, the woman who ran the post office, and Margie at the pub. The lady at the tea shop was far too meek. And—

Voices interrupted his reverie. Angry voices. He'd taken several steps toward his car when he realized he wasn't alone. There was an old truck and a dark sedan parked in the MacClausens's driveway. A group of rough-looking men were standing on the erstwhile lawn arguing.

"I told ye, we met the shipment on the beach and delivered it to your man Smithy, untouched. We dinna open the bloody thing!" a punkish-looking young man insisted. He resembled Mac and sounded... well, he sounded like a liar, if Simon were any judge.

"There's a bloody kilo missin'! Do you think I'm a fookin' idiot?" shouted a large man in a leather coat. His face was pitted with acne scars. "I know you two bawbags took it! What the fook ye dain? Tryin' to skim off a bit for yerself on the side?"

In the next blink, Simon saw the gun the man with acne scars held in his hand. He realized he'd stepped into a very bad and potentially violent situation. Unfortunately, before he could turn around or hide, the men spotted him.

"Who the fook is that?" The big man with acne scars demanded.

"Fook if I know. Who the hell are ye?" the younger man spat out. "And what the fook are you doin' at my house?"

"Sorry. I, um... I was interviewing your father."

"Interviewing?"

"What the fook, Jamie! He's some kind of bloody reporter! I swear to God, can't you two gits do anythin' right?"

Simon tried to backpedal. "No! I'm not a reporter. I was just... asking your father about the local legends, is all."

But the large man strode up to him and grabbed Simon's coat, hauled him up to his toes. "You're one unlucky bastard, is wha' you are."

"Look, I don't know who you guys are, and I don't care! Just let me go, and I'll get out of your hair."

The big man looked at an older man who was standing by the car and hadn't said a word. The older man shook his head grimly.

"Right. Jamie, Liam, grab the rope that's in the trunk o' the car."

Simon felt a surge of panic. Surely he wasn't going to die over this. Not over something as stupid and accidental as walking out of a goddamn trailer. He struggled against the man's hold. "Please. I won't say a word, I swear to—"

There was an intense pain in the back of his head and the world went dark.

~9~

"HAYDEN. I need a word."

It was Angus. He hurried across the road to the small car park at the post office. Hayden shut the door of the Rover and turned to the man wearily. He'd been up all night with the team from the NDWA. What a farce. He'd got some sleeping pills from Doc Gorden, and they'd given two to his mother last night after supper. They'd knocked her out cold. He'd also taken the precaution of adding an exterior lock to her window and the front and back doors of the house. It was a fire hazard to be sure, but he couldn't risk her opening them from the inside while Ruth was asleep.

But he couldn't very well tell the dog wardens, or his boss in Inverness, that this killer beastie was his mother, and that he'd taken care of it. So he'd been up all night right along with the team. Of course, they'd found no sign of the creature that had killed that poor camper, Mr. Brauber.

"If you'll give me breakfast and coffee, you can have all my words," Hayden said with a tired smile.

"Come on, then. You look reet knackered."

Angus waited until Hayden was seated on a stool with a plate of food in front of him before leaning over the bar with a troubled look. "I'm worried about Simon. He didn't come down for breakfast this mornin', and Margie wanted to tidy up his room, so I knocked. He's na there. Don' believe he was back all last night."

I think it's best you go. Hayden remembered how terrible it had felt to say the words to Simon, to see the hurt look on his face. He swallowed hard. "Has he left town, ye think?"

"Och, no. All his stuff is still up in his room." Angus shook his head in a troubled way that meant *what do you make of that?* "Think maybe he got into some trouble? Like that couple from London done? That's what has me scared. 'N a nice man he is too."

Hayden took a sip of coffee and parsed it through his mind. He'd had two wardens in the Rover most of the night, and they'd driven out to several of the trouble spots—the Mitchell's farm, the Peaks, Loch Dale.

He'd not seen any sign of Simon's car all night. And he'd noticed it wasn't parked at the pub when he came in either.

"When was the last time you saw him?"

"Yesterday 'bout noon. He came back from a walk lookin' like someone'd stabbed his ma, and I asked him about it. He wanted to know about the MacClausens, so I set him up on the phone with Mac. Could be he went out that way."

Angus gave Hayden a knowing look, as if to say if there was trouble, Jamie and Liam MacClausen were probably not far from it. Hayden was overcome with a strange physical sensation. A prickling itch ran up his spine. His shoulders suddenly felt tight inside his shirt—like they might just bust the seams. The hair on his head stood up on end. He thanked God he kept it short. Hopefully, Angus wouldn't notice.

He took another big gulp of coffee while he tried to get back some control.

Simon went out to see the MacClausens. Alone.

Though Jamie and Liam were troublesome, there was no reason to be particularly alarmed at that idea. Yet Hayden was. He'd felt something was wrong there when he'd staked out the place a few nights ago. And Simon *was* missing, wasn't he?

"I'll go out there right now." Hayden pushed aside his plate and stood up.

"You're dead on your feet, lad. Do ya want company? I can close down for an hour."

Hayden considered it. But the truth was, he had more than one secret to protect. "No, Angus. I'll be fine."

HAYDEN WENT out to the MacClausens. There was no sign of Jamie and Liam, or Jamie's truck. Mac swore up and down that he'd only had a "wee chat" with Simon the day before, and that Simon had left afterward. But he seemed edgy and nervous. He admitted that he might have been "a little tippled" when Simon left.

He was hiding something. But what? As for Mrs. MacClausen, she wouldn't even look Hayden in the eye. She claimed she hadn't seen Simon leave, but her face was pale and drawn with worry.

Hayden stood outside their trailer and looked around, trying to see what wasn't there. There was no sign of overturned earth or blood in the yard—thank God. He walked around the property and found some tire tracks in the damp earth out back. They were small tires, consistent with Simon's rental car. They certainly weren't the fat tires from Jamie's truck.

There was an old shed a hundred yards behind the MacClausens's trailer. The door was locked. Hayden peeked in a cobweb-covered window. The shed was so full of junk it was doubtful it could hide a full-sized adult, dead or alive.

Dead or alive.

Hayden turned away from the shed's window and got that strange sensation again. Standing there in the midmorning drizzle and cold, looking toward the trailer, he felt it like a crawling thing. It felt like his flesh was trying to escape his bones. A terrible and anxious feeling bubbled deep inside him. He felt the hair on his neck go to attention, like the ripple of a caterpillar.

Something is wrong. Must do something.

Simon was missing, and this sense of wrongness was related to that somehow. What had happened to him? Was he dead? If he was, the last thing he would remember was Hayden telling him he didn't want him anymore.

I was scared. I pushed you away. Maybe I should have trusted you.

Why had Simon come out here to talk to Mac? Was he still determined to write that bloody book no matter what Hayden had said?

His mobile buzzed in his pocket. With a sense of hope, Hayden got it out. But the screen didn't say "Angus" or "S Corto." It said "Ruth."

"Aye?" He answered.

"Hayden? Oh, Hayden, love, you'd best come home!"

HAYDEN REACHED for his mother just before she put her hand through the plate glass of their living room window. He grabbed her wrist. "Ma— stop it! Calm down. I'm right here."

"I'm sorry I had to call you, Hayden, but you see how she is." Ruth hovered behind them, at the end of her rope. "She's been gettin' worse and worse since this mornin'. I can't control her!"

Hayden saw all right. His mother's hair stuck out all over as if it hadn't seen a comb in a decade. She wore crumpled pajamas, and her eyes were wild. She stared right through him, not recognizing him at all.

"Out!" His mother said insistently, tugging to free her hand. "Out! Out!"

Hayden didn't think she was telling him to leave. No, she wanted out of the house herself. She fought with him, trying to get out of his hold. But bloody hell, she was strong. It took everything he had to hang on to her.

"Ma, no! Ye canna go out like this." Hayden turned, searching for Ruth. "Can we give her more o' those bloody sleepin' pills?"

"I tried, Hayden. She near bit my hand off, then sent them flyin' across the room. She won't take 'em."

Bloody hell, when it rained, it poured. He couldn't deal with this right now. Not with Simon missing and his own sense that something—

Fuck. *Fuck.*

"Ma. Mother! It's Hayden. Look at me. *Ma.*"

He spoke to her urgently, shaking her by the arms. And her eyes did turn to his face, some sense coming back into them. "Hayden? I have to. I have to. Please."

"I feel it too. Ma, listen to me. If you let Ruth get you dressed, I'll take you out in the car, ye ken? My friend Simon is missin'. Somethin's happened to him. Can you show me where he is?"

Hayden's mother blinked at him for a long moment as if struggling to process what he'd said. Then she nodded and relaxed, suddenly calmer. "You'll take me? Now?" She looked so hopeful it broke his heart.

"I'll take you. But first get dressed, aye? And we'll go."

"Hayden, you can't—" Ruth warned.

"Just do it, Ruth! And hurry."

SIMON WORKED hard to keep the fear at bay. *Angus will notice I haven't been back. He'll tell Hayden,* Simon assured himself. *Hayden will come looking for me.*

He refused to believe that Hayden would abandon him. Whatever Hayden's reasons were for pushing him away, he wouldn't ignore the fact that Simon was in trouble. *Keeping people safe.* That was Constable MacLairty. He was a good man. He was probably looking for Simon right then.

Even if he is, how is he going to find me?

He wasn't still at the MacClausens. He was being held in a small cabin, probably a hunter's cabin. He was tied to an old iron bed, which was ridiculous in a way, because the bed was light enough he could move it around if he shifted hard enough. But the ropes were tightly wound around the frame, and it wasn't like he could get the thing through the door.

Anyway, *they* were outside. He knew because there were cracks in the rough board walls that let in the howling wind. They let in voices as well.

"I'm not gonna do it!" a voice said adamantly. It was a voice Simon was starting to recognize as belonging to the elder MacClausen son, Jamie.

"You'll do it and shut up about it," a rough voice replied. That was the man with the acne scars, Simon thought. "This is all your fault. We wouldna come out to this godforsaken rat hole in the first place if you hadn't nicked that kilo. 'N that reporter was at *your* house, you fookin' dickhead."

"How was I supposed to know he was there?"

"Just shut your hole and do as you're told. We got a sweet deal here, and we're not riskin' it for no yank. We'll deal with fancy pants here, and then I'll deal with you and your twat of a brother."

"I am not gonna murder a man in cold blood, Fergus! Runnin' drugs is one thing, but I ain't no killer!"

The men continued to argue, but the blood rushing in Simon's ears made it hard to hear. They were arguing about who was going to kill him. *They were going to kill him.*

This couldn't be happening. What a ridiculous reason to die. At least if the Black Dog had gotten him, it would have been a romantic death, one that made sense with the books he wrote. But this... to have blundered into a drug ring. No one would ever know what had happened to him. Simon Corto, author—vanished.

And Hayden. Simon heard himself voice a hysterical little laugh. Hayden MacLairty—big and gorgeous as the Scottish mountains, and as earthy and as grounded too. Simon could picture a life with that man. He could picture walking from their little cottage to the village in the morning for a cup of coffee with Angus and to pick up their mail. He could picture writing in some cozy little room that overlooked their back garden and the sea beyond, the window cracked so he could hear the sound of the waves. He could picture a big bed with a down comforter and Hayden large and warm and hard to wrap up in it with him. He couldn't imagine any life he wanted more.

He would give up New York in a heartbeat for Hayden, if the man had only asked.

If Simon had only lived long enough to ask Hayden himself.

He could feel a blind fear encroaching, and he decided to get angry instead. *Angry.* Those fucking low-life scum. If they thought they were going to conveniently dispose of him without one *hell* of a goddamn fight…!

He struggled again with the rope, determined to fight for his right to live. He was tugging hard on his right hand, which seemed a tiny bit looser, when he heard the sound. He paused, listening. It might have been the wind or a distant engine. Then he heard it again and his body broke out in goose bumps and his stomach rose up into his throat. He knew that sound, that low, menacing growl.

It was the Black Dog.

It was outside the cabin. He listened hard, afraid to even breathe. There was the sound of a single gunshot, and then for a moment there was nothing. The men's voices had fallen still. Then… screaming.

~10~

HAYDEN'S MOTHER motioned at every crossroads, indicating which way he should go. She was silent and intense, her eyes large and her hands nearly digging holes in the Rover's glove compartment lid. But in truth, Hayden could sense in advance which way she would indicate. He felt it too—a tug pulling at the center of him, from somewhere behind his navel. Inside his wool coat, his shoulders had bunched so hard they'd split the seams of his shirt some miles back. He couldn't care less.

I'm changing. I'm changing too. He wondered if he would lose control. Would he become the Black Dog? It should have been terrifying, but he was so enraged at the idea of Simon being taken, hurt. There was no room left in his mind for anything but action. People didn't do this. Not on his land.

If I change, I wouldn't accidently hurt Simon, would I?

Is he even still alive?

They pulled off onto a rough, dirt track that went into the woods. This was game lands, regulated by the Scotland Game Board and open at certain times of year for hunting by permit only. It wasn't open season on anything right now, but Hayden could see fresh tire tracks in the dirt—big tires. *Jamie's truck.*

"Ma, you stay—" he began, but he had the Rover moving slowly over the rough ground, and before he realized what she was about to do, she'd opened the door and jumped out. She moved fast—and in a moment was gone into the trees. The way she moved—decisive, strong. She looked nothing like his ailing mother now.

"Bloody hell!" he cursed. He stopped the car and nearly went after her before he thought better of it. Better to follow the tire tracks. He had a feeling when he found Jamie's truck he'd find Simon. And maybe he could beat her to wherever they were headed.

HE SAW a flash of red through the trees and the nearly hidden driveway. He cut the engine, deciding to approach on foot. He crouched low and went through the trees, his shotgun in his hands. This was no longer about a rogue dog or vermin control, and he really ought to call in the Armed Response Team. Hayden wasn't trained for this. But Simon could be dead by the time they got there. He couldn't allow that.

In front of the cabin was Jamie's beat-to-shite truck and an older black BMW. Jamie was arguing near the cabin with a tough-faced man in a leather jacket. Leather jacket was waving around a handgun. Liam hung back warily.

"Just take the bloody gun and get it done! If I have to shoot him meself, you're next!" the stranger shouted.

"Have it your way," Jamie said calmly. He reached out and took the gun. Hayden moved faster, in a run now. Two things crossed his mind— that Simon was still alive, probably being held in that cabin, and that he wasn't going to be alive for very long. Hayden would shoot Jamie if he had to, by God he would.

He burst from the trees, shotgun raised. At the same moment, Jamie raised the handgun and fired a shot directly into the face of the man in the leather jacket. The man crumpled to the ground like a heavy sack of laundry.

For a moment, Hayden just stared, shocked. No one moved.

"Down! Put the gun down!" Hayden screamed, coming back to himself. He braced himself into a firing stance still twenty feet from the cabin, shotgun locked on Jamie. Jamie was looking down at the body on the ground, his face blank. He looked up into Hayden's eyes. That was when they heard the growl.

The growl was like the sound of the earth, like the rumble of an earthquake, if the earth could be alive and furious. Jamie swung around, half raising the handgun. He and Liam stared as the Black Dog stalked out from the trees. It was late afternoon, and despite the gloom of the skies, it was a shock to Hayden to see the thing in daylight. It was taller than a Great Dane or a wolfhound. But it was bulky too—its body thick and roped with muscles like the most ferocious fighting dog. It looked hungry, its jaws slavering, and it seemed deranged, the glint of madness in its red eyes. The sight of it caused Hayden's blood to turn to ice. It was like looking Death in the eye.

Liam gave a sob and fell to his knees. Jamie made an effort to raise the gun, but his arm was shaking so hard he couldn't do more than wave it around an inch or two. And then, thinking better of it, he dropped the gun and fell to his knees in surrender.

"Oh, God, Jamie!" Liam sobbed. "Da said if we brought trouble 'round, the Dog'd be on us! He was right! It's the Devil himself, and we're done for!"

Jamie just stared at the beast with huge eyes, his skin blanched white. Liam babbled as it stalked closer, drooling with anticipation.

It's going to kill Jamie and Liam. His mother was going to kill them.

As angry as Hayden was with the two brothers, he didn't want that for his mother, didn't want the burden on her shoulders. And he didn't much care to see the two idiots torn limb from limb either, or face the circus that would cause. The thought finally snapped him into gear. He blinked and slung his gun back over his shoulder.

"Calm now! Calm." He approached the Dog slowly, his hands raised. "Stand down, now. Hold."

The Black Dog didn't look at Hayden, but it did stop its menacing growl. It approached the body on the ground warily, sniffed at the bloodied head as if scenting the dead man.

"Where is Simon Corto?" Hayden asked the boys, never taking his eyes from the dog.

"We didna hurt 'im!" Liam insisted. "You can see for yourself! And Jamie.... Jamie.... Oh, God, Jamie shot Fergus! But he had to! Fergus wanted us to kill Corto and—and we was just tryin' to make a little money, Hayden. We dinna mean no harm!"

"Is there anyone else here?" Hayden barked.

"N-no. It was just Fergus. That reporter, h-he's in the cabin."

Hayden stepped past the useless git and went to the cabin door. "Simon!" he called out.

"Here!" came the anxious reply.

BY THE time Hayden freed Simon and helped him from the cabin, the Black Dog was gone. Apparently, it had decided the danger was over and it would let Liam and Jamie live. Hayden was inclined to agree. They were foolish lads, always had been, but he'd be surprised if they didn't fly a bit straighter from now on. They were absolutely terrified of the Black Dog.

And maybe there was more substance to Jamie than he'd thought. He had killed Fergus, after all. Hayden never would have expected that.

Hayden listened to Liam and Jamie's rambling confession—running all over each other to tell Hayden everything about the drug shipments they'd been helping to pass through from the coast to points south. Hayden was pretty sure Inverness would be able to apprehend the higher-ups with the information they'd provided. And Jamie wouldn't be able to back out later either—not if he wanted to claim the shooting of Fergus was self-defense. It was a claim Hayden was happy to back up.

By the time Hayden and Simon were driving back to Laide, it was pitch dark. Simon had been quiet through most of it.

"I heard it," Simon said, when they were on the road. "From inside the cabin. I heard the Black Dog."

"Aye. Well."

"It can't be you," Simon turned to look at him, his voice puzzled. "I know it isn't you. You were on the cliffs."

"It's not me," Hayden said quietly.

"But you know who it is. That's why you wanted me to leave. Mac said it was a woman."

Hayden said nothing. He was torn between the comfort and reassurance he was aching to give Simon and his loyalty to his family, this place.

"Hayden," Simon said in a very serious voice. "I would never do anything to hurt you. I know you must sense that, or you wouldn't have been so open with me the other night. The way we were together... I trust you, and you have to believe you can trust me too."

Hayden cleared his aching throat. It felt like it had swollen to twice its size with the words he wanted to say, wanted to say but shouldn't. "It's not that I don't trust you, Simon. But what about when you go back to New York? Years'll pass, 'n you'll forget what you felt for me. And this story.... It'll be a terrible temptation. Why would you stay loyal to me 'n keep mum on something as big as tha'?"

Simon reached over and put his hand on Hayden's shoulder. "Pull over."

Hayden sighed.

"*Pull over.*"

Hayden found a wide place in the road and pulled onto the shoulder. They were right at the coastline there, and out the window were the cliffs and the half-moon reflecting on the sea. Hayden was struck again by how much he loved this place. And it wasn't fair that he had to choose between this and the man who might well be the love of his life. But in the end, he could make no other choice.

"Hayden." Simon unsnapped his seat belt and scooted closer.

Hayden looked into Simon's brown eyes, dark in the light of the moon, and he saw only love there. Simon took a deep breath.

"I want to stay here. With you. And I want us to be together. What I feel for you... it's beyond solid. I can be loyal to you and yours. Is it a risk? Yes. For both of us. But it's worth it. Don't give up without even trying. I know you're stronger than that, Hayden MacLairty."

Hayden's chest warmed with a burgeoning affection so strong he only now realized how hard he'd been keeping it captive. He touched Simon's curly hair. "You have some sweet words there, Mr. Corto."

Simon smiled. "A good imagination too. Aren't you the lucky one."

Hayden laughed. "You'd really do tha'? You'd stay here with me?"

Simon nodded. "You have no idea how much I want that. Do you want that?"

There was only one answer in Hayden's heart. He pulled Simon into a passionate kiss. It felt so right, Hayden wondered how this place could ever be home again without the man in his arms.

~Epilogue~

Two years later

SIMON AND Hayden walked side by side ahead of Becca MacLairty's hearse. Ahead of them were bagpipers, their melody ringing out over the hills like a mournful cry. Ruth walked with them, and Hayden's six older brothers, all of them kilt-clad, and their wives and children and babes in arms too. Behind the hearse came the entire population of Laide, it seemed, and all the towns around.

Becca, Simon thought, would have been proud of the large procession.

At the small cemetery at the end of town, the parson gave a lovely blessing. He talked so movingly of Becca's love for the land and her sense of duty to it that Simon was sure the pastor must know the truth. All of Becca's sons put a fistful of dirt on her lowered coffin, and Hayden nudged Simon to do so too. He let the grains of dirt fall from his fingers and felt a wave of grief.

He'd never known Becca when she was completely well, but he'd loved her all the same. She was Hayden's mother, after all, and an Amazon in her own right. She was good and loving and often as innocent as a child.

"And do you know what happened to my dog, Bandi? Mama said Bandi ran away, but the neighbor's son told me. Papa shot him."

"Becca." Simon remembered the day he'd finally been unable to bear that story anymore and had taken her hands in his. *"If your papa had loved Bandi as much as you loved him, as much as Hayden loves you, he couldn't have shot that dog. He would have found a way to keep Bandi away from those chickens and keep him safe."*

Becca had stared at Simon for a long time. Then she smiled a wobbly little smile and asked about dinner. She'd never told that story again.

Becca had died of pneumonia in the end. It had happened fast. From one month to the next, she'd caved in on herself even as Hayden seemed to grow bigger than ever before. Simon knew Hayden felt guilty about that, felt like he was somehow sapping his mother's strength, even though there was nothing he could do about it.

After the graveside service, Hayden and his brothers stood in a line so that their friends and neighbors could pay their respects. Simon stood off to the side with the wives and watched, worried about how Hayden was holding up, and proud of how strong and able he looked, how gracious he was to the mourners he greeted, even in his grief.

"That's odd," Linda, Jackson's wife muttered.

"What is?"

"You'd think Hayden was the local nobleman or something, and not just a constable." She watched with a puzzled frown as the mourners greeted Hayden last, and with little bows of their head. One old man kissed Hayden's hand, tears of gratitude in his eyes.

Simon had heard the whispers a few times in the crowd. *Coimheadair.*

"He's a good man," Simon said, trying to sound casual despite the pride swelling in his chest. "They respect him."

"Well, he certainly was a saint looking after Becca all these years. I used to feel sorry for him, bein' stuck here in dumpy old Laide. But then he found you. Still don' know how he managed that. Or how the two of you can bear it in this backwater, especially being gay."

Simon looked at her, bewildered. Could she really be so blind? How could she not see how magical this place was, or Hayden himself? The locals had even embraced Simon—after a perfectly understandable period of shock.

How could it not be obvious it was Simon who was the lucky one?

"I wouldn't live anywhere else for all the world," Simon said with conviction.

Linda laughed. "You sound like Janice. She's absolutely obsessed with Laide. Has been since we brought her out to meet Gran when she was only two years old. 'Laide-this' and 'Laide-that' and 'when are we going to Laide?'. I swear! I don't see the appeal myself. Oh, I suppose it's picturesque enough if you like the country and you don't mind it being bloody Baltic half the year."

Simon scanned the crowd and saw Janice, Linda's youngest, sitting off by herself. While the other children played half-heartedly on the grass or took a stroll around the headstones, Janice, aged six, was watching Hayden and the mourners with fascination.

Simon felt a sudden pang. This was what funerals were for, he supposed. To say good-bye to the people you loved, and to remember, too, that life was a cycle. Not all that long ago, Becca had buried her own father and mother here, and Ruth's father, the previous *Coimheadair*. And someday, it would be Hayden who was lowered into the ground—horrible thought, though it was—and another would be standing up to take his place. Maybe even Janice.

It was a good reminder to appreciate every moment of what he had while he had it. He cleared his throat. "You're welcome to send Janice up anytime for a stay. We'd love to have her."

"Really? God, don't let her hear you say that, or I'll never get her to stay home! I'd better go check on my brood, now that I think of it."

Linda wandered away in mother mode. Simon watched her go and felt a hand on his elbow. He turned to look up at Hayden. His eyes were red and puffy, but they held a calmness Simon was grateful to see.

"How are you holding up?" he asked.

Hayden hesitated. "She's in a better place. Guess I have to believe tha' anyway."

"I think so."

Hayden nodded. His face was serious, and there was a trace of anxiety in his eyes. Simon squeezed his hands and leaned in close. "You're going to be the best *Coimheadair* there ever was, Hayden. Don't doubt it."

Hayden huffed in disbelief, but he smiled. "I'll be happy if the Black Dog is never needed, that it never comes to tha'. And if I ever… if I ever get… out of hand, out of my head. You'll take care of it, won't you, Si? Promise me."

Simon wanted to protest, but he could tell Hayden meant it as a serious request. It deserved a serious answer. "I promise you that I will always love you as much as I do right now and as much as you ever loved your mother. And I will do anything it takes to support you."

Hayden nodded, his face going a bit red. "Guess we'd better get home. There'll be a hundred people in and out o' our bit for the wake."

"Aye," Simon said without thinking.

Hayden gave him a cheeky smile. "'Aye' is it? We'll make a Scotsman of ye yet, Simon Corto."

That ship has long sailed, me lad, Simon thought with a sense of utter rightness. But he only smiled and took Hayden's hand.

ELI EASTON has been at various times and under different names a minister's daughter, a computer programmer, a game designer, the author of paranormal mysteries, a fanfiction writer, an organic farmer, and a profound sleeper. She is now happily embarking on yet another incarnation, this time as an m/m romance author.

As an avid reader of such, she is tickled pink when an author manages to combine literary merit, vast stores of humor, melting hotness, and eye-dabbing sweetness into one story. She promises to strive to achieve most of that most of the time. She currently lives on a farm in Pennsylvania with her husband, three bulldogs, three cows, and six chickens. All of them (except for the husband) are female, hence explaining the naked men that have taken up residence in her latest fiction writing.

Website: http://www.elieaston.com
Twitter: @EliEaston
E-mail: eli@elieaston.com

By ELI EASTON

Blame it on the Mistletoe (Audiobook Only)
Closet Capers (Dreamspinner Anthology)
Heaven Can't Wait
The Lion and the Crow
A Prairie Dog's Love Song
Puzzle Me This
Steamed Up (Dreamspinner Anthology)

GOTHIKA
Claw (Multiple Author Anthology)
Bones (Multiple Author Anthology)
Stitch (Multiple Author Anthology)

SEX IN SEATTLE
The Trouble with Tony
The Enlightenment of Daniel
The Mating of Michael

Published by DREAMSPINNER PRESS
http://www.dreamspinnerpress.com

Stitch

Gothika #1

By Sue Brown, Jamie Fessenden, Kim Fielding, & Eli Easton

When a certain kind of man is needed, why not make him to order? Such things can be done, but take care: Much can go wrong—but then, sometimes it can go wonderfully right. Imagine...

In *The Golem of Mala Lubovnya*, a seventeenth century rabbi creates a man of clay to protect the Jews, and the golem lives a life his maker never imagined, gaining a name—Emet—and the love of a good man, Jakob Abramov. But their love may not survive when Emet must fulfill his violent purpose.

In *Watchworks*, Luke Prescott lives as a gentleman in a London that never was. His unique needs bring him to famed watchmaker Harland Wallace. Romance might blossom for them if Harland can come to terms with loving a man and keeping him safe.

In *Made for Aaron*, a young man in an asylum for being gay met the love of his life, Damon Fox. Twenty years later, Aaron thinks his life is over when Damon dies and then disappears from the hospital. Aaron is determined to find the truth, but secrets hide the unthinkable.

Reparation unfolds on the harsh planet of Kalan, where weakness cannot be tolerated. When Edward needs help, his life becomes entwined with exceptional cyborg slave, Knox. But when Knox remembers things he shouldn't know, the two may pay a blood price for their taboo alliance.

http://www.dreamspinnerpress.com

Bones

Gothika #2

By Kim Fielding, Eli Easton, B.G.
Thomas, & Jamie Fessenden

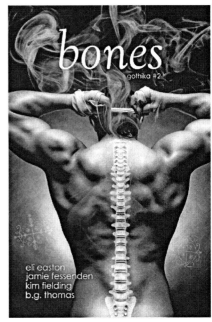

Vodou. Obeah. Santeria. These
religions seem mysterious and dark to
the uninitiated, but the truth is often
very different. Still, while they hold the potential for great power, they can
be dangerous to those who don't take appropriate precautions. Interfering
with the spirits is best left to those who know what they're doing, for
when the proper respect isn't shown, trouble can follow. In these four
novellas, steamy nights of possession and exotic ritual will trigger
forbidden passion and love. You cannot hide your desires from the loa, or
from the maddening spell of the drums. Four acclaimed m/m authors
imagine homoerotic love under the spell of Voodoo.

The Dance by Kim Fielding
The Bird by Eli Easton
The Book of St. Cyprian by Jamie Fessenden
Uninvited by B.G. Thomas

http://www.dreamspinnerpress.com

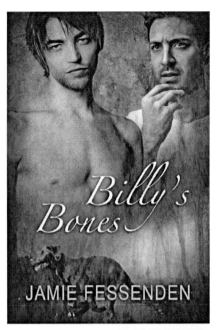

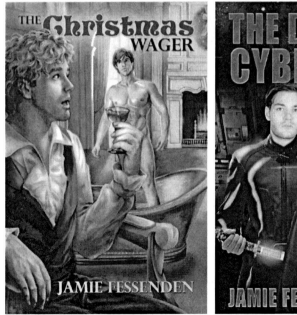

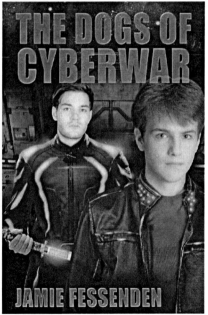

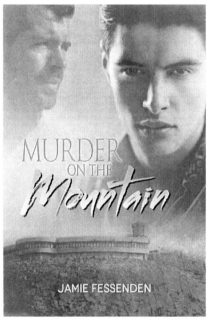

http://www.dreamspinnerpress.com

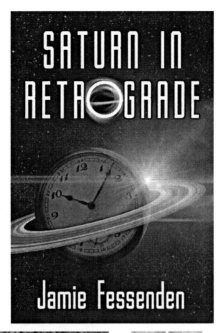

http://www.dreamspinnerpress.com

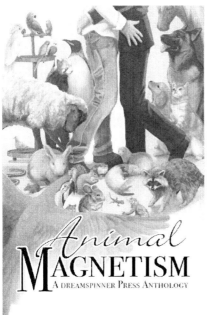
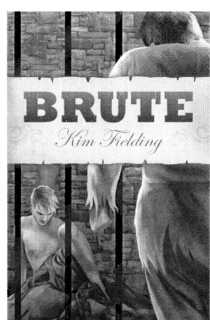

http://www.dreamspinnerpress.com

http://www.dreamspinnerpress.com

http://www.dreamspinnerpress.com

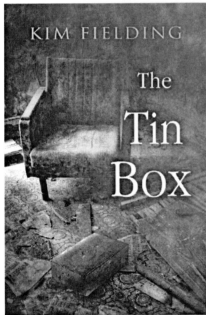

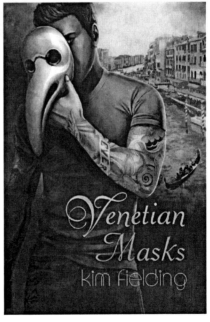

http://www.dreamspinnerpress.com

Good Bones

Bones: Book One

By Kim Fielding

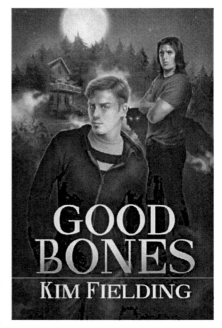

Skinny, quiet hipster Dylan Warner was the kind of guy other men barely glanced at until an evening's indiscretion with a handsome stranger turned him into a werewolf. Now, despite a slightly hairy handicap, he just wants to live an ordinary—if lonely—life as an architect. He tries to keep his wild impulses in check, but after one too many close calls, Dylan gives up his urban life and moves to the country, where he will be less likely to harm someone else. His new home is a dilapidated but promising house that comes with a former Christmas tree farm and a solitary neighbor: sexy, rustic Chris Nock.

Dylan hires Chris to help him renovate the farmhouse and quickly discovers his assumptions about his neighbor are inaccurate—and that he'd very much like Chris to become a permanent fixture in his life as well as his home. Between proving himself to his boss, coping with the seductive lure of his dangerous ex-lover, and his limited romantic experience, Dylan finds it hard enough to express himself—how can he bring up his monthly urge to howl at the moon?

http://www.dreamspinnerpress.com

Buried Bones

Bones: Book Two

By Kim Fielding

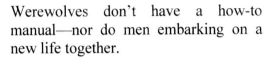

Werewolves don't have a how-to manual—nor do men embarking on a new life together.

It's been a few weeks since Dylan Warner wolfed out and killed Andy, the crazed werewolf who originally turned him and later tried to murder Chris Nock. Architect Dylan and handyman Chris are still refurbishing Dylan's old house as they work out the structure of their relationship. They come from very different backgrounds, and neither has had a long-term lover before, so negotiating their connections would be challenge enough even if Dylan didn't turn into a beast once a month.

To make matters worse, Dylan's house is haunted, and events from both men's pasts are catching up with them. Dylan has to cope with the aftermath of killing Andy, and Chris continues to suffer the effects of a difficult childhood.

In his quest to get rid of the ghost, Dylan rekindles old friendships and faces new dangers. At the same time, Chris's father makes a sudden reappearance, stirring up old emotions. If Dylan and Chris want to build a lasting relationship, they'll have to meet these challenges head-on.

http://www.dreamspinnerpress.com

Bone Dry

Bones: Book Three

By Kim Fielding

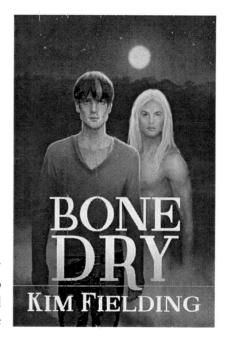

Ery Phillips's muse is MIA. He's pretty sure his job as a graphic designer is to blame, because let's face it, what kind of muse wants to draw grocery store logos and catheterized penises?

When Ery's friends Dylan and Chris head off on a European vacation, Ery jumps at the chance to stay on their farm, hoping a stint in the country will encourage his muse to reappear. To be sure, the farm has attracted a few oddities—Dylan is a werewolf and the place was recently haunted—but Ery isn't canceling his plans just because his friends warn him that there's something strange going on in their pond. What he doesn't expect is Karl, a beautiful naked man who appears at the water's edge.

With Karl as his inspiration, Ery creates amazing paintings and begins to achieve the success he had previously only dreamed of. But Karl comes with certain challenges, causing Ery to question his own goals. Creating the life of his dreams with an unusual beloved may be more challenge than Ery can handle.

http://www.dreamspinnerpress.com

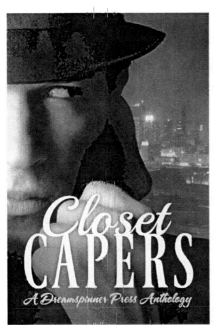

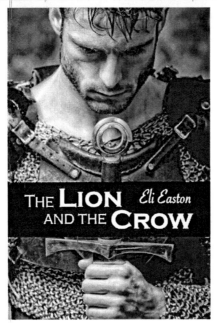

http://www.dreamspinnerpress.com

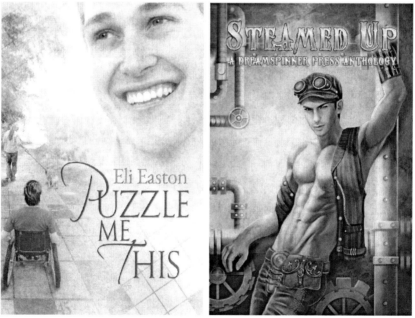

http://www.dreamspinnerpress.com

Blame It on the Mistletoe

By Eli Easton
(Audiobook Only)

eli easton

When physics grad student Fielding Monroe and skirt-chaser and football player Mick Colman become college housemates, they're both in for a whole new education. Mick looks out for the absent-minded genius, and he helps Fielding clean up his appearance and discover all the silly pleasures his strict upbringing as a child prodigy denied him. They become best friends.

It's all well and good until they run into a cheerleader who calls Mick the "best kisser on campus". Fielding has never been kissed, and he decides Mick and only Mick can teach him how it's done. After all, the physics department's Christmas party is coming up with its dreaded mistletoe. Fielding wants to impress his peers and look cool for once in his life. The thing about Fielding is, once he locks onto an idea, it's almost impossible to get him to change his mind. And he just doesn't understand why his straight best friend would have a problem providing a little demonstration.

Mick knows kissing is a dangerous game. If he gives in, it would take a miracle for the thing not to turn into a disaster. Then again, if the kissing lessons get out of hand, they can always blame it on the mistletoe.

http://www.dreamspinnerpress.com

The Trouble With Tony

Sex in Seattle: Book One

By Eli Easton

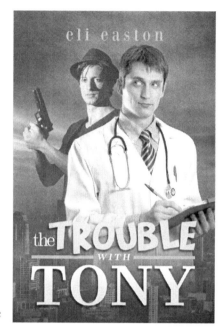

As part of the investigation into the murder of a young woman, Seattle P.I. Tony DeMarco poses as a patient of Dr. Jack Halloran, the therapist who treated the victim at a Seattle sex clinic. This isn't the first time Tony has gone undercover, but it's the first time he's wanted to go under cover with one of his suspects. He can't help it—Jack Halloran is just the kind of steely-eyed hero Tony goes for. But he'll have to prove Halloran's innocence and keep the doctor from finding out about his ruse before he can play Romeo.

Dr. Halloran has his own issues, including a damaged right arm sustained in the line of duty as a combat surgeon in Iraq and the PTSD that followed. He's confused to find himself attracted to a new patient, the big, funny Italian with the puppy-dog eyes, and Tony's humor slips right past Jack's defenses, making him feel things he thought long buried. But can the doctor and the P.I. find a path to romance despite the secrets between them?

http://www.dreamspinnerpress.com

The Enlightenment of Daniel

Sex in Seattle: Book Two

By Eli Easton

Business tycoon Daniel Derenzo lives for his work until his dying father reminds him life is short. When Daniel starts to reevaluate his world he experiences a startling revelation—he's attracted to his business partner and best friend, Nick, even though Daniel always believed himself to be straight. In typical type-A fashion, Daniel dissects his newfound desires with the help of the experts at the Expanded Horizons sex clinic. He goes after Nick with the fierce determination that's won him many a business deal.

Nick Ross was in love with Daniel years ago, when they were roommates in college. But Daniel was straight and Nick patched his broken heart by marrying Marcia. Two kids and fourteen years later, they go through the motions of their marriage like ships passing in the night. But Nick's kids mean the world to him, and he's afraid he'll never get joint custody if they divorced. If he can trust his heart to an awakening Daniel, they all might find their way to a happily ever after.

http://www.dreamspinnerpress.com

The Mating of Michael

Sex in Seattle: Book Three

By Eli Easton

Everyone admires Michael Lamont for being a nurse, but his part-time work as a gay sex surrogate not only raises eyebrows, it's cost him relationships. Michael is small, beautiful, and dedicated to working with people who need him. But what he really wants is a love of his own. He spends most of his time reading science fiction, especially books written by his favorite author and long-time crush, the mysteriously reclusive J.C. Guise.

James Gallway's life is slowly but inexorably sliding downhill. He wrote a best-selling science fiction novel at the tender age of eighteen, while bedridden with complications of polio. But by twenty-eight, he's lost his inspiration and his will to live. His sales from his J.C. Guise books have been in decline for years. Wheelchair bound, James has isolated himself, convinced he is unlovable. When he is forced to do a book signing and meets Michael Lamont, he can't believe a guy who looks like Michael could be interested in a man like him.

Michael and James are made for each other. But they must let go of stubbornness to see that life finds a way and love has no limitations.

http://www.dreamspinnerpress.com

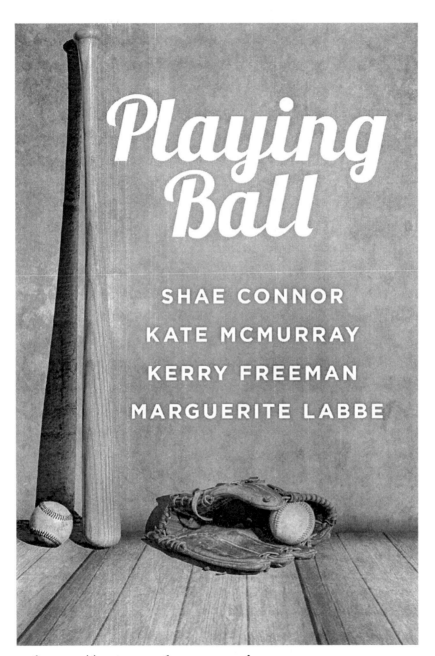

Playing Ball

SHAE CONNOR

KATE MCMURRAY

KERRY FREEMAN

MARGUERITE LABBE

http://www.dreamspinnerpress.com

FOR **MORE** OF THE **BEST GAY** ROMANCE

DREAMSPINNER PRESS
dreamspinnerpress.com